Deep blue. A winter evening. On the fringes of the lake. Lynette Meyer stood there with Pete's axe in hand. She had furiously chopped a wide hole in the thick ice and was now standing back from it and watching as *they* appeared from beneath, smiling their big empty smiles.

They came up one by one through that wide hole she'd chopped in the ice, using her dead husband's axe.

They turned to the east and made their way single-file through the knee-deep snow, heading for Many Pines Inn.

Also by T. M. Wright
published by Tor Books

T. M. WRIGHT

THE ISLAND

TOR
HORROR

A TOM DOHERTY ASSOCIATES BOOK
NEW YORK

This is a work of fiction. All the characters and events portrayed in this book are fictitious, and any resemblance to real people or events is purely coincidental.

THE ISLAND

Copyright © 1988 by T. M. Wright

A TOR Book
Published by Tom Doherty Associates, Inc.
49 West 24 Street
New York, NY 10010

Cover art by Hector Garrido

ISBN: 0-812-52765-8   Can. ISBN: 0-812-52764-X

Library of Congress Catalog Card Number: 87-50887

First edition: March 1988
First mass market printing: December 1988

Printed in the United States of America

0 9 8 7 6 5 4 3 2 1

This book, very special to me, is for my children.

ACKNOWLEDGMENTS

To the following people, my thanks:
Chris, my wife, for helping me find the right tune, and for sticking around.
My editor, Harriet P. McDougal, for giving me the chance to write this book.
Bill Thompson, for a beginning.
Terry Boothman.
Greg Basile, for all the fish.
Bob and Nancy Garcia, for their friendship.
Shirley Jackson, Herbert Lieberman, Joan Samson, Herbert Gold, and Elizabeth Coatsworth for, respectively, *The Lottery, Crawlspace, The Auctioneer, He/She,* and *The Enchanted,* all of which contributed, in varying ways, to the way I have told this story, and to my desire to tell it.

BOOK ONE
THE PEOPLE

ONE

January, 1987: In The Adirondacks

By half past eight in the evening, several dozen fishermen had set up small tents and lean-tos as protection against the cold on Seventh Lake. They did not speak much, although their voices carried well on the still air. For these men, fishing through the ice was a solitary pastime, and even where there were clumps of two or three of them at the same lean-to, there were only occasional whispered references to the cold, or to the dark, or to the stillness, all of which suited them, and wrapped them up and shielded them temporarily from what they saw as the torment of their daytime jobs, their wives, and the general wretchedness of their existence.

Here and there, a small fire had been built and white smoke drifted nearly straight up, dissipating, finally, at an altitude equal to the height of the dark trees on shore.

A group of six friends was fishing in a small area a hundred yards from shore. These friends were Pete Meyer, Sam Hanks, Harry Stans, Frank Weaver, Tom Lord, and Jim McFee; all were dressed in thick dark sweaters layered one on top of the other, at least two pairs of pants, and black rubber boots with buckles. They were fishing for bullhead and brown trout.

* * *

Pete Meyer, who had trundled over from his lean-to, said to Harry Stans, "Harry, I saw something in the hole."

Harry was sitting on a small stool, like a milking stool, and he had his eyes trained on the hole he'd cut in the ice. The water beneath was black. He said, without looking up, "You saw something in the hole?"

Pete Meyer gestured toward the spot where he'd been fishing, twenty yards away. "I saw a woman's face in the hole."

Harry Stans looked up at him, blinked, nodded dully, but said nothing.

Pete Meyer said, "I did, Harry."

Harry said, his eyes again lowered, and with a little quaver in his voice from the cold, "What can you see in this lake, Pete? You can't see nothin' in it."

"I saw a woman's face," Pete said. "It came up into the hole and then it went away."

"Drowned woman?" Harry asked, with a little spark of interest now.

"No," said Pete Meyer.

Harry looked up at him, cocked his head, looked back. "Sure it was a drowned woman, Pete, and they'll find her in the spring."

"She had her eyes open, Harry."

"Course she had her eyes opened. She was drowned. Drowned people have their eyes open."

"And she moved her lips at me, too."

Harry shook his head dismally. His gaze was still on the hole he'd cut in the ice. "You can't see nothin' in that water, Pete. You didn't see nothin'. You saw some dead fish come up and float away."

Pete shook his head, vigorously at first, then less vigorously; at last, he merely looked befuddled.

Harry said, "Am I right, Pete?"

"Don't know," Pete muttered. "Maybe you are."

"It was a fish," said Harry.

"A fish with green eyes?" said Pete.

Harry smiled. He felt a little tug on his fishing line. He said, "Fish got green eyes, some of 'em."

Pete started back to the hole he'd made in the ice. Suddenly, he felt very cold. Colder, he thought, than he'd felt in a long time. It had little to do with the weather, he decided, which was cold enough, for sure, but not as cold as it had been on Tuesday, and not nearly as cold as it had been on Sunday. He was as cold as he was, so bone cold, he realized, because of the thing he had seen through the hole in the ice. If it was just a fish, then it was a hell of a fish, a fish with a woman's face and green eyes and red lips that moved —lips that tried to talk to him, but could say nothing through that inch or so of dark water between them and the bottom of the hole.

Pete shuddered. He glanced to his right at the black outline of the Many Pines Inn on the lake's eastern shore, a half mile off; the inn was dark—no one stayed there in winter.

He looked away. He was at his lean-to; then, a few steps more, he was at the hole he'd made in the ice. He bent over and peered hard into it. He whispered, "Are you in there, honey, are you still in there?" He saw no movement in the black water, only the dull glint of something just below the surface, like the smooth silver skin of a fish.

He straightened. He heard from far to his left, "Jack's gone in!"

Another voice called, "Jack?"

The first voice answered, in confirmation, "Jack!"

Pete looked at the hole in the ice.

The second voice called, "Can you see him?"

There was no answer.

Pete said to the hole in the ice, "You in there, honey, are you still in there?"

"Can you *see* him?" called the second voice.

"No," the first voice answered.

A glint of something blond came and went just below the surface of the water beneath the hole in the ice.

"He's gone in," called the first voice. "Get something. Get a pole."

"I got my net," said a new voice.

"Net's good," called the first voice. "Bring it quick!"

Beneath the hole that Pete Meyer had made in the ice, the surface of the dark water broke very briefly, as briefly as if a bass had come up for a fly and, seeing nothing, had gone back down.

"Damn!" said a new voice. "Jack's gone in, Jack's gone into the lake!"

Pete Meyer leaned closer to the hole. He put his big hands on his knees. He smiled. He whispered, "You got him, honey?"

Another glint of something blond came and went just below the surface of the water. It was slower this time. It suggested that something was rolling below, and Pete cocked his head at it in confusion. He put one knee on the ice and leaned still closer to the hole. Around him, men were shouting curses and commands as they ran to the spot where Jack had gone in.

Pete whispered, eyes on the dark water churning up, "This is real strange."

A light snow started. It was composed of spindly, translucent flakes the size of dimes; the flakes settled gracefully onto the surface of the water and sizzled up.

"Real strange," Pete whispered.

Around him, curses and commands had changed to commands only as men told other men the best ways to find a victim of the lake.

"Pull the net along just below the water. Yeah, like that," one man yelled. "Maybe you'll snag 'em."

And another man yelled, "Someone's got to go in! Someone's got to go in after Jack!"

"I'm going in after Jack!" yelled another man, and his voice was shrill with excitement.

Pete looked up, away from the hole. He saw a dark shape go into the lake fifty yards away. He heard a harsh, crackling splash, then a muted scream as the icy water closed around the man who had jumped in.

Pete smelled soap. He thought that it was coming up from beneath his chin, from within the hole he'd made in the ice. He thought that that was strange, too, because smells did not carry well in the frigid air above the lake in winter.

But it was not unpleasant. He even thought he liked the idea of smelling soap out here.

He looked again at the hole. He smiled. He saw two dime-sized, spindly snowflakes hit the churning, black water—first one, then, quickly, the other.

He started to straighten, to back away from the hole because, suddenly, he was very, very cold, as if something even colder were watching him from below, from beneath the surface of the water. He got his knee off the ice, got his back straight.

The green-eyed head of a woman pushed through the hole and as it broke the surface, its mouth opened wide as if to scream.

The ice around the hole heaved upward; first the woman's shoulders, then a long, naked arm appeared above the surface of the ice. Her mouth opened still wider, the way the mouth of a snake opens wide to accept its prey.

Pete felt himself bathed in the frigid water of the lake as the woman rose up out of it. A grunt of surprise and desperation came from him and he went over on his back and crab-walked, grunting, away from her. He felt the top of his head hit the lean-to, saw the dark wool of the lean-to come down on him and cover his face and chest.

He screamed. He felt a hand close around his ankle and clutch hard at him through his rubber boot.

He tore at the dark wool of the lean-to that covered his face; it clung to him and he felt as if he were blind. He screamed again and he knew that no one could hear the scream, that the wool covering his head was making him all but mute.

He felt the hand around his ankle close tighter. He felt himself being dragged back, toward the break in the ice where the woman had come up.

Three Days Later

When Lynette Meyer answered the knock at her cottage door, she had a small child at each hand. One, a boy of six, had a thumb stuck far into his mouth and was sucking mightily at it; the other, a girl of two, dragged a faded rag doll behind her. The boy wore faded blue dungarees, scuffed black shoes, a button-down pink shirt, and a blue, pullover sweater; the girl wore a long, threadbare gingham dress, red sneakers, and a white, cardigan sweater with several buttons missing.

Lynette Meyer said to the tall, gaunt man who had knocked on her door, "They ain't found him, yet, ain't that right, Harry?"

Harry Stans grimaced, started to speak, and Lynette cut in, shaking her head, "Ain't gawna find him, neither, and that might be all right, 'cept he knew how to fish."

"God, yes, and I'm sorry," said Harry Stans.

Lynette, short, chunky and strong looking, dressed as warmly as her children in two sweaters, a long white dress, gray socks, and house slippers—because the heat in the cottage was provided solely by a small wood stove in the kitchen—shook her head again, but with a sad smile on her plump mouth. "Before long, Harry," she said, "he'll come outa there"—she glanced toward Seventh Lake, a quarter mile north, visible through a break in the pines that crowded the steep slope to her cottage—"and we'll put him in the ground." And with that, her children following, she stepped backward away from the door and closed it.

Late that afternoon, she set Jolene and Pete Jr. to coloring with some stubs of crayons she had saved for them in a drawer that was out of their reach, sat in a small, overstuffed chair in what had served as the living room and bedroom for her and Pete, and she wept quietly until darkness came.

TWO
Late Summer, 1987

The owner and manager of the Many Pines Inn was a big, happy-looking man of forty-nine with thinning brown hair, gentle soft brown eyes, and a square, intelligent face. His name was Arnaut (pronounced Arno) Berge. He spoke, he explained, "with a little Armenian in my accent," because so many people found him difficult to understand. He was not Armenian, though. All of his life he had struggled mightily to master the flow and subtlety of the English language. It had been a struggle that had seen him advance by very slow degrees, so, telling people that he was Armenian was simpler and easier than telling them the truth.

Two children appeared before Arnaut on what he called the Great Lawn—just a stone's throw east of Many Pines' rambling main building—and asked him about using the inn's cavernous game room. He said, "Your Mum and your Daddy, they are where?"

"Asleep," answered a thin, broad-mouthed, white-faced boy of nine named Alec. "They were up real late," he added. "Foolin' around, making lotsa noise."

His sister, Cindy—a feminine miniature of himself, four years younger—giggled at that, and, upon a scornful look from her brother, put her hand over her mouth and continued giggling quietly.

Arnaut Berge's smile slipped a little, then reappeared. "I see," he said. "Then when they come awake you can go with them together and make employment of that room."

After a moment's deciphering what Arnaut Berge had told him, Alec protested, "Why can't we go there now?"

"It is for adult supervision," Arnaut answered. "Adults at all times must be constantly with you there."

Alec cocked his head. "Huh?"

"Because," Arnaut explained, "there are dangerous items in that room of some consequence."

Alec shook his head.

"You don't understand me?" Arnaut asked.

"They got a pool table in there, I saw it," Alec said.

"And . . ." started his sister.

"Space Invaders, too," Alec finished for her.

Arnaut decided on a new approach. "Have you breakfast within you?"

Alec smiled at that. He patted his flat belly beneath his Izod polo shirt and explained loudly—bathing Arnaut in an unpleasant mixture of smells —"Blueberry pancakes and sausages."

"Good," said Arnaut and checked his watch. It was 10 A.M. Many Pines' morning was well underway. At the boat dock, north, across the Great Lawn, several people in bathing suits were waiting under a hot late August sun to go water-skiing, or for a ride on Seventh Lake in *Martha,* the inn's small ferryboat, named after Arnaut's deceased wife. South, on the far side of the parking lot, the inn's four tennis courts had been in use since just before 7 A.M. The small, white-sand bathing beach, west of the boat dock, was filled to capacity, although it wasn't crowded; it was never crowded. Arnaut believed that no one liked crowded beaches or crowded inns, so he accepted no more than eighty guests at Many Pines at one time, leaving a little over a third of its rooms and cottages empty. That morning, there were sixty-eight guests at the inn, a dozen due to leave that afternoon and half a dozen others due to arrive for a week's stay before the inn closed on Labor Day.

Arnaut said to Alec and Cindy, "You can go to the beach."

Alec shook his big white head vehemently. "Don't know how to swim."

Arnaut grimaced a little at that. To his way of thinking, any child who didn't know how to swim before he could walk had a fool for a parent.

Cindy chimed in, "Me, too."

Arnaut let his smile return. Again he checked his watch. 10:02. He heard one of the water-skiing boats chug out toward the center of Seventh Lake. The lake was precariously shallow for water-skiing except near the center, where its depth, a local rumor had it, was uncharted. Arnaut had lived near the lake for fifteen years and had been owner and manager of the Many Pines Inn for ten years, so he knew better.

He put a big hand on Alec's bony shoulder. "You can go now and to use the game room, in there being of dangerous and expensive equipment, remind you, if there are also adults in there of whom there must be supervision."

Alec shook his head in miserable incomprehension of what Arnaut had told him.

Arnaut looked at Cindy, who was smiling sweetly. "Do you understand?" he asked her. Her sweet smile did not alter.

Alec said quickly, "You mean we can go and use the game room?"

Arnaut's smile broadened. "Yes. Oh yes. With the supervision of the adult people in there, of course."

Cindy said, parroting him, "Of course."

"Yeah, thanks," said Alec, took his sister's hand and led her back to the main building.

* * *

A mile away, on the southeast shore of Seventh Lake, Lynette Meyer was sitting on a rock at the water's edge. She had her bare feet in the water and had stripped down to her panties. She was on a section of shoreline that was well protected by brush from prying eyes, although she wasn't sure, anyway, of what use modesty was to a person like herself. Her body was certainly long past being attractive to any man, she thought, even to Pete, rest his soul. Before that awful night in January, he'd taken to making love to her in the pitch-dark—"Don't know what good it would do at a time like that to have to *look* at you, darlin'!" he explained; it went exactly counter to the way they'd made love in the first few years of their marriage, when she'd been forty pounds lighter and as close to being sweet and innocent as was possible for someone who couldn't remember ever *being* sweet and innocent.

She looked down at the two fleshy rolls of her belly and thought that if Pete were still around, there might well be another child in there. And if there were, then God help *her* and God help *it* because once it plopped out of her and into the world it would surely starve to death in a couple of days.

"Damn it almighty," she breathed, and let her head go back so she could feel the hot sun on her neck. She liked that feeling. It reminded her of Pete, who used to kiss her there, and his breath was always hot. Now there was no one, not even Harry Stans, Pete's best friend, who had come around for a while but lately made bad excuses about why he couldn't anymore. ("Gotta clean my tackle box, you know," and "Gotta go in to Eagle Bay"—the nearest town, fifteen miles north—"and get my tires rotated.") Lynette knew why he wasn't coming around. He'd found someone else. Someone thinner and prettier. (Lynette stopped herself there; chunky as she was, she knew she was still damn pretty), that woman's name was Myrna.

"Myrna," Lynette whispered. Pretty name. And from what she, Lynette, had seen of her she was a good and deserving woman. More power to her. And more power to Harry, too. A person had to take what she could from the world because the world for sure wasn't giving anything away.

Except maybe hot sunlight on the neck.

And the feel of cool water on feet bone tired from carrying a sick child about all night.

And, from time to time, the voice of a dead husband from out of nowhere to whisper to her the words he had whispered years ago.

In the water skiing boat, a man named Steve Volich saw Lynette from a distance of a quarter mile and riveted his gaze on her. He was at Many Pines with his brother-in-law, Larry, who'd come water-skiing with him, and his wife, Gloria, who'd chosen to stay on-shore and sunbathe.

Steve Volich said, without taking his eyes off Lynette, "Hey, Larry, look at that over there."

Larry looked up from adjusting the straps on his life preserver and called, above the growl of the inboard motor, "Did you say something, Steve?"

"Yeah." He glanced back at his brother-in-law, and, smirking, gestured with his chin at Lynette. "I said there's a woman over there with her titties hanging out."

The two men were among a group of six people who had chosen to go water-skiing that morning. The boat's pilot was a young, well-muscled, blond woman named Barbara who had a very dark tan and a clipped, officious way about her that was the result of shyness, but which most people mistook for brisk efficiency. She was closest to Steve when he made his pronouncement about Lynette and she said nothing.

Another young woman, sitting in front of Steve, glanced back and said, in clear annoyance, *"Titties! Titties!* Are you twelve?"

He gave her a flat, macho smile. "Puberty's gaining on me real fast."

Larry said into Steve's ear, "Yeah, I see her, but she's fat, Steve. F-A-T!"

Steve shrugged. "So what?" he said. "Parts is parts!" and they both laughed.

The boat's engine slowed while they were laughing. The boat came to a bouncing halt, and Barbara said to the six people who were looking to her for an explanation, "This is the starting point," put the ignition at idle, and continued, "Who among you has never been water-skiing before?"

The woman sitting in front of Steve answered, "I've been out only once, Barbara, when I was a kid, but I remember I got the hang of it pretty fast."

"Yes," said Barbara, "I see." She gave her a small, forgiving kind of grin, then said to the rest of the group, "Anyone else?"

A tall and painfully thin man standing at the bow of the boat in black Speedos said, "What's that down there?"

Barbara looked at him. "Sorry?"

He glanced back at her. "There's something down there," he called, and pointed to indicate an area twenty feet or so to starboard. "I don't know—it looks like the roof of a house, I think it looks like the roof of a house, Barbara." He gave them all a flat smile, as if in apology. "But it couldn't be . . . *that.* It's . . . something else, huh?"

"No."

"No?"

"It's the roof of a house," Barbara said.

The man in black Speedos gave her a quick, quizzical smile, then turned around and looked to starboard again. A young man and woman joined him, then Larry, Steve, and the woman who'd been sitting in front of him. Barbara watched them gather at the bow, listened for a few moments to their exclamations of surprise, then called to them, "It came from over there." They looked back at her almost in unison. She raised her long, well-muscled, nicely tanned arm and pointed at a small island covered with pine trees. "Dog Island," Barbara told them. It was only hollering distance east of the boat, which put it not quite a mile south of the Many Pines Inn.

Barbara went on, in her tone of brisk efficiency, "The house rests on a natural rock ledge, seventy-five feet down. The cold at that depth preserves it." The little group turned in awe to look starboard again. Barbara continued, "It's been there for quite a long time. Ten or eleven years, anyway."

"An entire house?" said the tall man incredulously.

Barbara nodded. "Yes. Furniture, rugs, dishes, linens." She paused a moment. "You can see the house only because the water here"—at the center of the lake—"is too acidic to support the growth of algae. It is, ironically, *too* clean to support the diversity of life that it once did, and that is quite unfortunately true of many Adirondack lakes." She smiled a tight-lipped smile, as if pleased with her little speech.

"Jees," said the thin man, "a whole house."

"A whole house, yes, sir," Barbara said.

Steve asked, "Are there any bodies down there—I mean, did anyone drown?"

"A family of four was in the house when it went down, sir," Barbara answered. "However, and very tragically, all of them had apparently been dead for several days."

* * *

Lynette Meyer saw the little group looking starboard over the bow of the waterskiing boat and she grinned knowingly. She'd witnessed the same scenario a dozen times in the past couple of years. *Local color*, Lynette imagined people thought of it—four poor souls dead from a leaking gas refrigerator, and a whole house sitting at the bottom of the lake. Lynette wasn't aware that it rested on a rock ledge nearly a hundred feet from the bottom. She had never actually seen the house, although she'd once been in a rowboat with Harry Stans and her husband, Pete, over the spot where it lay. And though they had coaxed her and cajoled her, she had refused to look. "Not int'risted," she'd told them. "Let those poor children down there rest in peace."

"Ain't just children," Pete said.

And Lynette reiterated, "And I ain't int'risted."

She watched now as the group slowly drifted away from the bow, watched as one of them, a woman who, Lynette thought, had the kind of body *she'd* once had, climbed down over the side of the boat, got her water skis on and took the towline from Barbara.

Lynette put her head back again, closed her eyes and let the hot morning sun caress her neck. Then she listened as Pete, making no more noise than a leaf falling, came to her down the brushy hillside that led to her cottage.

"Hello, darlin'," he whispered, and put his lips on her neck. "Hello, my darlin' sweet," he said, and she felt his hands move softly over her shoulders, then onto the high slopes of her breasts. In life, she thought, he had never touched her so lovingly and so sweetly. So maybe it was good that he was dead.

". . . clothes on!" she heard distantly. She opened her eyes. Pete's touch evaporated. She focused on the waterskiing boat and saw a man on it who seemed to have his hands cupped around his mouth. She heard, "Put your clothes on." Then, a moment later, ". . . scare the fish." She grimaced, reached to her right, got her shirt off the side of the rock she was sitting on—the shirt was a size too large for her; it had been Pete's—got her jeans and her house slippers from the upper part of the rock, put them on, and trundled up through the thick brush to her cottage.

When she got there, she found that her daughter's fever of the night before had returned.

THREE

The interior of Many Pines' main building was like a maze. It hadn't always been that way. A succession of owners since the building's construction in 1893 had added several wings and nearly thirty-five additional rooms to the inn's original twenty, and their construction efforts had been hurried, at best. Consequently, one eight-foot-high hallway suddenly became a seven-foot-high hallway where it joined the main building with one of its wings; at two points, on the east and west side of the main building, there were doors which were kept permanently locked because they led absolutely nowhere. This was the handiwork of the inn's third owner, who had calculated that two additional wings would allow him to accommodate dozens of additional tourists each summer. He hadn't calculated on a miserable, rainy summer and dozens of cancellations, so the frames he had erected for the additional wings had to come down when he found himself on the brink of financial ruin.

From above, with its roofs lifted off, the inn's hallways would not have looked so much labyrinthine as anarchic, as if the mind which had conceived them were disoriented and, aware of it, amused by it—as if it had created some perverse joke, a human ant farm.

There was also no real plan in the layout of the inn's lakeside cottages, which, like the inn itself, and despite their prettily sculptured knotty pine doors, bore a sturdy utilitarian look, as do so many Adirondack buildings.

The cabins had been part of the inn's rustic ambiance since the turn of the century. It was thought by the original owners that people came to visit the Adirondacks out of a strong, if temporary, need to get away from things artificial and to be part of what was *real, organic, natural*—the terms changed with the decades. Five cottages were built first. Each was a rough-looking, two-room, Lincoln-log affair with no indoor plumbing and a massive stone fireplace as the only heat source. Two of these cabins burned in the forties and were replaced by larger, frame buildings sporting rough-hewn pine clapboard and Adirondack-style gingerbread trim—short, narrow pine logs stripped of bark and arranged under peaks and roof edges in various triangular patterns. Three more of these buildings were constructed a decade later, and five years after that, all eight of the lakeside cabins were equipped with oil-fired furnaces, electricity, and indoor plumbing. It had been decided by the inn's third owners that rustic was fine, but Spartan was a pain in the ass for guests.

Cabin furnishings—which Arnaut Berge occasionally had to augment or replace with pieces culled from yard sales or antique shops in the area—were not as comfortable as the furnishings in the rooms at the inn. Beds were comfortable enough, but other furniture, as one guest put it, "looked to be a mixture of Salvation Army, art deco and fifties modernist; a thoroughly drab combination." But this very drabness, it was found, was what people who stayed in the cabins were looking for. They had come to the Adirondacks not for furnishings but for air and view, and to get close again to nature, for however short a time. Arnaut did not mind that some guests referred to the cabin furnishings as "rustic tacky."

The only compromise he made to style was in the use of Adirondack chairs. These were made of wide, flat wooden slats with huge, rounded flat wooden arms, and seat backs which sunk a good four or five inches lower than the seat fronts.

When he took over the inn in 1977, Arnaut knew that it was going to provide him with a myriad of continual challenges, from keeping up with building codes, to satisfying fire inspectors, keeping guests happy (and warm on cool Adirondack summer nights), fending off the continuous onslaught of insects that had gotten into the inn's woodwork and were intent on building a future for themselves, and keeping the area's wildlife no closer than shouting distance. This was difficult. More than once, on early morning tours of the inn's grounds, Arnaut had come upon a deer, a brown bear, a raccoon, or family of opossums that had wandered into the tennis courts or even into the small open area between the cabins and the inn. He usually managed to easily shoo these trespassers away. He knew that although many of his guests enjoyed seeing them from a distance, they would be uneasy, at best, about sharing their "civilized space"—the space around the inn—with them.

Arnaut's idea of the purpose of Many Pines —beyond its promise as a money-maker—was to get city people in touch with their real roots. He thought of the inn not only as his home, but as the place where he would want to be put to rest.

The floors in all the inn's hallways had been inlaid with small octagonal ceramic tiles laid out in a black and white checkerboard pattern. These floors had proved very hard to care for and keep clean. The current caretaker, Francis Carden, spent much of his time repairing or replacing tiles that had worked loose over the decades since they'd been put down. He had once calculated that there were at least a thousand feet of these floors at the inn and that he had, in the eighteen months he'd been its caretaker, repaired at least three hundred feet of them.

He also spent much of his time repairing the gray stone tile roofs. There were three roofs and their pitch was precipitous, but once he was up on them he found the view engrossing. Several times, he had gotten carried away with it, had started sliding toward the edge and had been able to stop his slide only by jamming the claw of his hammer into the top edge of a metal tile anchor.

The view he had on the roofs was at once panoramic and also oddly claustrophobic, as if the land and lake around the inn were suddenly going to curl in on itself. To the south, the land was flat and green for a good mile and a half; to the west, a high, pine-covered hill—called Bear Mountain by local people—crested steeply; to the north, Seventh Lake seemed to rise slightly at the horizon, as if the lake were, impossibly, higher than the land level. Carden guessed it was an illusion created by the fact that the mountains beyond the opposite shore were at a good distance and lost in a bluish haze, while closer mountains, to the extreme west and east, were much more clearly delineated. This gave the lake a compelling, forward look.

A mile to the west of the inn, there were small summer cottages with steep white, black, and pink roofs set brightly against the lush, flat green of the mountains beyond. These cottages were laid out like Monopoly pieces along the shore.

Across the lake, a mile and a half northwest of Many Pines, there was a year-round tavern called The Squeeze Inn. Its clientele consisted of vacationers in the summer, and year-round people in the spring, fall, and winter.

It was an observation by Francis Carden to Arnaut,

toward the end of Many Pines' summer season, that led to Arnaut's decision to reopen the inn after the New Year.

"You know," he said, "this time next year you're going to lose the west wing to termites. And the year after that, the north wing is going to crumble from dry rot."

It was not the first time that Arnaut had heard of the termites and the dry rot that plagued the inn, but it was the first time he had been given to believe that the problems were so immediate. He said, "You're kidding."

Carden shook his gray head. "I don't kid about things like that, Arnaut, because I don't want to be the one your inn falls down on."

"I was unaware—" Arnaut began.

"You are now," Carden interrupted.

"What's the salutation?" Arnaut asked.

Carden, who often got the general drift of what Arnaut was talking about on the first go around, answered, "The solution is to rebuild, Arnaut. Either rebuild or load this sucker up with chlordane."

"Chlordane?"

"Insecticide. It'll kill the termites. It'll also probably kill anything else that comes around."

Arnaut looked confused and sad. "I don't want to do that," he said. "And I have no money to rebuild."

Carden shrugged. "Then what you got to do is stay open a while longer."

From that point, the idea was formulated to reopen the inn during January and February for cross-country skiing. Several other inns in the Adirondacks lake region had done it and it had proved successful.

Lynette Meyer could hear herself whimpering as she woke in her small, overstuffed chair. She opened her eyes wide. It was a hot early evening, the sun gone, except for a dull, peach-colored smudge through a break in the pines. The heat wouldn't last, she knew. The thin air in the Adirondacks could not hold it long.

And the dream clung to her. She threw herself forward in the chair so her elbows were on her knees and her face was in her hands. "Dammit almighty!" she breathed. The dream clung hard to her.

It had a color. Deep blue. The color of cold. And a time and place. A winter evening. On the fringes of the lake. She was there with Pete's axe in hand. She had furiously chopped a wide hole in the thick ice and now was standing back from it and watching as *they* appeared from beneath, smiling their big empty smiles.

She whimpered again. She wanted desperately to chase the dream away.

Her son said to her, "Mama, Jolene is real sick."

And they came up one by one through that wide hole she had chopped for them in the ice.

"Mama?"

And turned to the east and made their way single file through the knee-deep snow that crowded the shoreline, to the place of warmth, to Many Pines, empty for the winter, where they could lie very still for a good long time and no one would know the difference.

"Jolene is real sick, real sick, Mama."

"Yes, Pete, yes."

"And she's real hot, too, Mama. Like she's on fire!"

Forty-Five Minutes Gone

The wail of an ambulance siren was an uncommon occurrence around Seventh Lake and it made Arnaut Berge look up from the letter he was writing to his daughter and listen a few moments. He guessed that the ambulance was going west, toward the little group of year-round cottages on the other side of the lake. He got up, went to a window that looked out on Route 43, a couple of hundred feet away and clearly visible beyond the inn's tennis courts and parking lots. He saw the ambulance. The words EAGLE BAY VOLUNTEERS were painted in bold red letters on its side. In a moment it was gone, and Arnaut waited for the noise of its siren to dissipate almost completely before he went back to his desk to finish his letter. Whatever tragedy the ambulance had been responding to, it was almost without a doubt some accident—a fall, a car crash, perhaps a hunting accident—because the people there, in those cottages, were dirt poor, certainly, but everyone knew that they were also robustly healthy. It was the hard work that made them that way; hard work all year long just to eke out an existence in these mountains. Arnaut could not imagine that one of them was ill. Illness simply did not strike mountain people. It struck the kinds of people who came to Many Pines on vacation—the middle-aged professionals who supposed that the mountain air would clean their lungs out and renew them for their battles with civilization. Arnaut did not think these thoughts in so many words. He knew that the people who came to his inn were not strictly of a type—not strictly middle-aged professionals with heart problems or alcohol problems or high blood pressure. There were the others, too. The young ones whose parents had come to Many Pines and had passed the word on about what a "change of pace" it was, and the old ones who had come to Many Pines years and years ago, when it had belonged to someone else. Arnaut liked it when these old people came to him and told him that the inn was "just as good" as they remembered. He liked the idea of keeping pleasant memories alive, and he regretted, now, as he'd already said in his letter to his daughter, having to close the inn until January. Labor Day traditionally marked the end of the tourist season in the Adirondacks. After that the nights were too cold and the days too short. A hard freeze often set in then.

He continued writing, "So there has been an ambulance coming by and I hope for no bad that it has responded to but I think otherwise, it being the way I have of seeing things. You know that, Mary." He paused. He could hear the ambulance again, on its return trip. He waited for the siren to wind down, then continued writing: "Closing the inn is not a good thing for me and so, also, to tell these people who have worked here all summer that the work has fled. For such reasons it's advantages to us that I am throwing it open again in January." He thought a moment. Mary liked his letters. "The longer the better," she'd told him. "They're so quirky." He wasn't sure what she meant, but he was perfectly willing to accommodate her. He continued writing: "So there is the fact of the winter people who will be coming in four months for the skiing trails and I hope it is not a woebegone experience for me to have them—and this is the first time because of the money for the repairs to the inn."

HISTORY—JULY 1, 1976

Anita Mosiman leaned over the kitchen sink and opened the window that Ben, her husband, had shut. She felt a cool breeze move into the house. "Well, *I* like it here," she protested. "All of us do." *All of us* included herself, her father, Joe Archer, and her children, Max, eight, and Catherine, six. Apparently —miserably, Anita thought—it did not include Ben, though it had been his idea in the first place to move here. She glanced back at him. He was sitting on a high wooden stool behind a counter where breakfasts and lunches were eaten; dinners were usually eaten at a round oak table in one corner of the big living room. He was bent over, with his crossed arms on the countertop and his chin resting on his wrists. He was scowling. Anita went on, "What's not to like, Ben?"

"Mosquitoes," he grumbled. "And black flies."

Anita shrugged. "So who likes mosquitoes and black flies? *I* don't. But I don't dwell on them, I don't let them get inside my brain and nibble away at my good times."

Ben grumbled, "And sweating in the day and freezing at night, and spiders in the damn john, and worrying myself nauseous about the kids floating off into the lake and never coming back—" He stopped. Anita had held her hand up.

She said, "All of which is worlds worse, of course, than worrying about the kids going to the playground and never coming back, and trying to coexist with next-door neighbors who've got their big ears plastered to the walls, and . . . and having to quadruple lock the damn doors, and . . ." She stopped. He was grinning at her. She hated being grinned at when she was angry. She turned away.

He said, "I'm going to tell you something, my love. It may surprise you—hell, it may knock your socks off, but here it is: I made a *mistake.* I thought this would be a wonderful place to live, I thought it would open my head and clear my sinuses and get me in touch with . . . with whatever. But I was wrong, I was wrong, and I'm admitting it now so we can get our fannies in gear and our lives straight. We were never meant to live here, Anita. We are city people. We need crowds and noise and car exhausts and pizza parlors and . . . and tension."

She gave him a confused look.

He straightened on the stool and nodded briskly. "That's right," he declared. "Tension! You know what's going to happen to us out here, in the middle of this lake, Anita, our blood is going to turn to . . . to water. We're going to turn into . . . cocoons!" He stopped. He liked that. He continued, "There is no damned tension here, Anita! We need tension. People need tension!"

She said, "Cocoons, Ben?"

He gave her a shrug. "Well, you know . . ."

"Cocoons?" she said again, and smiled.

He said, "It fits."

She sighed. "Can you give us another week?"

He looked embarrassed. "It's not my decision alone, Anita, don't lay that on me."

Max, their eight-year-old, burst into the room through the side door. "Catherine's missing!" he declared. "I can't find Catherine!"

Joe Archer, Anita's father, came in. He had a wide-eyed, helpless, apologetic look about him. He shook his old head miserably. "She ain't in the lake, Anita, she ain't in the lake! Gawd, she must be in the house . . ."

"Damn you!" Ben shouted at him, got off his stool, came quickly around to Max, leaned over, took hold of his thin shoulders. "Where did you last see her, Max? Now think!"

Anita stood by openmouthed. She was feeling helpless and trying hard to fight back the panic that was building inside her.

Max stammered, "Near the pond . . . near the pond . . ."

Joe Archer, who had been looking at his grandson's lips and so realized what the boy had said, cut in, "No, Ben, no, she wasn't nowhere near the pond, not nowhere near it!"

Catherine appeared in the open doorway that Max

and Joe Archer had come through. She smiled a huge, devilish smile. "Couldn't find me, huh?" she teased.

Barbara, the waterskiing instructor, surprised Arnaut in the gazebo. It was a quiet place. In summer there was often the steady drone of honeybees flying from their hive—down the slight slope to the lake—to a growth of cultivated wildflowers between the gazebo and the inn. But in the evening, in early September, there was only a fluid, comfortable coolness. The gazebo never got as cold as the outside air—a phenomenon Arnaut had noted more than once—even though it stood at the end of a narrow peninsula that pushed a hundred feet out into Seventh Lake.

"Hello," Barbara said.

Arnaut chirped, "Hello," and grinned sheepishly. "You gave me a shove."

"A shove?"

"A startle."

"You mean I gave you a start?"

"Yes."

She touched his arm. "Sorry," she said. "It's beautiful here, isn't it?" She nodded to the west, where the sky was a fragile pale blue touched gently by rust. "Especially now."

He nodded. "It is beautiful. It's very . . . temporary. You can see that." He was standing at a waist-high treated pine railing that circled most of the perimeter of the gazebo. He had his hands on the railing and Barbara could see that he was gripping it very hard. "Something wrong?" she asked.

He shook his head, put his hands in the pockets of his jacket, gave her a smile. "Thank you. No. Only thoughts."

It was clearly an invitation for her to ask, "What thoughts?" She said, "Oh, then I'm disturbing you."

Again he shook his head. "Who's disturbed? It's

good to have company." He took his hands from his pockets and put them on the railing again. He looked out at the lake. His gaze fell on Dog Island. He lingered on it.

Barbara said, "What thoughts?"

He did not hesitate. He said, eyes still on the island, "Thoughts about my wife."

"Oh," Barbara whispered, uncertain what he wanted her to say but feeling that he merely needed to talk.

He nodded to indicate the lake. "An accident killed her here. Eight years ago."

"I know. I'm sorry."

He turned his head, gave her a brief, flat smile of thanks, looked at the lake again. "And so I come in here to be with her."

"I understand that."

"Not that she came in here, ever," Arnaut said. "Of course she couldn't have." He smiled at Barbara again; she looked away. He looked back at the lake. "She couldn't have come in here because there was no gazebo then. When she was alive. There were trees here. That was all. She liked to walk within them. She dwelt within them happily."

"And still does?"

Arnaut gave her a quick, broad smile. "That pleases me. Yes. And still does." He tapped his temple. "But maybe just in here."

Barbara smiled back. "And that's all right."

"Of course it is. It's all right." He gave her an apologetic smile, as if he had sounded gruff, though he hadn't. He went on, "If she walked here in . . . realism, in all her . . . physicalness, maybe I would hardly say a thing to her. Not hello. A grunt only, perhaps."

Barbara said, "And I understand that, too. It's better that the dead exist just in memory. I don't know if we'd have any idea how to deal with them otherwise."

During their short conversation, the sun had set, the pale blue sky touched gently with rust had changed to gray, and then, more quickly, to black. It was the way such things happened in the Adirondacks. And the only light on Barbara and Arnaut was what filtered through the pines between the inn and the gazebo—a soft, creamy light, like the luminous hands of a watch, the kind of light that seems to flow rather than reflect.

Arnaut said, "The lake has vanished."

Barbara said, "Not entirely."

Arnaut said, "I think sometimes that she is there, in that lake, drowning again and again."

The whisper of a breeze pushing over the surface of the lake slid up the short slope and into the gazebo, gave them both a chill, and was spent. Across the lake, the lights of a house winked on, off, then on again, as if someone leaving had decided to stay.

Barbara said, "Oh," and there was no inflection in it, no hint as to what she meant.

Arnaut said, "It would be an awful way to exist, of course."

Barbara nodded.

Arnaut said, "It was near the island. That island. Dog Island." He nodded to indicate it, though it was not visible because of the darkness. "They found her there. At shore. On Dog Island."

Barbara said, "I'm sorry. I *am* disturbing you. Excuse me," and she began to leave.

Arnaut reached out, took her arm. She stopped, looked at him. "No. You're not," he said, and she heard a pleading quality in his voice. "I am more disturbed . . . I think I am more disturbed without you here. Because you were right. How would we deal with them? How can I deal with her? I can deal with her only here." He touched his temple. "Because she is alive here." He looked in the direction of Dog Island. "There she is not."

Barbara shook her head. "It's chilly. I'm sorry. I'm going to go in." With a little twist of her arm she was free of his grasp, which hadn't been tight, and in a moment was gone.

Arnaut listened to her walk over the bed of pine needles on the path to the inn; her footfalls made a sound like wet paper being crumpled. Early in the morning, in late spring and summer, he had listened at his window and had heard just such sounds often. He knew who made them. Martha. His wife. Back from Dog Island. Back from the lake to walk.

FOUR
Early January, 1988

"The cold and me—why we're old friends, Mr. Berge," said the fat man at the registration counter. His name was Walt Roman and he puffed his chest out when he talked.

"Arnaut," Arnaut corrected.

"For sure," Roman bellowed. He looked confused. "What's that?"

"Arnaut. It's my name. Arnaut."

"It is?" The man glanced at his wife, a thin woman with short, graying, curly hair who was looking at a display of postcards at one end of the registration counter. "Mitzi, this guy's name is Arnaut. Fancy that!"

She glanced over, nodded, said, "That's nice," and continued rummaging through the postcards.

Arnaut gave them both a flat, noncommittal smile. He wasn't sure what "fancy that" meant and he wasn't at all sure, either, how well he and this man were going to get along.

The man explained, "My damn cousin's name is Arnaut. Arnaut Peters. Used to be Petersak but he didn't want no one knowing he was Polish so he changed it."

"I'm Armenian," Arnaut said.

"And that's all right by me," the man bellowed. "You be anything you wanta be, Arnaut."

Arnaut said, handing Roman the key to Deer Cabin, at the middle of the row of eight cabins along the lakeshore, "Please I hope your stay with us at Many Pines is memorable, Mr. Roman."

The man's face lit up. "You're a character and a half, Mr. Arnaut."

"No, just Arnaut. My last name is Berge. My entire name is Arnaut Berge. Thank you."

"You betcha. Arnaut it is." He pocketed his key, looked at his wife again, who'd selected several post-cards and was holding them the way she might a poker hand. "Keep 'em, Mitzi," he said. "I'm sure old Arnaut here can stand the loss, right, Arnaut?"

Arnaut nodded at once. "Certainly. They are of no value. Keep them, Mrs. Roman."

"Mitzi," her husband said. "Call her Mitzi."

She said, "You got the key, Wally?"

"I got the key."

She put the postcards on the counter. "Then let's get outa here, okay. It's stuffy."

Mitzi and Walter Roman were followed, a quarter of an hour later, by a young couple with an infant in a portable bassinet. The couple were a good match. They could have been twins, Arnaut thought—both were tall, he a touch over six feet, and she barely an inch shorter. Both had long, oval faces, turned-up noses, wide, full mouths, and skin as flawless and creamy as a five-year-old's. They were like oversized pixies, Arnaut told himself. Each of them also wore a constant look of surprise or excitement that altered only as much as the benign expression on the face of an animal changes from minute to minute.

Arnaut thought at first that these large pixies were not very bright.

The man stuck his hand out. Arnaut took it. The man let go almost at once. "We are the Glynns," he explained. He stuck his hand out again, again Arnaut took it, shook it a moment, and the man let go. "My name is Jeff. My wife's name is Amy." She balanced the portable bassinet precariously on one thin arm and tried valiantly to offer Arnaut her free hand, but the counter was too wide and her angle too restrictive so while Arnaut was saying, "That is okay, please, the baby will drop," she was withdrawing her hand and taking the bassinet in both arms again.

"We made reservations," Jeff Glynn said.

Arnaut nodded. "You are in the room behind you."

The man looked through the glass door, past the driveway at another door, the east wing of the inn; the door had the number 8 on it. He looked back at Arnaut and asked, "Is it quiet?" then nodded to indicate the bassinet his wife carried. "Our child is a light sleeper."

Arnaut answered, "No, it is not always the highest elevation of quiets. In summer it is a distraction of cacaphonies owing to the cars lumbering past all the while, and so I only seldom let it out." He grinned a small, secretive grin, having, he was sure, uttered one of his few masterfully constructed sentences, and went on, "But today, so much out of season, that is somehow not the same. Now it is the unearthliest of quiets."

Glynn frowned. His wife said pleasantly, "It sounds wonderful, Mr. Berge."

"Yes," said her husband, though clearly unconvinced. "But we do, of course, have the right to switch rooms if we aren't satisfied?"

"You have all sorts of rights," Arnaut said smiling, "being the guests of Many Pines Inn."

"I'll take that as a yes," Glynn said, accepted the key from Arnaut, and, as his wife struggled after him with the bassinet, went to room number eight.

Jean Ward and her brother, Dave, arrived moments later.

It was not the first time that Lynette Meyer had been on Seventh Lake in a rowboat, but it was the first time she'd been out so late in the year—when ice had already formed around the shoreline—and being on the lake itself was like being in front of an open refrigerator. It was also the first time she'd been out on the lake alone. Pete had taken her out a couple of times, to keep him company as he fished, and Harry, when he'd been courting her, had taken her out one mild spring day to read poetry to her. That had come off badly because he did not read well, the poetry he'd chosen had not been to her liking—"The boy stood on the burning deck . . ." and "The Cremation of Sam McGee"—and it had been very much out of character for him, anyway. He apparently had believed it was the romantic thing to do, and he'd done it, she realized, hoping that it would get her into bed with him. But she'd sat tight-lipped and gloomy through it all, until he rowed back to shore, made some lame excuse about why he couldn't stay (he was clearly embarrassed) and had gone home.

Today she was dressed as warmly as possible, in several sweaters and a gray wool coat that had belonged to Pete, and though she was accustomed to Adirondack winters, she shivered as she rowed.

She was on Seventh Lake because she was giving thanks, and what better place to do it than where God could see her—in the middle of a clear lake under a clear blue sky with clear thoughts and clear words.

"Thank you, God," she said. She lifted her head and focused on nothing, because there was nothing to focus on. She was not far from Dog Island. Many Pines was visible a mile off, on the eastern shore. Lynette's small cottage, where Pete Jr. was taking a late afternoon nap, was three-quarters of a mile west.

"Thank you, God," she said again. It was her idea that God did not particularly care if words of thanks and appreciation varied from one moment to the next. Perhaps it was even better if they didn't; perhaps the repetition made the thanks and appreciation seem even more sincere. "Thank you, God," she repeated. "Thank you, God!" She conjured up a smile now, and imagined that it looked plump and meaningful with the afternoon sunlight on it. "Thank you, God, oh, thank you, God." She felt her smile enlarge, and so she closed her eyes to ride the flow of her good feelings and thankfulness. "Thank you God, oh, thank you, thank you!" She shivered with the intensity of her good feeling. She threw her hands into the frigid air. "Thank you!" she yelled. "Thank you, thank you!"

She felt the boat quiver on the smooth, cold surface of the lake. She let her arms drop and looked first left, then right, over the gunwales. She had a quizzical look on her face as she smiled, and the picture that gave her of herself ruined the moment she was enjoying so she stopped smiling and took the oars in hand. Giving thanks for the life of her daughter Jolene was done and surely God was pleased.

Jolene would come home sooner or later. Better later, after the winter was through, which, considering the care she needed, was the most likely time she'd be back. (If she was going to come back at all. "How can you see to the upbringing of two little children, dear?" the nurse had asked. "You can hardly see to your own needs. And now there's bound to be a welfare case-worker coming to visit; this is a clear case of neglect, you know.")

Again the boat quivered, as if something had swum beneath it and had arched its back for a moment, not quite touching the underside. Lynette stopped rowing, held the oars up, half a foot above the surface of the lake, and again looked right and left over the gunwales. She saw ripples no wider than a child's fingers.

The boat quivered again, and again, and there were more ripples, the size of her own fingers now, and she peered intently at them because they had an odd color

and texture, not the smooth blue of the water but black
and geometric, as if, she thought, she were looking at
the tiles on the roof of a house.

"Damn it almighty!" she breathed, dipped the oars
into the water once more and began rowing. Damn it
almighty! Why in hell had she come out here? She
knew this spot. Why would she want to see that house
down there? She wouldn't, she had no *need* to see it
and no *desire* to see it! Let them rest in peace, let them
rest forever down there in peace!

She rowed faster, and as she rowed she thought
beneath her anger and her confusion that the same
thing under the boat was arching its back continually,
sending tiny shivers through the hull.

On Dog Island, at dusk that same day, a man named
John Kennedy (who had explained a thousand times in
his forty-three years that he was in no way related to
"the real John Kennedy," and that his middle name
wasn't Fitzgerald, either, it was Warren) had made the
quick hike from the island's northwest side to its south
side.

He had crab-walked down a short and muddy slope
which led to the perimeter of the island (it could not be
called a shore; there was no shore, per se—the island
dropped off precipitously at its edges; twenty feet out
the water was nearly twenty feet deep) and he was
looking at the back wall of a white, two-story clapboard house. He was on the island because for years
he'd had a love affair with islands. He thought they
were romantic, that they suited his independent way of
living. He had first seen Dog Island three hours earlier,
on a flight over Seventh Lake in a seaplane on his way
to The Squeeze Inn, at the Lake's northwest side. His
wife was scheduled to meet him there at 8 P.M., which,
he realized, gave him more than enough time to rent a

boat and explore Dog Island (he thought it was a fitting name because, from above, the island looked much like the profile of a dog).

The back wall of the house he was looking at bore two windows, one beneath the peak of the roof and one to the left on the first floor as he faced the house. Both windows were bare of curtains. The bottom half of the attic window stood open. On the ground at the center of the back wall there was a large black tank for propane. The tank bore a patina of rust along its top edge. The rust ran in rivulets down the sides through the black paint from beneath a thick, moist layer of pine needles. One of four thin green metal legs screwed into short pieces of thick wood that held the tank up had rusted away completely. John supposed, upon seeing this, that the leg had rusted because it was closest to the water and that the tides brought the water level up close to the bottom of the tank.

The house stood on short, thick, rectangular stilts. John could see only two of these stilts from where he stood. He thought fleetingly as he looked at them that the years had taken their toll and that before long the stilts would crumble and pitch the house into the lake.

FIVE
January 10

Walt Roman and his wife, Mitzi, lay side by side in their bed in Deer Cabin. It had taken him longer than usual to recover his breath after orgasm and that concerned him. He asked, "Mitzi, honey, would you say that I'm an asshole?"

She didn't answer, so Walt rolled to his side—a gargantuan effort for him because of his massive belly—and tried to see her in the darkness. He saw little—the outline of her small nose, the severe slope of her forehead. He said, "I mean it. Am I an asshole?"

She smacked her lips and took a couple of deep breaths. It meant, he knew, that the topic at hand was either not to her liking, that it was boring, or that it had been discussed before and so needn't be discussed again. She said nothing.

"I'm not kidding," Walt insisted. "I need to know."

Again Mitzi smacked her lips. "Sort of," she said.

This took him aback. He had wanted her to confirm what he suspected about himself, that he was outspoken and congenial to a fault, but that he was not, after all, an asshole. He rolled to his back and closed his eyes. "Sort of?" he whispered. "You wanta explain that?"

"Sure," she said aloud, clearly relishing her words. "Everyone's 'sort of' an asshole, Walt. Even me. It's just that some people, like you, are *more* sort of . . . assholish than other people and that's because of your upbringing, I guess, which you can't be blamed for."

"So that's what you think? You think I'm an asshole?"

"I think you're my husband."

"Shit, that's not what I asked."

"It's what I have to say, Walt. Now go to sleep."

He said, "Don'tchoo even wanta know why I asked? Huh? Don't that concern you?"

"I know why, Walt."

"You know why?"

"Yes. I was with you there too. Remember? I heard them talking, too. You think I'm deaf?"

There were sixteen people, eight couples, at the inn. Several of these couples were there for only a week, several others for two weeks—to accommodate their vacation time; when they left, others were due to arrive, and a few, Walt and Mitzi Roman, Jeff and Amy Glynn, Dave Ward and his sister, Jean, were there for the season.

Walt Roman said, "You know, it's only assholes that call other people assholes behind their backs."

She said nothing.

"Don't you think that's true, Mitzi?"

"I think," she said, "that we came here to do some cross-country skiing and we haven't seen a snowflake yet."

January 11: Night

Dave Ward said to his sister, Jean, seated next to him on an ancient, green aluminum settee on the screened-in porch of their four-room lake cabin, five hundred feet east of Many Pines' main building, "That's why I say we should've gotten a room at the inn, because we'd be closer to the other people. Don't you *want* to be closer to the other people, Jean?"

Jean hugged herself for warmth, though she was

dressed warmly enough—in jeans, blue ski mittens, and a blue ski jacket. She said nothing.

"Huh?" Dave coaxed.

"That's a dumb question," she said.

They were on the porch because they had started a fire in the fireplace and had neglected to open the flue. The cabin had quickly filled with smoke and now, its front doors and windows open, was airing out.

Dave Ward fidgeted on the settee and said, in paraphrase of comments he'd made several times, "This damn thing is damned uncomfortable. Why the hell don't they get some damned *civilized* furniture?"

The cabin was a very short stone's throw from Seventh Lake. On the night before, when the wind was up, Jean and Dave had heard the comforting rhythmic white noise of the waves from their bedrooms at the center of the cabin. Tonight, the air was very still and the lake was calm. The ice at the shoreline had thickened and widened.

Dave nodded to indicate a long string of plastic lanterns, each with a yellow Christmas tree bulb inside. The lanterns were hung over a walkway made of wooden slats, like apple crates taken apart and laid end to end, that led west past seven other cabins—theirs was farthest from the inn—to the main building. Dave said, "Now why the hell would that guy do that?"

"What guy?" Jean asked.

"You know what guy. That guy. That Arnaut guy. Why the hell would he want to go and hang those stupid lanterns up?"

"I like them," Jean said. "They're nice. They're romantic."

"No, they're not. They're stupid. They're not bright enough. Someone could trip and fall and that guy would have a damn lawsuit on his hands."

"Then that would be his problem, wouldn't it?"

Dave grinned at her. "I'm pissing you off, right?"

"Right."

"I'm raining on your damn parade, right?"

"Right."

"I've been raining on it ever since we got here, right?"

"Wrong."

His smile faded. "Wrong?"

"You've been raining on my parade a lot longer than that, Dave."

His grin returned. He let his gaze follow the line of yellow lanterns that curved gracefully as it followed the wooden walkway toward the main building; the walkway itself curved to follow the shoreline. He said, "You wanta fucking elaborate on that, Jean?"

"No," she said.

"I think you oughta elaborate on it. If you got some complaint, then I think I oughta hear what it is."

"No. No complaints. I'm tired, that's all. And I'm cold."

He looked at her. His grin became a sneer. "The whole world's tired and cold, sis." He stood quickly, which, because he was stocky and tall, caused the settee to slide backward an inch or two on the porch and made Jean lurch forward, thinking the settee was going to topple. "Christ, Dave!"

"I'm going to go and find Jeff," he said, referring to Jeff Glynn, with whom he'd shared a few beers that day at Many Pines' bar.

Jean said nothing.

"Maybe we'll go into Eagle Bay or Old Forge"—two towns within an hour's drive of the inn—"and see if we can find some action."

Still she said nothing. She wasn't looking at him; she was looking at the walkway. There was a man on it, in front of the neighboring cabin. The man was looking at her. He was tall, in his fifties, she guessed, and his stance was very erect. He was dressed casually, in a white shirt, bulky yellow sweater, and baggy gray pants, as if for an afternoon of early spring gardening. She cocked her head slightly at him, then gave him a tiny nod. He stayed still.

Dave rattled on, "You wanna come with me? A little *action* might do you some good, sis." He grinned.

She said nothing. The man on the walkway turned his head an inch so his gaze was on Dave.

Dave went on, certain now that he was annoying Jean, "Okay. Have it your way. But it might be morning by the time I get back. I can't promise you it won't be morning."

"Why would I care what you do with your time?" she asked.

He chuckled. "Because I'm going to be having lots more fun than you." And with that, he turned, went down the porch steps to the wooden walkway, and started toward the main building. He stopped, looked back, and called, "Don't wait up!" Then, after nodding at the man watching him and saying, "Hi, pal, you're gonna freeze your nuts off dressed like that," moved at a half walk, half dance toward the main building, his shoes making hollow, clop-clop noises on the wooden walkway.

The man looked briefly at Jean. She thought there was something vaguely questioning about him, as if he had lost his way from one cabin to another and was too embarrassed to ask her for directions.

She said, in an effort to put him at ease, "Hello. Quiet evening, isn't it?"

He said nothing. He turned his gaze briefly in the direction that Dave had gone, then looked back at Jean. A very slow smile came to him, as if there were pleasure in him that started at the point of zero and ascended, as slowly as mercury in a thermometer, to the point of fever.

Jean asked him, "Are you okay, sir?"

He said nothing. His smile of pleasure was broad but apparently toothless and she could see no gleam whatever in his eyes.

He turned toward Many Pines' main building and his face, in three-quarter profile, was well illuminated for only a moment by one of the overhanging lanterns. Jean saw that she had not guessed his age accurately, that he was decades older than his fifties, that there was a latticework of lines on his face and that his skin seemed to have no pigment at all—neither pink, nor gray, nor white—but came close to translucence, and she imagined that she could see the stiff line of cheek and jawbone beneath. Then his back was to her and he was making his way in slow, shuffling steps toward Many Pines' main building.

After several moments, Jean went back into the cabin. The smoke had cleared. She went to the fireplace, sat cross-legged in front of it, and stoked the fire rhythmically. She enjoyed the dancing sparks, the quick flames, the warmth.

She was nearly asleep when she heard her brother calling to her. She had a small windup alarm clock on the dresser near her bed and when she glanced at it she saw that it was close to 1:30.

"What do you want?" she called.

"Jean?" she heard again; she realized at once that there was confusion in his voice. "Jean?"

"What *is* it?" she called again.

"Jean?"

She got out of bed, put on a white terry cloth robe, padded through the cabin's short hallway in her bare feet, through the small living room—there were still some live embers in the fireplace, she noticed—and then to the porch. The plastic lanterns had been turned off and she could see little except the crisp outlines of snowflakes against the light of a long fluorescent tube outside the inn's main entrance five hundred feet away. "Dave?" she called, and hugged herself tightly for warmth. "Dave, where are you?"

"Jean?" he called back. This time she sensed more than confusion in his voice, she sensed fear and —improbably, she thought—amusement, as well, like someone calling from a roller coaster. She flicked the switch for the floodlight at the center of the porch roof. It illuminated the beach in front of the cabin and several yards of lake beyond. Dave was there, in the lake, in his jeans and shirt and denim jacket. He was facing her and had his arms wide as if to balance himself. The water was at his knees and he was walking slowly backward, his body leaning first right, then left, in time with his slow, short, awkward steps.

She smiled. "What the hell are you doing, Dave? Are you a polar bear?"

He shook his head, gave her a quivering smile. "I don't . . ." He was shivering and it made his voice unsteady.

"Dave, give me a break, okay? I was *asleep,* for God's sake."

He continued shaking his head as he backed out of the light of the flood lamp. It illuminated him from his nose down, now. "Jean, *why* am I *doing* this?"

Her smile broadened. "You're joking, right?"

"Please, Jean. I'm not joking. Please. Come out here!"

She opened her mouth as if to speak, then closed it, unsure of what to say.

"Jean, believe me." The light from the flood lamp illuminated him from his neck down, now, as he moved backward through the dark water. (A wide perimeter of most of the lake froze solid enough by late December that cars could be driven on it, but there was motion in the water around the inn, due to the action of underground springs, and so there were large areas where the ice got only paper thick, and other spots where it never froze at all.) The water was midthigh on Dave Ward. "I want to come out of here, Jean," he pleaded. "I really do *want* to come out of here!"

"Then do it, for God's sake!" She was beginning to sound frantic, she realized.

"I can't!"

"Is there a current, Dave? Is some current drawing you out?" She started down the steps, stopped halfway. "Dave?"

"There's no current. It's not a current. Help me, Jean. Please! Come out here!" He was pleading with her. She thought he was at the point of tears.

She shook her head. "You're trying to be funny and you're not being funny, Dave. You're being an ass. I'm freezing to death!"

The flood lamp illuminated him from the area of his navel down. The water was at his groin. She saw him slap the water as he struggled to keep his balance. "My God, Jean, I don't understand this, I don't fucking understand . . ."

"Just put one foot in front of the other, Dave, and walk the hell out of there." She went quickly to the bottom of the steps. She could see the dark outline of his torso, his head turning quickly as if he were looking for something to grab onto.

"Christ, Jean, I'm trying that, I'm fucking *trying* that and it doesn't work, my goddamned . . . my goddamned legs won't do what I tell them to do."

She ran to the edge of the lake; there was a short stretch of broken ice.

He had backed completely out of the light of the flood lamp, now. She saw only the path he'd made through the ice near shore, and the dark outline of his shoulders and head against the slightly lighter sky at the far horizon. She called, "Walk *toward* me, Dave, toward my voice, can you hear me?"

"Jean, my God, you're missing the point . . ." There was silence.

She stood quietly for several seconds. She called to her brother, once, then again, and again. She paused. She heard behind her, "Miss Ward, there is a problem?"

She turned quickly. Arnaut Berge was there, on the walkway. She pointed stiffly toward the lake. "My brother, he's . . ."

Arnaut was in the lake within seconds, searching frantically for Dave Ward.

January 12: An Hour Before Sunrise

"And so," Arnaut comforted, "my thought is surely rising with your brother."

Jean was beside him on the hard, armless red vinyl couch in her cabin. She was looking at the lake through the cabin's big front window. "You've had experience with this sort of thing, haven't you, Mr. Berge?"

"Arnaut," he corrected. "Yes, my wife died in this lake."

"You tried to save her?" She looked quickly from the lake to him. "I'm sorry. That was crass."

He nodded, though not in agreement with what she'd said. "I tried to save her, yes."

Jean looked at the lake again. "Was it like Dave?"

"Your brother will come out of this shining new," Arnaut told her.

"That's not what the doctor said."

"The doctors all tell us the very worst of things so we will not be too disappointed and they will not look too bad. But I know that your brother will come out of that hospital and you will take him home. I know such things as that."

"And?"

He looked at her. "I'm sorry?"

"If he lives and I take him home, will he be the brother I came here with?"

Arnaut shook his head. "You are being trepidatious and so I am out in the ocean."

It took her a moment to decipher what he'd said. "Five minutes without oxygen," she said, "and the brain dies. That's what the doctor told me. Dave was down there a lot longer than that, Arnaut." She nodded dully toward the lake.

Arnaut understood. "Yes," he said, "but you are not considering the freezing at those depths where I pulled him up from, which the same doctor said was of great service to him and brought his . . . his . . . metabolism sliding into . . . negativity. And so the needs of his brain were like those of a small animal."

She gave him a sad smile. "I know what you're trying to do, Arnaut, and I appreciate it—"

He cut in, shaking his head, "I don't humor anyone, especially being of the experience I am with my wife also who drowned. I'm telling you what I *see*"—he tapped his forehead meaningfully—"and I am asking you to hear me."

She nodded, clasped her hands in front of her, shook her head. "My God, he looked so *helpless,* Arnaut. He looked like a baby being swept out to sea."

"Yes," Arnaut said. "I understand." It was the truth.

She looked earnestly at him. "I'll stay until this

situation . . . is resolved."
"And then?"
"And then I'll go."

Mary Berge nearly always smiled when she read her father's letters because his style of writing was often like his style of speaking—disjointed, roundabout, almost anarchic, as if the words he used bore little relationship to what he wanted to say.

The letter she was reading now, in her dorm room at Cornell University, in Ithaca, New York, where she was majoring in elementary education, was no exception. "More to the good it will be seeing you," it read in part, which she translated easily as, "It will be good to see you." The letter also read, "The sun on the daylight delights the water, and then there is the evening turnaround," which meant that the days were pleasant and the nights very cold. His shorter sentences were better. For example, "I miss you," and, "The food here is wonderful. Come have some," which, beyond its literal translation, was an appeal for her to take a few days off and come to see him. She had not seen him at Christmas, although she had planned to, because she had decided to spend Christmas with her boyfriend, at his last-minute insistence and pleading. He—his name was Chuck—had taken the opportunity to tell her good-bye. Now, reading her father's letter, she smiled both wistfully and regretfully and thought that her father, at least, would never hurt her that way.

But, her thoughts hurried on, if her father's letters were amusing, they were also disturbing—though now, after so long, only in a small way. They were a hard reminder that her father was a mystery to her, that he appeared normal in every way except in the way he talked, and there was no real, or clear reason for the way he talked. It was as if that . . . abnormality reflected the mystery within him, the mystery of his spirit, his soul, his deep inner self. The kind of mystery that most people kept hidden, even from themselves.

She had tried often to understand the sort of mind that could make such a Rube Goldberg kind of mess of the language; she wondered if his thoughts came to him in the same way, and his perceptions, too. If, perhaps, when he looked out on Seventh Lake he saw it inverted, or, talking with someone, saw lips move in reverse to what was being said. She was not unaware of the fact, either, that many of his written and spoken pronouncements were poetic—"The sun on the daylight delights the water," for instance—as if his mind were dancing, as if, at the bottom of it all, he was having a marvelous time.

The letter she was reading now went on to tell her that he had reopened the inn to accommodate cross-country skiers. It was a first for him, but there were major repairs necessary to the inn and keeping it open during January and February would help pay for those repairs.

The letter ended, "It will be experiential. The inn is cozy of itself. But nothing moves these nights. Not animal, nor the images of us. All are sleeping."

HISTORY—AUGUST 16, 1976

Max Mosiman maintained that he had grown beyond the silliness of Big Bird pajamas, now that he was eight years old and almost a *preteenager!* But, his mother reminded him, his Aunt Carol had bought the pajamas for him for his birthday two weeks earlier, and he had no other pajamas (having worn his GI Joe's threadbare) and the nights were cold here, even in summer, so he was expected to wear them.

He had tried ripping them—his mother, he decided, would not force him to wear torn pajamas —but the fabric was very strong. He had also waited until well after she had said good night, then had wriggled out of them while still under the blankets (sound carried well in the house and she knew when he was out of bed). But, at last, he had had to admit that sleeping in the silly Big Bird pj's was far warmer and more comfortable (considering the clamminess of the sheets and the room) than sleeping naked.

Tonight, however, he was not sleeping at all well. He wasn't sure why. Catherine, his sister, wasn't yakking at him from her bed at the other side of the big room. The house was quiet, except for an occasional cough from his grandfather's bedroom, just below. He wasn't too cold, or too warm; he did not itch; he wasn't spooking himself with imaginings of what might be in this corner, or that corner, or in the closet, or under the bed. And he was tired, he knew that he wanted to sleep, that he *could* sleep if only his eyes would stay shut and his mind stop racing from here to there.

He realized at last what was happening to him. He was awake and he was dreaming at the same time. A switch somewhere in his head had refused to close and so what usually happened to him when he was asleep was happening to him while he was awake.

He thought, in so many words, *It's like being crazy.* And once he thought that, he began to enjoy it.

He dreamed of walking on the island, as his father so often did, though always alone. He dreamed of walking the same paths his father walked, only much faster, as if the earth beneath his feet were moving, too, pulling him along at running speed as his feet paced out the speed of a walk. Often in such dreams, he had watched himself jump and come down ten feet away, and then, after another jump, twenty feet, then forty, fifty, his body arching higher and higher each time until, at last, he was all but flying.

This dream did not become that. As his feet paced out the speed of a walk, the earth moved him along at running speed. And he stayed firmly earthbound, cemented to the island.

Held by it.

Embraced by it.

His breathing grew labored, as if the air were being sucked from the room.

The dream dissipated.

"Max?" said Catherine in the bed across the room. "You okay?"

"Uh, yeah," he answered.

"You havin' trouble breathing again, Max?" He was still recuperating from a pesky flu that had kept him coughing and breathing heavily, through his mouth, for what had seemed to Catherine like forever.

"No," he said. "I ain't havin' trouble breathin'."

"Max, I can hear ya and I'm gonna go and get Mom."

"I'm all right. It's okay."

Catherine said nothing for a moment, then, "I don't wantchoo to die, Max."

"Shit," Max whispered. His breathing still was labored and he was having a great deal of trouble getting words out, but, for Catherine's sake, he made a believable effort. "Shit," he repeated. "Who says I'm gonna die? I ain't gonna die. How can I die? It ain't . . . ain't like I'm . . . old . . . old . . . like Grandpa."

"He ain't old," said Catherine. "*Mama* is old. And Daddy, too. Grandpa just . . ." She hesitated. "He just *is,* that's all."

"Catherine, that don't . . . make . . . sense."

"You're still having trouble breathing, aren't cha, Max?"

"I ain't."

"I think you're gonna die. And if you do, Max, then I'll miss ya. I will."

Max said nothing. Catherine listened to his labored breathing a few moments, then sat up. "I mean it,

Max. I'm gonna go get Mama and tell her what's happening to you."

"Nothing's happening to me! I just had a bad dream is all."

Catherine hesitated. She supposed that her brother was lying to her, but she knew that if she actually did go and get her mother then Max would be mad at her for a long time.

She lay down again. She was dressed in pink flannel pajamas which were warm enough that she could lie on top of her blankets. She said, twiddling her thumbs as she spoke, "I don't like it here much. Do you, Max?"

He said nothing. She noticed that his breathing was quieter.

"Max?" she coaxed.

"Yeah?"

"You like it here?"

"I don't know. I guess so. I don't know."

Catherine glanced over at him. She saw little. Darkness on the island was nearly total. The only light in the room was what filtered in under the door from the hallway. In that light she saw that her brother was on his back with his hands folded on his stomach. She said, "You look like you're dead, Max."

"Shit!" he said again. He enjoyed the word. It was the only obscenity his parents let him get away with and he liked the feel of it coming off his tongue, as if it were something stolen and delicious.

Catherine said, "You look like you're lying in your coffin like that, Max. You look dead."

He said, clearly to get her off that particular subject, "Yeah, I like it here. I like it here a lot."

"I don't believe you."

"I don't give a shit what you believe, Catherine."

Catherine fell quiet. She didn't like it when her brother cursed because it seemed it was something that *he* was allowed to do, but which *she* wasn't, even in private. She could hide herself away in an animal hole on the farthest corner of the island, and she could whisper, *whisper,* the same word that her brother had just said aloud, and her mother and father would know. And when she got home they'd sit her down in a kitchen chair and take turns scolding her.

"But sometimes," said Max, "I don't like it here much."

"Me, too," said Catherine.

"Like, you know, I think I'd like to go to a *real* school." His mother taught both him and Catherine at home, though they were still waiting for official approval from the county school board. "You never went to a real school like I did, so you don't know, but it's fun running around with all the other kids."

"I went to nursery school," Catherine protested.

"It ain't the same."

Catherine said nothing.

"And that ain't the only reason I don't like it here much," said Max.

"Yeah?" said Catherine.

"Yeah," said Max. "I don't like it either 'cuz it makes me afraid, sometimes." He hesitated very briefly, then hurried on, "And don't you go repeatin' that to no one. Like Dad."

"Okay," said Catherine.

"You promise?"

"Sure." A brief pause. "I get scared too, Max. When me and Mama go out for walks, I get scared."

"Uh-huh," said Max.

"What do you get scared of, Max?"

"Bears," he answered.

"Ain't no bears here. Ain't no bears on islands at all. Or snakes."

"That's dumb."

"Ain't dumb. It's true. I read it in one of my books. And Mama told me it's true."

"Ain't true. I *seen* snakes."

"You have?"

"I have," he said resolutely. "I saw one of those cats with a snake in its mouth. Big snake, too. Big as a baseball bat."

Catherine let this sink in. It was important information, and confusing, too, considering what her mother had told her, and what she had read in her book. She trusted her mother and her books implicitly. No one and nothing else—not her father, not Max, not her grandfather, not even the evidence of her own senses—could give her information she trusted as much as she trusted information from her books and from her mother. At last she said, "If it was big as a baseball bat, Max, then the cat wouldn'ta been able to carry it. So you're lying and I ain't gonna talk to you."

Joe Archer, Max and Catherine's grandfather —Anita Mosiman's father—was nearly blind and deaf at age eighty-two and was also plagued by a number of ailments: the beginnings of arthritis in his hands, a bothersome cough that had been with him for nearly a decade (and which he chalked up to the effects of working once as an asbestos pipe fitter), a spastic colon, psoriasis. But, despite all these problems, he was usually cheerful and quick-witted, and it was clear from his square, pleasant face, his strong jaw, his playful pale blue eyes, his full head of bright white hair, and his ready smile, that he had once been quite appealing. Age had not destroyed that appeal; if it had dulled it, it had also refined it. His dealings with others were not colored by the bullshit of youth and middle age. All his chances for quick and easy satisfaction were beyond him and no longer mattered very much, except in his memory. What mattered most were the people around him—the people he loved, and the people who loved him.

He realized that his coughing could be heard throughout the house. Though it sounded distant to his own ears—as if he were coughing underwater—he knew that the house conducted sound well. Not simply because Ben, his son-in-law, had told him so, but because he had a sense of such things. He had lived in enough houses, he thought, to know the ones which kept secrets well, and the ones that didn't. This one didn't. It couldn't. It was, he had thought more than once, as if it were made of paper, as if it were designed as a house that could not keep secrets. Hadn't his own sleep, always unusually and unnaturally light, been interrupted by the unmistakable sounds of his daughter and son-in-law making love? They were sounds that disturbed him, and he wished that they didn't. He thought that those sounds disturbed him only because he was old and infirm, and so such pleasure was far, far behind him. He thought also that he was being paternal, and he resented it in himself. Surely his daughter—married ten years and in her late thirties—had the right to make love to whomever she chose. And wasn't that the key? She had chosen Ben Mosiman. And Joe Archer wasn't at all sure that she had chosen well.

He stuck his face into his pillow and rode out a long coughing fit. When it was done, he lifted his face and breathed heavily. God but it was awful to be dying. To be old and incapable and dying. To be waiting out the years inside a body that could do little more than shuffle about, a body whose hands could not even accurately gauge the heat of a stovetop coffeepot, because his sense of touch had dulled.

He wished he was stupid, then he wouldn't notice his own slow death. He even wished, at times, that he was senile and could lose himself in his past, in the arms of all the women he had loved. That would be a blessing. But most of the time he was thankful that his mind had not failed him in old age. He was less of a burden this way.

He coughed again. It was short and dry and it hurt.

"I think Grandpa likes it here," Max said.

"He told me he did," Catherine said.

"He don't want to go in the water. He closes his eyes when we go to shore in the boat. Didja know that?"

"Yeah," said Catherine. "I seen him. Mama says he almost drowned once."

"And he don't like the house much. He said it's flimsy."

"Flimsy?" Catherine said.

"He said it should be tore down and a better one put up."

Catherine looked past her brother and out the window near his bed. She saw a patch of black sky with a half dozen stars sprinkled on it. Beneath were the lights of the Many Pines Inn, three-quarters of a mile off, laid out narrow and flat on the horizon. She said, "He likes the island, though. He said that he wished he could see it better. He said—"

"I don't like it."

Catherine ignored the interruption. "He said it smells good to him. I think he meant the flowers smelled good, and the lake, too. But the lake smells like fish, don't you think, Max?"

Anita Mosiman lay on her back in a sweat from foreplay that had gone nowhere. She took a deep breath. She said, "That was interesting."

"No, it wasn't," her husband said.

"You're right. It wasn't."

"You're blaming me?"

"I didn't know the concept of 'blame' entered into it, Ben."

"Because if you are, then don't."

"I won't." She looked at him. They usually made love with a light on; this time was no exception, and she could see that he was staring at the ceiling. His narrow chin was set, as if he were making a resolution. His lips were drawn tightly together, and he was pouting a little. He looked at her, sighed, then looked away.

"Why are you staring at me?" he asked.

"Is there something you'd like to talk about, Ben? Is there something on your mind?"

"Good Lord, there's *always* something on my mind."

She smiled, despite herself. "I wasn't aware of that. I'm sorry." She shrugged. "Is there something on your mind now that you'd like to talk about?"

He reached to his left for a pack of cigarettes on a small wooden table near the bed. He said, lighting up, "Not everything can be solved with talk, you know."

"Everything?"

"And you're not nearly as clever as you believe, either. You think you can draw me out with your one-word, evocative questions."

"Evocative questions?" She smiled again; she wasn't sure why. Clearly her husband had something on his mind, so, clearly, it was not the time to be amused by his insecurities. She fought the smile down. "Talking often does help, though," she said. "Won't you admit that?"

He pushed himself up to a sitting position, adjusted the pillow behind his back. "Sometimes, yes," he said, and looked for an ashtray on the bedside table. "Sometimes it doesn't. Sometimes we just want to be alone."

"Like we are on this island?" Anita asked.

He adjusted the blanket covering him to his stomach so it covered him to his chest. "Cold," he whispered. Then he pushed a box of Kleenex tissues to one side, found a glass ashtray behind it, put the ashtray on his lap. "I'd rather not talk now." He flicked a short length of ash into the ashtray. "Besides, we never really *talk*, do we? We don't *talk*. We . . . do something else. We . . . circle around each other."

"I'll listen then," she offered, and sat up in the bed, adjusted her pillow, folded her arms beneath her breasts.

"That's distracting if you're offering to listen," he said.

"My breasts? Do you mean my breasts are distracting?" She smiled again, first to herself, then, turning to look at Ben, as if in response to what he'd said.

"Yes," he answered, looking briefly at her breasts. "They're always distracting. You know that."

"I do now," she said, and pulled the blanket up so it covered her. She folded her arms again. "I'm sorry. I don't want to distract you. I want to listen."

He said, "It's part of the art of conversation, you know. Listening." He took a long, noisy drag on the cigarette, butted it out, and immediately lit another. "Don't tell me I smoke too much," he said. "I *know* I smoke too much."

"Then you'll stop if you want to," she said.

"That's a smart ass answer. You *know* it's a smart ass answer. It's just the sort of thing you say all the time."

"I do not give smart ass answers. I'm sorry if you believe that I do, Ben."

He shook his head, as if in disbelief, took a drag from the cigarette, and went to pull it from his mouth; the filter end got stuck on his dry lips and his fingers raked along the lit end so the tip fell off. It hit the side of the ashtray, then bounced onto the bed. "God-dammit!" he hissed, and swiped at the smoldering tip to get it onto the floor. It burned quickly through the soft cotton blanket and down onto the sheet. He pushed the blanket away, jumped from the bed, and swept the tip to the floor. He watched glumly as it burned out on the hardwood then he stuck his burned fingers into his mouth. "Dammit all the hell!" he mumbled.

"Does it hurt?" Anita asked.

"No," he answered sharply, fingers still in his mouth. "It'th thumbthing I do for fun."

"Cold water will help. Then a bandage to keep the air away."

He sighed, got back into bed, lifted the blanket and made a show of studying the hole left by the lit end of the cigarette. "You know, they shouldn't make blankets that burn this easily. It's a hazard."

"Smoking in bed is a hazard."

"Another smart ass answer."

Joe Archer thought that Dog Island would be a fine place to live out his days, as long as he didn't have to get too damn close to the water. The island had a nice, comfortable feel. It would be a good place to be buried, in fact. He was thinking especially of an open area at the center of the island that was fringed by pines and alive with butterflies and spiders and chipmunks. Violets and daisies grew in crazy abundance there.

Another coughing fit wracked him. He pushed his face into his pillow; his back and rear end rose slightly with each cough. At last, the coughing subsided and he rolled to his side. "Dammit to hell!" he breathed.

He got out of bed and went to his door. He was dressed in yellow boxer shorts and a white T shirt and when he flicked on the overhead light he saw himself in a long mirror on the back of the door. He scowled. If someone got up and saw him like this, they'd have bad dreams, for sure. He got his long, red velour robe from a coat tree near the door, put it on, and went into the kitchen.

The vision he had of surroundings that were more

than an arm's length away was as if he were seeing a huge and faded painting whose colors had run and blended; it was a sort of madras view of the world. The kitchen table was a pale blue rectangle with shimmering silver edges; the propane refrigerator an off-white oblong with a squat brown blob on top (an old Radio Shack table radio, seldom used; here, in the Adirondacks, it got mostly static). The windows, tall narrow rectangles—two at the east side of the kitchen, one on the south wall, near the back door—were big dark ovals, like mouths stretched wide in a yawn. Joe had thought once that it was like seeing the world through Vaseline. And he thought that if he didn't know better, he would think that it was incomplete, in the process of construction, that it was being pushed up out of the earth and Mother Nature was not yet certain about what exactly she was producing. But when he walked into the edge of the refrigerator, or slammed his knee into the side of the table, or, barefoot, banged his toe into the leg of a chair, he knew that it was a world which was painfully real, and all-too-complete. Better, he had also thought, if it were a dreamworld whose hard edges parted easily for him, like water, a world where there were no certainties, where the windows could indeed be mouths yawning, and the brown table radio a sleeping, furry animal. But that was not the world he tried to move about in, and only when he was sitting in his old chair in a corner of the kitchen, and out of harm's way, did he try to convince himself otherwise.

He did not go to that chair now. He was hungry. It was likely that he'd peer into the refrigerator—trying to make out from the mixture of shapes and colors he saw there what he was hungry for—that the empty feeling would leave him suddenly. It often did, as if the aged walls of his stomach and colon had suddenly fallen in on themselves, like wet paper.

He also knew that just a few bites of whatever he pulled from the refrigerator—it was like pulling a surprise from some deep hole—would be enough to satisfy him. And then he could go and sit in his chair, put his head back, and pretend. Lying in bed brought on the coughing fits. Sitting in his chair prodded his imagination and that made him happy for a time.

"Your father's up," said Ben Mosiman.

Anita nodded in the darkness (she had padded naked across the hardwood floor to turn the light off. "Maybe you can just stand there like that a few minutes," Ben had suggested, her finger on the switch and her body at right angles to him.)

She said now, "I know he's up. I heard him."

"He'll injure himself stumbling around all alone down there."

"For God's sake, Ben, he's not blind."

"He might as well be."

"Go to sleep."

"What do you think he's doing? Do you think he's hungry?"

"What*ever* he's doing, Ben, he has a perfect right to do it. It's his house, too."

Ben said nothing.

Anita said, reading his silence, "Well, it is. He lives here, so it's his house just as much as it is ours. Christ, you're always so damn worried he's going to *do* something to himself."

"Or to us, Anita. He could get into a lot of trouble down there."

She sighed. "He's not a child. He's not stupid."

"I never said he was stupid."

"And if you keep it up he'll hear us."

"*Hear* us? Don't make me laugh. He couldn't hear—"

"Can it."

"Well, he is nearly deaf, Anita. You know that. You can't deny it."

As Joe had guessed, his hunger had dissipated as soon as he'd opened the refrigerator, and now he was in his chair in the corner of the kitchen, and he was pretending.

It was not his daughter's kitchen. It was the kitchen of his first lover, Charlene. He was nineteen and she was twenty-one, recently widowed, and strangely playful. She was short, vivacious; she knew how to move, how to laugh, how to flirt. Her eyes were the eyes of sex.

"Have you ever done it on the kitchen table?" she cooed.

He had no answer for that. It was the agonizing promise of the gift of something wonderful and brand new, and he could only grin dumbly in response.

She answered for him, "Of course you haven't. I doubt that there are many who have. Kitchen tables are for other things." And as she said this, she began to strip, her fingers moving slowly and lovingly over her buttons, as if she were touching *him.*

She kept her distance. She did not come too close.

She let her blouse slide to the floor. She wore no chemise. She said, "Help me with my dishes, Joe."

"Like that?" he said, still grinning.

"I never fuck unless the dishes are clean," she cooed.

His grin increased. It was the first time he had heard a woman use the word *fuck.* He stood, followed her to the sink. His hands went twitching to her breasts; she pushed them gently away. "Dishes," she told him.

"Yes, dishes," he said.

"I'll wash, you dry."

"Anything," he said.

It was a warm, spring day; she had the window open over her sink. In a house not far away—none of the houses on her narrow city street were far away —another woman was apparently also at her sink, with her window open. Joe watched her a moment, thinking she might look up from her work and see them. That would embarrass him, he knew. But he hoped that she would look up.

"She's a very private person, that woman," said Charlene.

"She might see us here," said Joe.

"If she did, she would only look away and continue her work."

A soft, moist breeze was pushing through the open window. It carried the smell of laundry with it —bleach, soap—and Joe found that he liked that smell.

In his old chair in a corner of the kitchen in the house on Dog Island, he smiled, remembering it.

Charlene said, "She saw me once."

"Saw you?"

"Naked."

"You were naked at the window?"

"I am now."

"Not completely."

"To your eyes, I am, Joe."

He thought about that. He wasn't sure what she was talking about, but he had an idea, and the idea titillated him.

He watched her bring a saucer up from her sink full of suds. She scrubbed hard at the saucer—though it looked clean—so her breasts moved left and right. The breeze through the open window had caused her nipples to erect; they were large, very red, the aureola dappled with tiny raised areas that Joe stared at, intrigued.

A finger's worth of suds fell from the saucer, as she

held it up to study it, onto one of her nipples. "Oh," she murmured, and pushed the little dollop of suds away with her fingers.

In his old chair in the corner of the kitchen in the house on Dog Island, eighty-two-year-old Joe Archer got an erection as he remembered Charlene and her sudsy nipple.

"You liked that, didn't you, Joe?" she said.

He nodded enthusiastically.

She smiled a little and handed him the saucer she had just cleaned. "But you've got to dry."

"I'll dry," he whispered hoarsely, and took the saucer from her.

Without a word, she unfastened the buttons at the side of her skirt and let the skirt fall to the floor. She wore nothing beneath. She gently kicked the skirt away and busied herself with another saucer from her sink full of suds.

Joe was breathing heavily and his lips and throat were going dry. He was happy on his island of memory.

Above, in Max and Catherine's bedroom, the conversation had become one-sided.

"Know what Dad told me, Catherine? He told me he thought the island was alive. I don't know what he meant. Islands can't be alive." He hesitated. Catherine's breathing was slow and nasal; she was asleep. "Dammit," he whispered and rolled to his side so he could look out the window to the left of the head of his bed.

He focused on the lights of the Many Pines Inn; he decided they were like the lights of a stern-wheeler in the distance. He had seen pictures of stern-wheelers in the textbook on American history that his mother taught from.

He liked the idea that the inn looked like a stern-wheeler. It got him to thinking that suddenly the lights would grow brighter and closer, and brighter still, and closer still, and at last rear up to the dock and the captain of the stern-wheeler would disembark.

"I'm afraid we haven't got the money to eat there," Max's father had told Max about Many Pines. Max didn't care, though it was clear to him that his father did. He didn't care because eating was eating. It didn't matter much if you did it at home or on a picnic or in a restaurant.

He realized then that he still could not sleep, and that his waking dreams were winding down. (He thought that the idea of Many Pines being a stern-wheeler that paddled across the lake and docked at their dock was a waking dream, and a good one.)

He thought about waking Catherine, glanced at her, decided to let her sleep, rolled over and focused once more on the lights of Many Pines. He whispered to himself, "I wonder what winter's gonna be like here."

Joe Archer couldn't remember Charlene's last name. He didn't think it was important. First lovers and first loves often existed in the memory only as first names, smells, and parts of the anatomy: hair, buttocks, breasts, a smile. He remembered a discussion he'd had with the men he'd worked with as a pipe fitter.

"Perfume," one said. "That's what I remember. Cheap perfume, *real* cheap perfume." He smiled as if through a mouthful of something tasty.

"Her ass," said another.

"Yeah, her ass," said another.

"She smelled of oranges," said yet another. "Oranges, you know . . ."

"I remember that we talked, I remember we talked," said someone else.

"Yeah, but'dja ever fuck?" said his buddy.

"Sure." He shrugged, nodded. "But I don't remember that. I remember we talked."

And Joe told the story of Charlene's naked dish washing. He did not name her. He thought that that would be dishonorable. The other men said his story was wonderful and most confessed that they had no memories to match it.

"Sure you do," Joe said, which started each of them remembering, and, before long, smiling in secretive ways.

Now, in his old chair, in the house on Dog Island, his smile flattened, his erection subsided, and he slept.

"I didn't hear him go back into his room," said Ben Mosiman to Anita. Their bedroom was on the second floor, near the children's room.

"Go to sleep," Anita mumbled.

"Maybe I should go down there," Ben said.

"Maybe you should leave him alone."

"You *think* we don't get along, your father and I. But we do, Anita."

She said nothing.

"You asleep?"

"Yes."

"I'm sorry."

"Forget it."

"I don't mean to keep you awake."

"Yes, you do."

He had no answer for that. He got back on the subject of her father. "I wish he wouldn't go walking around this island alone, Anita."

"*You* do," she said.

"I do, yes. But I'm much younger. I can *see.*"

From outside their open window came the soft hoot of a distant owl, then, seconds later, another. Ben said, "That's a nice sound."

Anita said nothing.

Ben announced, "I'm going downstairs. I don't like him sleeping in the chair all night."

"He's more comfortable sitting up, Ben. Leave him alone. Go to sleep."

Ben considered this. It was true that his father-in-law coughed more lying down. And it was also true that he—Ben—did not want to go padding around the dark house alone. He said, "Okay. He'll probably get up and go to his room, anyway."

Anita said nothing.

Ben thought suddenly that people who withdrew into themselves, into their pasts, as Joe so often did, were a lot like islands, that they were hard to reach by the people around them. He said, "Anita, your father is like an island. Do you know what I mean?" He smiled, pleased with the analogy. He got no reply. "Anita?" he said.

Still she said nothing.

He glanced at her. "Are you awake?" he asked.

Silence.

"Anita?"

Silence.

"Okay," he said. He rolled over, away from her.

Beyond the open window, Dog Island slept.

SIX
January 14

Muriel Fox put her skis up, took off her coat, set water on for tea and decided coffee would be better. The cold today had been biting, wounding—a bad day for cross-country skiing, too, with so little snow on the ground.

Her small house, filled with knickknack memorabilia, was very warm, the thermostat set high, but she did not feel it at once. She shivered intermittently with each recollection of the day, as if her memory of recent cold made her cold all over again.

She was thin, square faced, her skin hard, creased, and darkened by decades of exposure to the crisp slap of weather in the Adirondacks. Her brown eyes sparkled with humor, often without apparent reason, though this was only because she found humor in situations that most people considered mundane.

More than once in the last few years—since she'd reached her sixties—she had told herself that the human body ages, the blood slows, the heat within diminishes, and that it was time at last to accept all of that and stay indoors on days such as this. But she was a creature of habit, and her habit was to forget the weather and do what made her happy.

Cross-country skiing made her happy.

She fixed her coffee, took it to the living room and set it on a dark cherry table near her chair, which stood before the fireplace. She stared at the fireplace as waves of cold passed through her like sickness and made her shiver. At last, she decided that she did not need a fire, and she sat in her chair.

She knew that she was very lonely. She knew also the picture she presented to anyone who bothered to look—aging, feisty, stubborn. "She'll kick three or four times in the coffin before giving up the ghost," they would say. In spring and summer her spirit would tend her garden. In winter it would ski. In the Adirondacks, beautiful autumn came and went as quickly as a blush.

An act of defiance to what she saw as her cringing inner self—a conscious denial of what others would see as real and undeniable—had brought her here forty years before, alone.

She had been born as a kind of ice child, she maintained, because New England in winter had been her place and time of birth. So that was how she would grow, with a love for the bitter cold, and mere tolerance of warmth and summer sun. Let the others—the weak—prattle on about the awful approach of winter; let them babble about spending January and February in Florida. Let them sweat, let them stick to each other. For her, cheeks and foreheads and noses burned red by cold wind, and breath that stung and made the insides brittle were what living was all about.

It had not always been her way of thinking. As a child, on a visit to her grandfather's farm in Watertown, she'd gotten stuck, exhausted, in a winter storm when she was just yards from safety and warmth. Then sleep had overtaken her.

And when she awoke, hours later—in her bedroom, where her grandfather had taken her—struggling up out of hypothermia, her body felt as if it were indeed made of ice, that it was cracking here and there, coming apart, giving her pain such as she had never felt before.

For years afterward she went out in winter only when it was necessary, and she saw to it that it was seldom necessary. She waited inside her porch for the school bus and ran out when its doors were opening for her. When others her age went off sledding or skiing or ice skating, she stayed in and prayed for their safety, wishing the experience she had had on no one.

But she still was not a creature of warmth. She did not seek out the hot summer sun. If the ice child within her had been stilled, it didn't mean that a new child waited there to take its place. It meant that she was afraid of being who she really was, and so she spent the rest of her childhood and adolescence alone.

Often, her sleep was plagued by dreams of those hours of cold and exhaustion on her grandfather's farm. The dreams were always the same; she retraced her steps, lay down on the hillside, felt the sting of wind-driven snow against her cheek, saw the gray mouth of the barn open to her left, where the animals were, and warmth, and safety. But her joints were frozen shut, and even her lips would not move. She breathed hard through her nostrils, and in her dreams she saw them flaring. It was like a dream of death.

At twenty-two, she sought to defeat it. She went to live in the house she was in now. She did not move out of it, ever.

She married, had children, saw her husband die in his fifty-first year. She grew to again cherish the extremes of the Adirondacks, especially its winters. She decided that they were toughening her for a very long life. In her imaginings she saw herself cross-country skiing or building snowmen well past her hundredth birthday, greeting visitors (and there would be many; all of them to gaze in awe at the creature who could live so very long) with the broad, toothy, *boy-I-showed-'em* smile of healthy-as-can-be-considering-my-age, hundred-year-olds. If a woman could survive thirty-below-zero nights alone, then she could survive anything.

But she was not always alone. Men were attracted to

her for various reasons: her independence, her tough attractiveness, her probing intelligence, her wit. And after her husband died, while she was in her midforties, there was a parade of men to her door. She made lovers of a few of them, friends of a few others, and turned most away with a polite smile and an explanation that she "was seeing no one this year."

But men rarely came to see her anymore. She had outlived most of her lovers, and those she hadn't had moved away with families or younger women. Her friends mostly stayed at home. Once a week, sometimes only once a month, she was visited by a man named Leo Heinz. He lived in Eagle Bay, twenty miles from her home. He was seventy-five years old, fat, and losing his mind. For a long time she had stopped looking forward to his visits because she could see his pain, the torment he suffered at his own slow decay, and holding conversations with him was like holding a conversation with a talking doll. His storehouse of topics was limited to his children—two daughters and a son, all of whom lived in Syracuse, New York, and who came to visit him on Christmas and on his birthday in June—his work as a dentist, from which he'd retired fifteen years earlier, and memories of the time he and Muriel had been lovers. It was when he got on that topic that Muriel became very uncomfortable, because he invariably toddled into her bedroom and started to strip. "Let's do it, Muriel," he wheezed at her. "C'mon now. Let's do it," his voice high-pitched from too many chins and dry from too little saliva. Eventually, he'd realize that lovemaking was impossible for him and he'd mumble an apology—"Sorry, Muriel. I'm losing my mind"—gather up his clothes, and sit on the edge of the bed, red-eyed, close to weeping, until she could coax him back into his clothes.

He had not visited her for three weeks now and she was beginning to wonder if he had died. She thought that it would be for the best if he had.

She sipped her coffee, set the cup gently down on the table near her chair, and she sighed. "Bill," she whispered. "Oh, Bill." Bill was not her husband. His name had been Earl. She was, in fact, not at all sure who Bill was, exactly.

Lynette Meyer said to Harry Stans, seated across from her at her white enamel kitchen table, "What happened to Myrna?"

Harry sipped at the strong coffee that Lynette had made for him. It was very hot and he set the cup down quickly. "Ain't nothin' happened to Myrna," he said. "She's still around."

"Then what are you doin' here?" She lifted her own cup of coffee to her lips and hesitated with her eyes on Harry.

He explained with a slight, apologetic grin, "You know I always liked you, Lynette." He was very tall and very thin and his face was hollow cheeked, but he had a ruddy complexion and a playful glint in his eye. "I ain't never stopped likin' you."

"She throw'd you out, did she?" Lynette asked, and sipped her coffee.

"I wasn't livin' with her, Lynette." Harry picked up his coffee cup. He liked hiding behind it; that was, he supposed, just what Lynette was doing with hers. "How's your child?"

Lynette nodded a little. "Jolene is gawna be fit's a fiddle in the spring and she'll be comin' back to me. But that ain't what we was talkin' about, was it, Harry?"

"No," Harry admitted. "We was talkin' about us, I know."

Lynette shook her head. The coffee cup couldn't

hide her wide grin. "We was talkin' about you and Myrna. There ain't no *us*, far as I can see."

"Not for lack of wanting," said Harry.

Lynette looked out the kitchen window. She could see much of Seventh Lake from it. Dog Island was at the center of her field of view, and there were a number of boats around it. She had first seen them there an hour before, at a little past sunrise. She looked at Harry, again. "You're givin' me nothin' but crap, Harry, like the time you read that awful poetry to me out on the lake. All you want's to get me into bed 'cuz Myrna's cut you off, ain't that so?"

Harry shook his head meaningfully. "Myrna and me never done it, and that's the truth, Lynette. We never done it. She couldn't, you know, on account of she's got female problems."

"Uh-huh," Lynette said, unconvinced. "The only 'female problems' that woman ever had was *you,* Harry." She chuckled at her joke.

Harry chuckled, too, though clearly to be polite. "I ain't a bad guy, Lynette."

She shook her head again. "Never said you was, Harry." She looked out the window. "Those boats been out there all mornin', Harry. And there's a police boat there, too."

Harry looked and nodded. "Yeah," he said, "someone missin', you know. Man by the name of John Kennedy, like the President. Ain't that somethin'?"

Lynette grimaced. "That goddamn lake sucks people up like a damn animal, Harry."

Harry sighed. He sipped his coffee, found it was comfortably hot, now, and took another sip. He set the cup down. "People are stupid, most of 'em, Lynette." He realized his mistake at once when she gave him a hard look. "'Cept Pete, of course, who had a bad accident that couldn't be helped."

Her hard look softened. "No, Harry. Pete was 'bout as stupid as a dinner napkin, I'd say. An' couldn't swim, besides."

Harry looked surprised. "Sure Pete could swim. He *told* me he could swim."

"Then he lied. Wouldn'ta been the first time, Harry. He lied like a used car salesman, and he lied a lot. He couldn't swim. He didn't have no coordination. He couldn't put one arm out in front of the other, you know, like a person has to do in order to swim. He couldn't get it right. I think he could dog-paddle, after a fashion, and that was all he could do. He didn't tell no one 'cuz he was ashamed. So I figure when he fell into that lake with all his winter clothes on, that he sank like a stone."

Harry drank the last of his coffee, then looked longingly at the pot on the stove. "Got more a this, Lynette? I could use a whole gallon of it."

She nodded. "Sure, Harry. You want some muffins, too? I got some muffins from last night that Pete Jr. didn't eat. They're blueberry."

Harry looked pleased. "I'd like that, sure." He looked out the window. "Those boats are goin' away, now, Lynette. I'll find out if they located the guy and I'll let you know later tonight. I'll come over and I'll let you know." He looked hopefully at her.

She grinned at him. "You're bout's persistent as a summer cold, Harry." Her grin changed. "You come over when Pete Jr.'s in bed and we'll discuss it."

His face lit up. "'Bout 7:30, Lynette?"

She stood, took his coffee cup from him, gave him a stern look. "Harry, we'll *discuss* it. Just don't bring none of your goddamn poetry, okay?"

"I'll leave it home, Lynette. For sure I'll leave it home."

SEVEN
January 15

Linda Kennedy was a short, thin, red-haired woman with deep-set green eyes, a bulbous nose that she had complained about all her life ("Can you imagine Him giving someone a nose like this? He must have gotten out of the wrong side of the bed *that* morning.") and a mouth whose upper lip was all but missing, which gave her a humorless, rigid look, though she was neither humorless, nor rigid.

She did not share her husband's love for islands. She did not like them, especially if they were small, as Dog Island was, because she imagined that they were going to sink and the water rush over her. For the same reason, she did not like to swim.

At the moment, as she stood on a hog-sized hump of bare earth in a clearing at the center of Dog Island, under a frigid, bright blue January sky, dressed in a pair of jeans, a red shirt, and brown leather jacket, she was feeling playful. She had no idea why. Even before John's disappearance, the whole aura of the trip to Seventh Lake had been gloomy. He had asked her here so he could tell her he wanted out of the marriage. It was okay, she'd been expecting it for a long time. She had seen the signs: disinterest in bed, disinterest at the breakfast table, disinterest on a night out, disinterest in what she had to say, disinterest in what *he* had to say. Their lives together had become a monument to boredom, but it had been a cutting blow to ask her to the place of their honeymoon simply so he could beg out of the marriage. Not that that was unlike him. He got perverse delight, she thought, from such things. He had once taken a girlfriend—she knew that there had been more than a few—to a restaurant that he and Linda talked of as "their" restaurant, and had even contrived to be seated at "their" table. Years later, when he had felt in a confessional mood and wanted to get his "meandering" off his chest, he had explained that he hadn't realized it was *their* restaurant and *their* table until the meal was half done. And what could he do then?

She thought now, on Dog Island—on that hog-sized hump of earth, under a frigid blue January sky—that she was feeling playful because she was glad John Warner Kennedy was out of her life forever. And if he had drowned, that was too bad, it had probably been an awfully uncomfortable and . . . distracting way to die. But he was dead and that was that and so she could feel playful.

She called to her husband, "John, are you here?" The stand of pines around her absorbed her words, and so did two or three inches of wet snow layered on the bare earth. She repeated herself, "John, are you here?" louder, with her hands cupped at her mouth, and felt a little disquieted at first that the island soaked her words up, as if she were yelling into cotton. "John, goddamn you, are you *here!*" she yelled.

It wasn't good enough, she thought. The simple fact that John was *gone* wasn't at all good enough to satisfy her. He might come back, might surprise her, might pop out from behind a door one day. He liked that sort of thing, too—popping out from behind doors and furniture to scare her. And telling her a small lie in his persuasive way simply to see how far she'd go along with it. "Christ, someone got run over—I don't believe this, Linda, but some poor slob got run over right in front of the house."—"You're kidding. My God!"—A smile, a wink. "Yes, I'm kidding. Funny, huh?"

His sense of humor, she thought now, had been the same sort of humor that a cat probably feels when it's tossing a mouse high into the air.

This was not enough. He simply wasn't here, on this island. Alive, or dead. It was simply not like him, it would not have happened to him, it *could* not have happened to him. "John, you asshole, where in the hell *are* you?" The snow and the pines soaked her words up; she barely heard them. She tried to outyell herself. "John, answer me you idiot, answer me, answer me, answer me!" and the island soaked her words up.

It did not seem right under that bright and frigid blue sky to have her words soaked up that way. It seemed . . . unnatural, even a little perverse. And that was it. The island itself was perverse. The island was reaching out and snatching her words into itself, snatching them out of her mouth, reaching into her throat and squeezing her larynx.

She took a breath. She recognized the signs, could see the fear starting. It had been stupid to come out here in the first place.

She got down off the hog-sized hump of earth and started through the shallow, melting snow, past her own footprints—the brown of the earth showed in them—toward a path through the encircling pines fifty feet away. She stopped. She heard someone calling to her. She looked back. She saw the hump of earth; she saw a man standing just inside the perimeter of the pines beyond; she looked at him a moment—*No,* she decided, it wasn't a man, it was an opening in the pines that was shaped like a man. She looked away. And again she heard her voice being called. She looked back. "Linda?" she heard from nearby, and because she saw nothing, she thought once more that the island was reaching out to her, that it was calling to her, and she found comfort in that fantasy, because it *was* a fantasy—like the island sinking and the water rushing over her were fantasies; they were both so much easier to deal with than the voice she had heard. She shook her head. She should not have come here.

"Linda?" she heard.

She walked backward, away from the voice.

She didn't remember seeing the two-story white clapboard house when she had come to the island, so she decided that she had come from the wrong direction, which satisfied her to the extent that it allowed her to approach the house cautiously, down the same muddy slope from which her husband had approached it almost a week earlier. She saw what he had seen, too.

The back wall of the house bore two windows, one beneath the peak of the roof and one to the left on the first floor. Both windows were bare of curtains. The bottom half of the attic window stood open. On the ground at the center of the back wall there was a large black tank for propane. The tank bore a patina of rust along its top edge. The rust ran in rivulets down the sides through the black paint from beneath a thick, moist layer of pine needles. One of four thin green metal legs that held the tank up had rusted away completely. Linda supposed, upon seeing this, that the leg had rusted because it was closest to the water and that the tides brought the water level up close to the bottom of the tank.

The house stood on short thick, rectangular stilts. Linda could see only two of these stilts from where she stood. She thought fleetingly as she looked at them that the years had taken their toll and that before long the stilts would crumble and pitch the house into the lake.

It surprised her when she went up to the back door of

the house and knocked. She expected no answer. The house had the crumbling look of abandonment about it. But then she felt movement through the soles of her shoes on the narrow gray wood porch and she supposed that someone was getting up and coming to the door. She smiled, though it was a chore; she had no idea what she was going to say to whoever answered her knock. She waited. She knocked again, again felt movement through the soles of her shoes.

The back door had a window in it. There were drawn curtains on the window, but there was a half-inch opening at the center. Linda leaned over a little and peeked through this opening. She saw the side of a refrigerator within a half-dozen feet of the door. It was smudged and its color was that of dirty cream —clearly, Linda thought, from decades of use—and there was what looked at first like a diagonal ripple in its metal skin, as if someone had dented it.

Above the refrigerator, she could see a horizontal sliver of light and she guessed that this was the top of a window at the front of the house.

She straightened. She knocked again. She leaned over and peered once more through the opening between the curtains. She saw now that what she had thought at first was a dent in the cream-colored skin of the refrigerator was really a motionless bare arm, that someone had been standing at the door all this time.

She backed down the steps. "I'm sorry," she whispered. "I'm sorry. I didn't mean to . . . I didn't mean anything." Then she turned and clambered up the muddy slope. Fear gripped her all the while, and confusion, too, as if she had been glimpsing a nightmare in its benign early stages.

EIGHT

HISTORY—AUGUST 29, 1976

The mailman's name was Lucius Kellogg and he'd been delivering mail to people around Seventh Lake for a dozen years. Ben Mosiman had realized on the very first day's delivery that the man liked to chat. Kellogg had docked his twelve-foot mail boat, reached up and handed him a handful of birthday cards—it was Ben's forty-second birthday—and had asked, smiling, "I'd say you're from . . . Ohio, am I right?" Ben had started to answer and Kellogg had cut in, nodding, "I'd say Ohio, and I'm not never wrong. Well, hardly ever. You know, son"—Kellogg was in his midsixties—"I thought I was wrong, once, but I was mistaken." He'd laughed. "Say, you ain't got some coffee, have you?"

"Sure," Ben said.

"I like my coffee like I like my women, Ben—hot, sweet, and black." Another laugh. "Not really, Ben. I never had no black woman, but I heard it don't rub off, so I don't think I'd mind giving it a try."

Today, almost two months later, Kellogg's patter was the same; lots of bad jokes and ethnic references, and Ben was aching to see him go.

Kellogg said, "You heard about those damn tall ships come into New York Harbor for the damn Bicentennial thing, right?"

Ben nodded.

"Betchoo didn't hear that the Polish tall ship was a damn five hours late, huh?"

Ben shook his head and answered—trying to sound

half surly—"No, I hadn't heard that, Mr. Kellogg. Is there some significance to it?"

Kellogg shook his head. "Ain't no significance to nothin', I guess." It was clearly something he found uproariously funny because he broke into a long fit of howling laughter. When he was done, Ben said, "I'm sorry, Mr. Kellogg, but I've got some repairs to make on the house—"

Kellogg interrupted, "You hadn't oughta live here, you know."

It was something that Ben had heard before. "Yes, Mr. Kellogg, so you've told me, *ad nauseum.*"

"I mean it. It ain't safe, you know. It's gonna go—"

"As I said, Mr. Kellogg, I've heard it before. I'm in the process—or at least I *intend* to be in the process —of *making* it safe, if you'll let me have the time."

Kellogg shrugged, nonplussed by Ben's outburst. "Don't matter to me, Ben. But you got a couple cute kids and a cuter wife and you know no one in Eagle Bay can figure out what in the Sam hill you're doin' out here—"

"Trying to mind our own business, Mr. Kellogg," Ben cut in. "What we're doing out here is trying to mind our own damned business."

January 16

Arnaut had had three minor traffic accidents in fifteen years. He drove badly because his mind wandered, but when he tried to force himself to concentrate on what was going on around him he found that his speed dropped to below twenty, his eyes focused on the area directly in front of the hood, and a dozen cars, horns honking, were soon backed up behind him, unable to pass on the narrow, twisting Adirondack roads.

Today, he was driving to the little settlement of cottages where Lynette Meyer and Harry Stans lived. He was going to visit Tom Lord, a woodworker who made ornamental pine furniture which Arnaut offered for sale at the inn.

Arnaut sang as he drove. He sang loudly and well, his voice a rich low tenor. Today he was singing "The Water is Wide." He sang, "The water is wide, I cannot get over, and neither have I wings to fly. Give me a boat that can carry two, and both shall row, my love and I." He rounded a wide, slow turn, began the verse again, "The water is wide, I cannot get over, and neither have I wings to fly. Give me a boat . . ." and mashed his foot into the brake pedal. The car's rear end spun around on the road, wet from a snowfall the previous evening. A pickup truck appeared around the curve, swerved left and missed him by inches. Arnaut spun the steering wheel desperately, the car straightened, then fishtailed in the opposite direction. He felt a deadening thump from the right fender. The car stopped; Arnaut's upper body shot forward; his lap belt stopped him. He looked toward the shoulder of the road. A young deer lay there, head lifted, eyes glazed in shock and pain, its lower body twitching. Arnaut slid across the front seat, opened his door, got out. He heard from behind him, "Gawna take it?" He turned his head. A thin man of about forty, with long stringy black hair and several day's growth of beard, stood next to the pickup. The man nodded grinningly at the struggling deer. "Gawna take it?" he repeated. " 'Cuz if you ain't, I will."

Arnaut understood at once. He shook his head. "The animal is not yet dead, sir," he said. "The animal is suffering."

"Yeah," the man said, and stopped grinning. "I guess he is now, but judgin' by the way you hit him, he won't be for long."

Arnaut understood this, too. He said reluctantly, "Do you have a gun?"

The man shook his head. "Yeah," he said, "but I ain't got no shells for it."

Arnaut looked at the deer. It still had its head raised; its rear end still was twitching. Arnaut said, as much to himself as to the man behind him, "The animal is suffering."

"Maybe you oughta get your car outa the way, mister," the pickup truck driver suggested.

Arnaut ignored him. He was intent on the deer. He moved forward, so he was standing over it. It was very young, he realized, probably less than a year old. Arnaut shook his head. "Forgive me," he said.

The pickup driver said, "Car's gawna come round that bend and there's gawna be hell to pay!"

Arnaut took several steps to his left, leaned over, picked up a rock the size of a muskmelon, brought it back to where the deer lay. "Forgive me," he said again, and brought the rock down very hard into the center of the animal's forehead.

The pickup truck driver said, "It's for sure not sufferin' no more. I'll take it now, okay?"

Arnaut threw the rock down. "Yes," he said.

The pickup truck driver came around Arnaut's car, lifted the young deer by placing one arm under its belly and the other under its chest, carried it to the pickup, and threw it into the bed of the truck. "Thanks a lot, mister," the driver called. "This'll keep me and the missus in meat for a long time. Best move your car."

Arnaut nodded dully, whispered, "Yes," got into his car by the passenger door, and slid across the seat. He put the car in gear; he hesitated. He was reminded of his first encounter with the people who lived here year-round: it had been fifteen years earlier. He had gone into Eagle Bay for groceries and had walked into the firehouse looking for directions.

He saw two men seated in big, dilapidated, over-stuffed chairs; they were looking at a Montgomery Ward catalog. He nodded. One of the men, the closest to him, growled, "Go ahead, say it, Mister."

Arnaut shook his head. "Hello?" he guessed.

The man held the catalog up so its cover was to Arnaut. "No. This. This."

"This catalog?" said Arnaut.

"A *Montgomery Ward* catalog. Go ahead, get it off your chest."

Again Arnaut shook his head. "This conversation is at right angles to my comprehension."

"Huh?" said the man who had remained silent.

"He's trying to say he doesn't know what the hell we're talking about, Jim," said the man holding the catalog. "But he sure as hell does, and I sure as hell wish he'd get it off his chest. Go ahead, say it. Say *Monkey Ward catalog.*"

"But why would I say that?"

"Because," said the first man, *"everyone* does. They say *Monkey Ward* for *Montgomery Ward* because they think that's what *we* say. But we don't. We say *Montgomery Ward.* Okay?"

"Okay?" said Arnaut, shrugging.

"Okay," said the second man.

Now, fifteen years later, as he watched the taillights of the pickup truck recede, the memory made him smile.

HISTORY—SEPTEMBER 2, 1976

Joe Archer had his hand on the doorknob of his bedroom door and he was cursing repeatedly under his breath when his son-in-law, Ben, came in from an inspection of the underside of the house and, grinning, put a hand on the old man's shoulder. Joe Archer turned his head and gave him a stunned look.

Ben said, his lips forming his words in an exaggerated way, "Is your door stuck again, Joe?"

Joe nodded dismally, gave the door a feeble tug, then looked, pleadingly this time, at Ben.

Ben said, "It's the damned moisture, you know."

Joe nodded. "I know that," he whispered. "I'm not stupid."

Ben said, "I realize you're not stupid, Joe." He reached around his father-in-law to open the door; Joe let go of the knob, Ben took it, turned it, gave it a mighty tug. The door opened. Joe looked embarrassed. He studied his small, neat bedroom. It was at the south side of the house, behind the kitchen, and the view out its one window was of a short, muddy slope, and a cluster of young pine trees beyond. He shook his head—Ben had no idea why—and said, looking at Ben, "What did you find down there?" He nodded to indicate the underside of the house.

Ben sighed. "We have several problems, Joe. The biggest problem is that one of the stilts is cracked. Not completely. I think it will hold until we can make repairs. I'm going into Eagle Bay today for lumber. And I'm not sure, but I believe that the refrigerator's on the fritz." Because the house had been built several years before electricity had been brought to the island, the refrigerator, which the Mosimans had bought with the house, was propane powered. "Our ice cream melted, and the fish spoiled, I'm afraid."

"Fish spoiled?" said Joe Archer. "I can check that, Ben. I know about those refrigerators. I can check it. Might be leaking. We oughta throw it out, I'd say. Get a new one."

Ben shook his head briskly. "No, thanks anyway, Joe, but I'd rather have someone from Eagle Bay look at it. I realize you've worked with propane refrigerators, but . . . but you don't have the proper tools, do you? And without them—"

Joe Archer cut in, shaking his head, "I don't understand you, boy. I never did." And with that, he went into his bedroom and closed the door.

Ben sighed, went to the kitchen door, which opened onto the house's small boat dock, opened it, saw the mail boat coming. He waited. Kellogg pulled his boat up behind Ben's at the dock, climbed out, and brought Ben the day's mail.

Evening

Arnaut Berge could see Dog Island through the north-facing window in his office on the inn's second floor. He looked at it now and, because it was well after dusk, saw only a dark lump on the smooth gray surface of the lake.

He used the island as a point of focus when he was lost in thought or when he simply wanted to drift. It's what he wanted to do now. He wanted to enjoy this place and this time and this solitude. He so rarely had the opportunity for it. The inn was like a small child—in need of nearly constant care, even when it was all-but empty, and he usually found himself bustling from one task to another, then to yet another. Now he had some time to himself and he wanted to do absolutely nothing with it.

His mind wouldn't let him accomplish that, however. It was used to continuous exercise and now, with his gaze on the island—he found that the island shimmered and was lost if he looked directly at it, so he had to shift his gaze slightly to the right or left to keep it in view—his thoughts ricocheted from here to there: from Mary, his daughter, to his new charges at the hotel, to beach erosion—a problem in recent years because the lake's level was rising inexplicably—to the obscenity with the deer that day, to his continuous struggle with the language—he often tested phrases mentally, again and again, revising them until he hoped they were right—to his own aloneness or loneliness. He wasn't sure which word fit. The meaning of both words blended in his head and he supposed, after all, that his own phrase, *ache for another person,* fit best. He had had that ache from the instant of Martha's death and for years he had flogged himself with the fact of it. He had asked himself many times, *That's all she was for you, Arnaut? Only a body nearby, and a face and a brain, someone to let her cold toes slip over you and warm up themselves in the winter nights?* And every time he'd asked the question his immediate answer had been yes. Because it summed up what she was— another human being to share space on the planet with him. She'd done that, and she'd done it well. Now, except in his memory—which was wonderfully and colorfully selective, and showed him only the best of her and the best of their times together—she was gone.

He thought from time to time about Jean Ward. He had noted that he'd mentioned her in one of his letters to Mary, and he had seen her walking about, as if merely drifting, as he was trying to do now. *Ageless* was the word he had been groping for in his letter to Mary, when he'd written, ". . . she is the sort of person for which the years sit on neither this way nor that and it is becoming increasingly so with the days passing."

Ageless.

And that was becoming truer as time passed.

But Arnaut didn't know what that meant, or if it was important to his feelings about her, though he didn't know precisely what those were either. He found her good to look at, "graceful on the eyes" was the phrase he had used in a letter to his daughter. He liked her walk, her manner of speaking and conversation, which he called, "for both of us, not for one only," and he had looked at her and wondered about going to bed with her. He had not wondered what sort of *performance* she might give, he had wondered how she would *hold* him, and how he would hold her, how natural and spontaneous and long-lived it would be.

An hour earlier she had come to dinner in the main dining room. Dinners were served inside, on the second floor, in a very large room on the inn's south side; in summer they were served on a small terrace protected by a wrought iron gate. The terrace overlooked the beach and boat docks. He'd come out of the kitchen and had the taste of the evening's meal— Trout Almondine—in his mouth when she called to him from across the room. He went over to her table.

She said, smiling up at him, "The hospital says my brother is improving."

Arnaut said with, he realized, the wrong tone, "I'm happy," because she came back, "Oh, about anything in particular?" and her smile became quizzical.

He decided to improvise. "About living," he said, and smiled back, "and about your brother, too."

She was clearly embarrassed. "I'm sorry, I didn't understand you . . ."

"I think that no one always does. I write down sentences I have used in the days which are good . . ." He stopped. Her quizzical smile had become one of confusion. He went on, "See now, even that one there is not too . . . useful and has gotten you in the mud . . ."

"In the mud?"

"Mire?"

"I understand now."

"Good. I'm happy."

She nodded. "So am I. Very. I love your inn, Arnaut."

He had liked the way she said that. Now, with his eyes on Dog Island, he remembered it and smiled. The solitude, he realized, was for moments like this.

A knock came at his door; a voice called, "Mr. Berge?"

"Yes, come in," Arnaut answered.

There was the sound of someone trying the door, then, "I can't. It's locked."

Arnaut stood, sighing, crossed the room, opened the door. Jeff Glynn was at it with a bemused expression on his face. He gestured to his right and explained, "I'm sorry, I'm sorry, but there's . . . a man . . ." He stopped, let his mouth fall open slightly as if he were going to continue, closed it, gestured again, went on, "Downstairs. At the . . . near the game room, outside the game room, Mr. Berge, there's a man . . . outside the game room, near the door to the game room, and he's standing very quietly . . ." He shook his head as if in confusion.

Arnaut said, "What man?"

Glynn cocked his head. "What man? I don't know. I haven't seen him before. Just a man. An older man. And he's very still, I thought he might be . . . suffering, having . . . an attack of some kind, a heart attack maybe, and I thought I'd better come up here and let you know."

Arnaut nodded briskly. "Thank you. I will come after you."

"Huh?" said Glynn.

Arnaut gestured toward the stairway to the first floor; the game room wasn't far from where it terminated. "I will come after you and together we will go and accost this quiet man."

Glynn said, "Oh. Yes. I see. Thank you. So"—he moved his head to the right—"I'll go down there right now and I'll . . . show you?"

"That would be good," said Arnaut.

"Right," said Glynn, and he turned and went to the stairway with Arnaut behind him.

* * *

Glynn opened the door to the game room and called to his wife, Amy, who was playing table tennis with Muriel Fox—she was delighted that the inn was open so late in the year; during summers, she ate here often—"Amy, where'd that guy go, that guy who was out here? You saw him, right?"

Amy made a quick, masterful shot that got past Muriel Fox, who ran after the ball, cursing under her breath. Amy called, "See who?"

"The guy who was out here. The old man."

"I didn't see him go anywhere." She paused. "Who?"

Jeff shook his head. "The *old man* who was standing outside this door a few minutes ago."

"Old man?"

Muriel had retrieved the Ping-Pong ball and was standing expectantly with it at her end of the table. "Someone went through there," she called, and nodded to indicate a set of closed glass and dark wood doors at the far end of the huge room—"just a couple of minutes ago, Jeff. I saw him when I came back from the john."

Amy gave her a confused look. "I didn't see anyone."

"That's because you were too busy totalling up your score, dear," Muriel said.

Arnaut said, "Was he a guest?"

Muriel shrugged. "Who knows?"

"And he went through those doors?"

"Sure. I guess so. I didn't see him go through but he's not here now, so, *ipso facto—*"

"I'm sorry?" said Arnaut.

Muriel gave him a grin. "Since," she explained, "he is not here now, and since he was heading in that direction, and since he has not come back through here,"—she nodded to indicate their half of the room

—"then, *ipso facto,* hé must have gone through *there."* She nodded to indicate the doors at the far end of the room.

"It is not impossible," said Arnaut, smiling back.

"Who are you talking about?" said Amy Glynn.

"The older gentleman," her husband explained. He stepped into the game room. Arnaut followed. The big oak door closed slowly behind them.

Amy Glynn shrugged. "I'm sorry. I must have missed him. "There was a man here?"

Jeff Glynn sighed. "Yes, as we've been discussing for the past five minutes, Amy."

She gave him a flat smile. It looked playfully menacing on her pixieish face. "Don't do that, Jeff."

"Do what?"

"What you're doing."

"And I say," said Muriel Fox, "that we get on with this game."

"Just what is it that I'm doing, Amy?"

"You're talking to me as if I'm a defective."

"No one's defective." He was clearly astonished at her outburst. "No one's defective," he repeated, and looked back at Arnaut for support. "Did I say anyone was defective, Mr. Berge? Did you hear me say, 'Amy, you're defective'? Did I say that?"

Arnaut answered, "It is at right angles to the geography of this discussion that we have in our hands."

There were things in the game room which were deaf. There were spiders in several of the high corners and they could not hear, they could merely sense vibration. The same was true of the flies that happened into the webs that the spiders built. It was true, as well, of the entity which waited with consummate patience at the glass and dark wood doors; it was waiting for the doors to be opened. It existed in a world of confusion, where switches opened and closed at random, where tears fell into mouths caught in the climax of a laugh, where need was leftover from the world that had gone before, but was mixed together with lust, and with memory, longing, and pain, where pain was mixed with pleasure, and pleasure with guilt, hatred, love, and love with confusion.

It could not hear the conversation going on at the opposite end of the game room; it was deaf, and even if it were not, it wouldn't have cared to listen. So, as it had done for a very long time at many doors, it waited. It would wait a day, a week, a month. Just as it cared nothing for conversation, it owed nothing to time. And when at last the doors were opened, it would go through and it would find another door blocking its path, and it would wait.

HISTORY—SEPTEMBER 4, 1976

"See that lizard there?" Joe Archer said to his grandson, Max, pointing at what he saw only as a green splotch on the gray surface of the pond at the center of Dog Island.

"Yeah, I see it," Max said, and searched the ground for a rock to throw at it.

Joe went on, "You know why he's in that patch of sunlight? He's in that patch of sunlight 'cuz he wants to get warm. He's cold-blooded so he wants to get warm. Nothing in this universe wants to be cold, Max."

Max leaned over, picked up a half-dollar-sized flat rock and winged it at the lizard, missing it by inches.

Joe finished, "Because being cold, my boy, is like being dead."

NINE

Harry Stans shook Pete Meyer Jr. until the young boy woke, blinked at him and grumbled in the cold darkness, "Who is that?"

Harry said, "It's me, boy. Where's your ma at?"

Pete Jr. shook his head, grabbed the top of the heavy blanket covering him, and pulled it up to his neck. "Jees, Harry, I dunno."

"She ain't in the house, Pete. Tell me where she is."

"Dammit, Harry—"

"Don't you say 'dammit' to me. You're just six years old and you don't say 'dammit' to nobody. Now, you just tell me where your ma is at and we won't have no trouble."

Pete sighed. "She went out the back door. I heard her go out the back door. And I ain't six, Harry, I'm seven, and I'm gonna go to school and I can say 'dammit' whenever I want, my ma said so."

Harry sniffed. "Jesus, boy, what'djoo do, d'joo crap in your damn pants?"

"I ain't crapped in my pants, Harry, I breaked wind, and it ain't none your business."

Harry laughed quickly, sarcastically. He had never gotten along with Pete Jr. He'd always seen him as a barrier between himself and Lynette, even when Pete Sr. was alive. "An' where'djoo learn *that?*"

"My ma told me to say it. She said 'fart' ain't a good word to say."

Harry straightened. "Your ma has got a screw loose somewheres, boy."

"No, she ain't. And I'm going to tell her you said

that, Harry." Pete Jr. rolled over and pulled the heavy blanket up so it covered his head.

Harry Stans said, his voice a hard whisper, "You ain't gonna tell her no damn thing, Pete, okay?"

Pete Jr. said nothing.

"Okay?" Harry demanded, his voice hard and threatening.

"No," grunted Pete. "I ain't gonna say nothin'."

"Good. Now you told me your ma went out the back door? When was that?"

"Dammit, I dunno. I was sleepin', Harry. I don't feel so good."

Harry harrumphed, "If you was sleepin', then how in the hell'd d'joo know she went out the damn door?"

"'Cuz she woke me up. I know 'cuz she woke me up. Shit! She got Pa's axe outa the closet and she woke me up."

On still, cloudless nights in January, Seventh Lake was flat and dark and the sky overhanging it a dull gray-blue from starlight. It was a sky that was alive, a sky that breathed, and Lynette always told herself that she would surely be able to see by its light. But it was never so, unless there was a moon. Tonight there was no moon. Tonight she was blind except when she looked into the thin, flat ice near shore and saw the smeary reflection of bright stars in it. And when she brought Pete's axe down hard into the ice, the black water bubbled up from beneath, overflowed the ragged hole she'd made, and she smiled.

Sound on such nights as this carried clearly and well, so when Harry Stans came out of the back door of Lynette's cottage he heard the quick, brittle noise that Pete's axe made when it hit the ice, and he started down the steep path which led to the lake. The path was clear of snow, but Harry found that he had to move very slowly on it to keep from catching his foot on a frozen clod of earth and pitching forward. He guessed that Lynette was close to where the path ended and he guessed also, from the noise he was hearing, that she was chopping at the ice.

He called, "Whatchoo doin', Lynette?" and smiled to himself, as if at a private joke. She made no reply and he realized he had not called out loudly enough, that he had actually not wanted her to hear him, that he wanted to surprise her in this strange thing she was doing. *Hey, whatchoo' up to there? Why the hell you choppin' a hole in the ice? If you got some kinda problem, then you'd best talk about it with someone who'll listen.*

His heels hit a small patch of ice, and he sat down hard on a fist-sized rock. He let out a loud *whoop!* of pain, scrambled to his feet, and turned around so he was facing up the slope, with his hands on the path and his knees bent. He moved this way down the slope for a few moments, then he stopped. He could still hear the brittle noises of the axe hitting the ice and he realized that he was close enough to Lynette that she had surely heard him cry out. Why then hadn't she stopped chopping at the ice? Why hadn't she called to him, or, at least, stopped what she was doing and listened? He considered this question for a few moments and decided that he had cried out just as the axe had hit the ice and so she had not heard him.

He continued backing down the slope. When he got to the bottom, where the path terminated at a foot-high drop-off to the beach, he straightened and turned to face the lake. He could hear the axe hitting the ice rhythmically, every five seconds or so, but when he looked toward the sound he could see nothing against the black backdrop of the beach, although Lynette was close enough to him, he guessed, that he would not have to raise his voice to be heard by her. But he said nothing. In time, he thought, his eyes would adjust.

He heard the axe head bite into the ice over and over again. He stared hard toward the source of the noise and he thought once that, yes, he could see something fluttering there, like a moth in a dark window, that it was Lynette, a part of her, anyway, her arm raising up, and he realized in the next moment that his eyes were merely manufacturing it and he was seeing nothing.

He stepped down from the foot-high drop-off and moved a few steps over the snow-covered sand, heard it crunch underfoot. He stopped. He realized at last that Lynette had been moving away from him all this time, that she was now twice as far from him as she'd been when he had reached the bottom of the slope.

"Lynette? Whatchoo' doin' there?" he called. He got no answer, so he called again, more loudly, "Lynette, honey, whatchoo' doin' there?" He got no answer. "Goddammit, you answer me." He listened. He could not hear the axe biting into the ice. "Lynette?" he said.

Moments later she moved past him, toward the slope that led to her cottage.

"Lynette?" he said, going after her.

He got no answer.

"Lynette?"

Still he got no answer.

"Goddammit, woman—" He tripped on a clod of earth, fell face forward, absorbed the impact with his hands, scrambled up, looked frantically about as he brushed the snow off. Lynette was nowhere in sight.

HISTORY—SEPTEMBER 14, 1976

Anita Mosiman and her daughter, Catherine, were having a picnic in a clearing at the center of Dog Island. It was dusk, the air was unusually warm and moist for mid-September, the sky a light blue/orange. The whisper of a breeze caused an occasional flip-flop of light and shadow in the trees that circled the clearing.

Anita Mosiman passed a pear to Catherine, who was very fond of pears. Anita said, nodding to indicate their surroundings, "It's very nice here. It makes me feel good."

Catherine said, "It makes me think of Uncle Harry."

"What makes you think of Uncle Harry?"

"This island we live on, Mama." She pursed her lips, clearly annoyed at her mother's ignorance.

Anita smiled. "Why Uncle Harry? I don't understand."

Catherine took a huge bite of the pear. It was very ripe and full of juice; some of the juice slid down her chin. "He used to hug me. He hugged me all the time."

"And?" Anita coaxed.

"And?" said Catherine, chewing the bite of pear. "Whatcha mean?"

"And how does that remind you of this island?"

Catherine answered, shrugging, "I feel like it's hugging me, that's all."

Anita nodded. "Oh," she said. A honeybee buzzed over, hovered near an open jar of mustard for a moment, then flew away. "That sounds pleasant."

"Uh-huh," Catherine said, "But I didn't like it."

"You didn't like Uncle Harry's hugs?"

Catherine grinned. "That's funny. 'Uncle Harry's hugs.' It's funny. It sounds like you're talking about those little drinks you get at the store." She had a sharp, almost nasal voice that Anita hoped she'd grow out of. "'Uncle Harry's hugs,'—that's funny, Mama." She laughed. It was quick, high-pitched, vaguely forced.

"Okay," said Anita. There were times when she found her daughter's sense of humor annoying. "Very funny."

Catherine's laughter subsided slowly. She took another bite of the pear. She said, juice squirting from the sides of her mouth as she spoke, "Because he hugged too hard, Mama."

"Hugged too hard?"

Catherine nodded. "Uh-huh. He hurt me sometimes. But I didn't say nothin'. I didn't want to hurt his feelings."

"That was thoughtful of you, dear," Anita said. "But in a case like that, where you're actually getting hurt, I'd say—"

"Sometimes," Catherine interrupted—she interrupted quite a lot; Anita tried to ignore it because it was clear that there were many things happening in her daughter's head and so it was understandable if, from time to time, she was oblivious to what others were saying—"when I'm in my bed at night, Mama, it feels like I'm being hugged real hard, *real* hard, almost so I can't breathe. Almost."

Anita was concerned. Was her daughter having some sort of respiratory difficulty, something to do with the island's high humidity? Perhaps she had caught her brother's flu. "Does this happen often, dear?"

Catherine nodded, studied her pear, which was half devoured, and said, "All the time, Mama. Especially at night, I guess. And Max says it happens to him, too."

"He does?"

Catherine nodded enthusiastically. "Sometimes it sounds like he can't breathe at all, Mama, like there's somethin' in his throat, and I get scared and I call over to him to stop it."

Anita studied her daughter a few moments, thinking that she might be playing another of her jokes, which were often grim. She decided, at last, that Catherine was being completely serious. She buttered a piece of her homemade seven-grain bread, offered it to Catherine, who shook her head, said, "No, thanks, Mama, I'm real full," took a bite of it anyway, and set it on her paper plate. They had lain a seldom-used quilt down as a blanket. It was a patchwork of many bright colors that had been given to the family by Ben's grandmother. Anita watched as an impossibly large ant made its way across one of the cream-colored squares, its dead companion in tow. She reached down, flicked both ants off the quilt with her finger and said to Catherine, "I really think that something of such importance . . . that you should have shared it with your father and me, Catherine."

Again Catherine shrugged. She shrugged quite a lot, Anita thought. "It ain't—" she began.

"It's *not,* Catherine," Anita cut in. "Not 'ain't,' *not,* okay?"

"Sure, Mama."

"You were saying?"

"Can I have another pear?"

"I thought you were full."

"I am, but I want another pear. Pears aren't like food or nothin'."

"Or anything. Not nothing. *Any*thing."

"Can I?"

Anita sighed, reached into the picnic basket, withdrew another pear, and gave it to her daughter. Catherine took a big bite and said as she chewed, "It's *not* important, Mama, because it ain't nothing wrong with *him*. It's this island we live on."

TEN

Ben Mosiman remembered moving into the house and being afraid. It had been a nebulous fear. Its only basis was in the fact that the house was new to him and he had no idea of its personality or of the ghosts that might inhabit it. Old houses had ghosts. It was a given.

But he did not believe much in ghosts. He believed in his capacity to be made fearful, and he respected it. He knew that it was something immature in him, something that hearkened way, way back, but he had never been able to shake it, so he'd stopped trying. He'd lived in a number of houses and his fear of them had always dissipated before long.

As it did with the house on Dog Island. Soon he came to know it well. He came to know that it was simply an old house with few secrets, and that the secrets it did have were probably not very interesting. He *knew* that. He sensed it.

Over time, instead, he became fearful of the island. *That* was a fear which he tried to shake because, he told himself, there was no basis for it. Not in his childhood, and not in his imagination. It was only an island and it had no personality, no life of its own. No secrets.

But it probably did have secrets, he decided. It had age, and so a past, and so, secrets. But it could not harbor them, it could not keep them, as a house could.

He said once to Anita—when they had been at the island for a month and were beginning to settle into a routine—"I don't like to walk on the island. But I do."

She gave him a small, confused grin. "What does that mean?"

"Only what I said. There is no other place to walk but on the island. So it's where I walk. But I don't like to do it."

"You could get in the boat and go to shore. You could walk there."

He shook his head. "Too much trouble."

"Well, it's a nice island," she said. "It's pleasant."

Again he shook his head. "It's not pleasant."

"I think it's very pleasant. So do the children. They love it."

"It's not pleasant, Anita. It's not *nice*. It's . . ." *Scary,* he wanted to say, but was afraid of her reaction. And he didn't know what he meant, either. Because the island *was* pleasant, he knew what she was talking about. He said, "Do you like it? Do you take walks here?"

She gave him another confused look. "We walk *together,* Ben."

"Yes, but that's different."

She nodded. "I understand that."

"When you're alone it's very different than when you're walking *with* someone, Anita."

"Ben, I agree. I said that I agree."

"When you're alone you become more self-involved. You become more defensive, too. You know. But the irony is that you open yourself up, as well. Your senses become heightened. *Because* you're on the defensive, of course. It's a lousy trade-off. You want to be relaxed and comfortable and you become defensive and that makes you vulnerable."

"To what?"

"To anything."

"You're being very cryptic, Ben."

"The island . . ." Again he didn't say it.

"The island?" she coaxed.

But he never told her.

The island's effect intrigued him, became something of a mystery, titillated him, and he left the house often to walk.

There were paths on the island that had been laid down decades earlier by previous owners and their visitors. These paths traversed several acres of fields, meandered through woods and then circled back on themselves. Ben quickly found that if he started off on any path, it eventually lead back to its beginning.

He saw wildlife on his walks on the island. There were birds—a hawk, several owls, grackles, starlings —and also an abundance of field mice and squirrels. And there were two feral cats who dogged him, appearing now and then very briefly, eyes intent on him, wildly and quietly curious. One cat was very large, the size of a small dog, and the other was medium sized and muscular, its square head appearing much too big for its body. They were orange tabbies and even from a distance, as they scooted off with their tails high, as if in imitation of white-tailed deer, it was clear that they were male. It was no great feat for Ben to realize that they were cats which had once been owned by people who had lived at the house. He enjoyed watching them, enjoyed their eyes on him because they showed him intentions which he could understand. He could not understand the island's intentions.

Once, he had tried calling to the cats, had tried coaxing them to him with, "Here kitty, kitty, kitty." He soon decided that these tough guys were far beyond such pretty nonsense, and that if he actually did succeed in getting them within arm's reach, they'd doubtless quickly draw blood and scoot off. He'd had experience with feral cats as a child. There were three-inch-long scars on his left forearm to prove it.

He named the cats Heckyll and Jeckyll, and he called to them several times on his walks, "Heckyll, Jeckyll, where are you?" They appeared soon enough, eyes intent on him, bodies low—in the cat crouch.

He walked mostly in open fields, knees rising up over the tops of the waist-high grasses so he could negotiate the tall clods of earth that were everywhere, pushed up by field mice and moles. The island was very warm and humid in summer, and though the wooded areas were cooler, they made him afraid, so he went to them only on the last few hundred feet of his walks, on his way back to the house.

After six or seven weeks, his fear of the island changed. He continued to be afraid of it, but he grew to believe that he understood it, too, as if it actually were an entity to understand—like an eccentric uncle, a grumpy brother-in-law, even the dark side of himself.

He thought he understood that the island was in pain. He had no clear reason to believe this, only the fact that pain caused just such feelings in himself as he was sensing from the island—a grasping, self-protective stasis, immobility.

Once, he said to Anita, "What do you think of the idea that the island is alive?"

She gave him a philosophical answer. "How can anyone say it isn't? Or that the air and the water aren't? We have a very narrow view of what the word *alive* means."

This didn't satisfy him. He said, "That's not what I meant."

She cocked her head. "Oh?"

"I meant it literally."

"So did I."

He shook his head. "You didn't mean it the same way I did. I'm sorry."

"For what?"

"For nothing. For disagreeing."

"But we don't disagree. We agree. The island is alive, just as we are, just as the air and the water are."

He understood, then. She simply could not grasp the real meaning of his question. Even if he explained it to her, she would not grasp it because it was something she did not feel the way he did. And she did not feel it, he guessed, because she was not as perceptive as he, and never had been. Her perceptions were for her children; to know when they were troubled, or in the first stages of illness, to know when to leave them alone, and when to go to them with her arms wide. She had no real perception of anything else. Not even of him. She put up with him because she told herself that she loved him and needed him. But it wasn't true, and he knew it. She loved her children and her father. She tolerated her husband. She talked with him and laughed with him and slept with him, but he was merely a companion whom she did not love.

His perceptions were different, he told himself. And that was why the island *talked to him.* It was a phrase he first used when he had been at the island for three months and had come in from a walk to find the house empty; a note left on the kitchen table explained that the rest of the family had gone into Eagle Bay to shop. It was the first time he had been on the island alone—the first time he had been unable to get off it, in fact—and he was very afraid. He closed all the shades, drew all the curtains. He was shutting himself away from the island, shutting himself up inside his house, inside himself.

The island spoke to him before long. It spoke to him in low hoarse whispers, as if it could speak no louder. He told himself that it was telling him of its pain, telling him it was uncertain how to react to the trespassers on it: to him, and his wife, his children, and his wife's father.

He did not try to speak back to the island because he heard only a constant, low monologue from it, and he had no chance to interrupt. He sat quietly in his big red winged-back chair in the living room, with the shades drawn and the smell of the lake wafting in on a breeze that pushed through the screen door at the back of the kitchen. And he listened to the island talk.

Late September was dreary and cold, and he fancied that the island stopped talking to him. He was happy for that at first, and he made his walks—under almost constantly overcast skies—longer than usual, because, for the first time in quite a long time, he had only his own thoughts to deal with.

He also tried to get closer to Heckyll and Jeckyll. He supposed that the coming winter might kill them unless they and he established a sort of gruff but friendly relationship. But they would have no more to do with him than when they had first encountered him. They kept a respectable distance, bouncing off when he got to within twenty or thirty feet. He got close enough once, though, to see that the smaller of the two—Jeckyll—had sustained an awful injury to its eye. Perhaps, Ben guessed, Jeckyll had tangled with one of the owls that lived on the island, or with the hawk. When he again got close enough to see Jeckyll's eye, two weeks later, he saw that it had healed dramatically and he muttered something about the miraculous healing powers of cats.

He decided, during that autumn, that the island had stopped talking to him because it had simply gone to sleep. If it actually was a living thing, then surely it would want to hide from the awful cold of an Adirondack winter.

January 17

Arnaut said to Lynette Meyer, "I am sorry, Lynette, but expectancy of work for you here is zero." She had worked at the inn as a housekeeper several times during its summer seasons. Arnaut went on, "You've haphazardly walked mid coldness in these trying times without much fortune." He smiled an apology. "Am I clear?" He didn't wait for answer. "A phone call in the intermittent—"

"Phone's disconnected," Lynette said. "I saw you was open. I came over. 'Sure he's got work for you,' I said."

Arnaut frowned. It was clear to him that she needed his help. He stood from his desk chair, came around, put his hand on her shoulder; "We're open now, what?—No more than January and February. No longer. And there is abandonment almost here besides. Only sixteen guests. And there is Mr. Carden"—the caretaker—"and the cook, and then I do all the cleaning, which is not much, a sheet here, a pillow-case here, a floor to be swept." He shook his head. "Please accept my forgiveness. I will drive you back, at least."

Lynette shook her head. "No. I don't mind walkin'. I know you got work to do."

"This morning, I have snow to push at, which will wait, as it always has."

"I can do that. I can shovel snow."

Arnaut sighed. He knew that if he offered Lynette a job it would not only be temporary, it would be very close to charity as well, and that was a precedent he did not want to set. To say nothing of the fact that he could ill afford to hire her. He said, "You have a child?"

Lynette nodded sullenly. "A child at home, and one at the hospital in Eagle Bay."

"Hospital," Arnaut said; it was not a question, but Lynette said, "She was real sick. She's better. She'll be back with me in the spring."

"It is my hope," Arnaut said, feeling suddenly helpless in the face of Lynette's misery.

"Real sick," Lynette repeated. "She 'bout died in fact and we took her in the ambulance to the hospital and she 'bout died there, too, but she's better now and she'll come outa that hospital in the spring, and please can I have a job, I'll work cheap, I'll work real cheap. I'll work for my dinner and that's all, if you let me come work here."

"I can give you more than that," Arnaut said, trying, at the same time, to figure out how.

Lynette smiled at him. "You offerin' me a job, then?"

Arnaut hesitated. *Yes,* he realized, he was offering her a job. He said, "I'm offering you what I can, Lynette. A room, meals . . ."

"When?"

Arnaut realized that her mood had changed suddenly, from one of pleading to one of insistence, and it annoyed him. He shook his head quickly, in agitation. "When is soon, perhaps. Maybe Thursday."

"Good. Thursday."

He looked at her a moment. She was slightly shorter than he, but she stood before him now so resolutely, with such an aura of power about her that she looked taller. "Yes," he said. "In the afternoon. I will pick you up in the afternoon."

"No need. I have a friend. He'll drive my boy and me."

"Your boy?"

"Tomorrow. My boy and me will come tomorrow.

We'll be here in the afternoon. Thank you." And she turned and left the office.

HISTORY—OCTOBER 12, 1976

The Mosimans were having a picnic at the center of Dog Island when a storm came up. It heralded itself in much the way that most such storms did—the horizon darkened and the lake grew quiet and whatever boats were out headed for home.

Minutes before the storm struck, Ben Mosiman offered that "the sky *looks* threatening, sure, but it doesn't mean a whole lot. I have a *sense* of these things." So, the family stayed at their picnic site, certain, anyway, that if a storm did strike, the close-crowded pines would shelter them as they made their way to the house.

They were right about that, though Ben, with little Catherine tucked under his arm as if he were a father bird sheltering his young, repeated again and again, all the way back, "So I was wrong, sue me!" And they clambered into the house and settled down in front of a big window in the living room that overlooked the lake and gave them a wondrous view of the storm unfolding.

Max proclaimed loudly, to be heard above the noise of the storm, "That's just lightning, and it ain't gonna hurt me in here!" which was a one hundred eighty degree turnaround from the way he'd felt about storms only a year earlier.

Catherine was entranced by the storm. She sat quietly on her father's lap with her gray eyes wide and her mouth open.

Anita's father sat nearby with a stunned look on his old face. He was remembering similar storms from his childhood, before he'd gone deaf, remembering the racket they'd made and the thrill they'd given him.

Now, because his eyes were failing, he saw little more than a flurry of gray and foam in front of the window, as if he were watching laundry turn in a washing machine.

It was Anita who felt the stilt at the back of the house crack. She turned to Ben, sitting beside her, and said, "Ben, did you feel that?"

He glanced at her. "Sure," he said, unconcerned, "it was a wave hitting the bottom of the house. Haven't you felt that before?"

She thought a moment and said, "Yes," paused and went on, "That's all it was?"

He answered, "That's all it was. Trust me."

ELEVEN
January 18

A heavy snow fell on the evening of January 17th, so the following morning, Arnaut got his guests together for a morning of group skiing. Everyone was pleased. Mitzi Roman grumbled that it "was about time,"—a sentiment shared by more than a few of the other twelve guests (two couples scheduled to arrive had cancelled). Snowfall had been unseasonably light and their days of skiing had been few. But Mitzi cheerfully got into her ski clothes, collected her skis and poles and was the first one waiting outside the registration area, where Arnaut had asked them to gather after they had all enjoyed a hearty breakfast in the main dining room. Amy Glynn was next, her infant daughter, Samantha, very warmly bundled up on her back. Amy took several, long drafts of the frigid morning air and exclaimed, "Nothing like the cold to make you feel alive!"

Mitzi Roman echoed that sentiment, though not as enthusiastically.

It was a sunny morning, the sky a shallow, pale blue—a winter sky—and the snowfall the previous evening had left a good eight inches of fluff on the ground.

"It really is very beautiful here, don't you think, Mrs. Roman?" Amy said.

"It's nice," Mitzi agreed.

Walt Roman appeared then from the cabin he and

Mitzi shared. He was wearing a red ski jacket, baggy brown pants, black ski mittens, and a blue and white knitted cap, and he lumbered toward them down the snow-covered wooden walkway that followed the lakeshore, skis in one hand, poles in the other. When he saw his wife and Amy Glynn he lifted a ski pole and yelled, "Morning!" Mitzi could see that he was smiling, and it pleased her. This was only his second winter of cross-country skiing and she knew that he would never quite get the hang of it. Like Arnaut's lopsided way with the language, Walt had a lopsided and ungraceful way with his feet and legs. Walking was fine, but pushing himself along on two slippery rails was another matter entirely; he accomplished it by moving one leg only, usually his left, while pushing himself along with the ski pole in his opposite hand. Mitzi thought that this was a comical way to ski—she'd been skiing since she was a child—but she knew that despite his lack of grace and the inevitable exhaustion, Walt enjoyed the hell out of it, so she said nothing.

Jeff Glynn was the next to appear. He and Amy wore matching ski clothes—blue parkas, white pants, red ski mittens, and brand new Aladdin skis; his were gray, hers blue. Jeff smiled feebly, nodded, and explained that he'd had a touch of indigestion, but it was over now, and he was ready to ski. He'd done very little cross-country skiing; his milieu, he told Walt and Mitzi Roman, was downhill. It was, he went on, "much more challenging than cross-country," to which Walt Roman responded with a belly chuckle, "Son," he exclaimed, "I can barely walk and chew gum at the same time, so cross-country skiing is a real challenge for me."

Mitzi said, "Don't let him fool you, Mr. Glynn. He's very coordinated, despite his size."

"I'm sure he is," said Amy Glynn with a polite smile. Samantha gave a squawk then, and Amy positioned herself so Jeff could get a look at the child. "She's lost her pacifier, Jeff," Amy explained.

"Uh-huh," Jeff said, "you're right," found the pacifier in the folds of the infant carrier, and put it back in his daughter's mouth. Within moments, the child was sucking noisily at it. Jeff said to Amy, "Did you give her her morning feeding, Amy?"

"Of course I did, Jeff," she answered.

Mitzi Roman said, "You're breast-feeding, aren't you, dear?" She had seen Samantha being breast-fed in a corner of the dining room earlier that morning. Mitzi concluded, "I think it's wonderful."

Walt Roman attempted a cheerful smile at this, to match the mood of the morning, but as far as he was concerned, breast-feeding was a distinctly private matter and women who did it in public were simply inviting the stares of strangers.

A newlywed couple named King appeared from the inn's side exit, followed by an older couple named Westlake, who were laughing together as if at a private joke, and then Muriel Fox came out the door of the reception area. She had ski poles in one hand, skis in the other, and a brown wicker picnic basket hanging from her back like a backpack, wide leather straps tied under her arms and over her shoulders. She gave the group a bright smile, her dark eyes sparkling. "Wonderful morning," she chirped. "A simply wonderful morning."

"Nothing like the cold to make you feel alive," exclaimed Amy Glynn.

Muriel said, "You're bringing the baby?" There was a tinge of concern in her tone.

"Yes," said Amy. "She'll be fine. My mother used to do the same thing with me. Not that I remember it, of course."

"She did," Jeff Glynn offered, then explained, as if in

apology, "Samantha's bundled up well, and besides, she gets a lot of heat from Amy."

"Of course," said Muriel Fox, still smiling, though clearly unconvinced. She glanced about, "Is this all of us?" As she said it, a tall, thin man named Fred Armstrong came out the same door that the Kings and the Westlakes had come out of; he was followed by a chubby, middle-aged couple with round, red faces and cheery smiles.

"Where's Arnaut," said Walt Roman.

"Where's the lady in the middle cabin, too?" said Mitzi Roman. "The one whose brother had the accident."

"I believe her name is Jean Ward," Jeff said.

"Yes," said Mitzi Roman. "Miss Ward."

Amy Glynn asked, "How is her brother, anyway?"

There was silence all around for a few moments, then Jeff Glynn said, "I hear he's going to be fine. A touch of hypothermia, but he'll be fine."

"I'm glad," said Muriel Fox. "Lord knows this damned lake has claimed too many people already."

"Oh?" said Jeff Glynn.

"Has it really?" asked Fred Armstrong.

"Too many," Muriel repeated.

Arnaut appeared then, from the same door that Muriel had come out of, his seven-foot-long, powder blue Trac skis preceding him. He stopped halfway through the doorway and squinted into the bright sky. "Pleasant surprises," he murmured. "Cold, snow, and sun."

"Is Miss Ward going to come along with us?" Mitzi Roman asked.

"I don't know," Arnaut answered. "She was missing at breakfast."

"Missing at breakfast?" said Walt Roman.

Muriel said, "Here she comes," and pointed toward

the walkway, where Jean Ward had just come out of her cabin and was making her way quickly toward them. She already had her skis on, and, as Walt Roman had done, she raised one of her poles and called, "Morning!" Nearly as one, the group called "Good morning!" to her, and within minutes all had their skis on and had started across the snow-covered parking lot. Walt Roman struggled mightily at the rear of the group to get the same tenuous feel for what he was doing that he'd had the last time he'd been out, a couple of days earlier.

At Route 43, which led into Eagle Bay, they hesitated. The ski trails Arnaut had laid out for them started at the other side of the road, crossed nearly a mile of open field, then snaked through several miles of pine forest, through another mile of open field, more forest, and, at least, doubled back on itself so their journey ended where it had begun.

Arnaut explained, before they crossed the road, "We are taking turns in the picnic basket. Muriel is first, then I am second, then I am propositioning volunteers beyond that, deleting, of course, Mrs. Glynn, who supports her daughter all the way."

Everyone in the group understood this, and arrangements were made for Jeff Glynn to take the picnic basket third, followed by Toby King, then Jean Ward.

Finally, Arnaut said, "Quiet now," listened hard for the sound of traffic on the snow-covered road—it curved sharply only a hundred yards east—then, with a dramatic wave toward the open field, called, "We're off," and moments later they were moving with varying degrees of grace and speed over the field, through the deep fluffy snow, their breaths exploding into mist in the frigid air, their faces red from the cold and the exertion, their mouths drawn into flat smiles of pleasure.

HISTORY—OCTOBER 26, 1976

Ben Mosiman was on his way back to his house on Dog Island in his twelve-foot green aluminum boat when the motor cut out and would not restart. There were oars in the boat, and Ben reluctantly began rowing to the island, which was still a good half mile off.

The afternoon was chilly, the sky overcast with billowy gray clouds, but there was, strangely, no wind. He was dressed warmly and the only discomfort he felt was the rough oar handles—the grain had risen from the surrounding wood—against his palms and fingers. Within minutes, blisters started.

He had been to the post office in Eagle Bay to mail a package of Adirondack-made products to his parents. This included jams and jellies, some cheeses, several small wooden toys, and half a dozen chocolates. He had no specific reason for sending the gift. It was not his parents' anniversary, and it was no one's birthday. The package was merely something he had seen a couple of weeks earlier at a Eagle Bay gift shop and had decided it was something his parents would appreciate.

He got to Eagle Bay in the family's five-year-old Buick wagon, which he kept parked in a rented garage half a mile from the Many Pines Inn.

He had been over three months at the house that October and this was the first time he'd had to row the boat. He was not accustomed to rowing; the last time he'd done it had been as a child, on a fog-shrouded lake in Maine, but he told himself that there was no real trick to it; all that it required was perseverance, ease of motion, and timing.

He rowed with his back to the bow, so he had to glance around every now and then to be certain he was still headed for Dog Island. His view of the island was good; he could see his house, the boat dock, the half circle of pine trees behind the house. At one point, when he glanced around, he even saw a face at one of the second-floor windows. He supposed that it was Catherine's face, because her room was there and he knew that Max was out with his grandfather on a walking tour of the island.

Ben took his hand from the right oar and waved. The face in the window disappeared. He reached for the oar; the handle had drifted toward the front of the boat when he'd let go of it. He grabbed the oar partway down the shaft, shifted his grip to the handle, and began rowing again, slowly, with perseverance, letting the oars come up out of the water on the back stroke and dip straight in on the forward stroke. It seemed right.

After what seemed many minutes, he glanced around, expecting to find the boat dock very near, but it seemed to be at the same distance as when the motor had stopped. He cursed and told himself that this task of rowing was too much like work, that it made mere seconds seem like minutes.

He stopped rowing for a few moments, oars held up six inches from the surface of the water. The boat swung slowly around so its stern faced the island. He told himself that the island was *not* just as far away as when the motor had stopped. That was impossible. Clearly the problem was that distances were awfully hard to judge over water. What seemed like a half mile could easily be much more.

He began rowing again, at first faster, more furiously. He stopped this after a few seconds, realizing it was an approach that was all wrong, that it would soon lead to exhaustion and, because a wind had come up, that it could get him into lots of trouble if a storm were brewing.

He rowed with a slow and deliberate rhythm and glanced back at the house often to be sure of his approach. After several minutes, he stopped again and let the boat's stern swing around so it faced the island.

He was farther off. He was certain of it. But, he guessed, looking over his shoulder, he was no closer to the mainland, either. Perhaps he was being swept laterally away from the island, so his movement was parallel to both the island and the mainland. He peered over the side of the boat, thinking he might see the swirling movement of a whirlpool, or the rush of current. But the clear gray-blue water had only a slight ripple on it from the wind.

He looked at the house for a long while, hoping to see what he had assumed was his daughter's face reappear in the second-floor window. But the windows remained blank. He called, "Anita? Anita? Are you there?" He supposed that she could hear him, even over such a distance, even over the wind, too, which was gathering in intensity, pushing the tops of the pine trees near the house. But she did not appear.

He began to row again. He said to himself, "Now don't panic. That would be stupid," and though he rowed faster, he did not lose his timing—gurgle, swish through the water, lift, return, gurgle, swish, lift, return—and kept it up for two hundred strokes, which, he estimated, would equal a good eight or ten minutes that, in turn, should take him perhaps a quarter mile through the water, considering an average speed of two or three miles an hour. He looked over his shoulder at the house. He was no closer to it, nor was he closer to the mainland.

He shook his head. He grinned, suddenly nervous and confused. Obviously he was caught in some kind of freakish current. Obviously what he should do was row back toward the *mainland,* and see if that would get him out of it. "It's a good idea," he whispered, and turned the boat around so its bow was facing the mainland. He rowed again. Slowly, methodically.

And he saw, quickly enough, that he was getting farther from the island, closer to the mainland. He stopped rowing. He smiled, pleased. Surely he was out of the freakish current, now. But the smart thing would be to try and avoid it altogether. He angled the boat so its bow faced the eastern edge of the island; he began to row again. Five minutes later, he stopped. He was getting no closer. He took a quick, agitated breath. This was getting stupid. "Dammit," he hissed. "Anita!" he called, "Anita!" and he wondered what, should she appear, he would have her do. There was no second boat (though now he resolved that there would be). "Anita," he called again, knowing that if he was indeed in trouble out here then she would be able to radio for help on their CB.

He called to her repeatedly, over the space of several minutes, but she did not appear.

At last, he started rowing toward the house again.

On the island, Joe Archer and his grandson, Max, were on the last leg of a long walk. Joe was holding Max's hand, but it was Max who was leading, because his eyes were good, and Joe's eyes could show him only what was within swatting distance.

Joe smiled as he walked because he imagined that the day was very warm, though it wasn't, and that the sun was shining brightly, though it was hidden behind a mantle of billowy gray clouds. Several times he had remarked to his grandson about what a warm and bright day it was, and Max had agreed, because he knew that his grandfather was wishing, or remembering, or that his senses weren't working right. Max loved his grandfather as much as he loved anyone. His grandfather needed him and loved him and, best of all, treated him as something more than simply a nuisance.

A small pond lay in a little hollow not far from the

house. The pond was the summertime home for frogs, mosquitoes, and dragonflies, and it even sported a tiny growth of cattails. Joe Archer and his grandson stopped by the pond before heading home. To Joe, it looked like a huge and fuzzy gray mirror, and he said so to his grandson.

Max said, "It's not a mirror, it's the pond, Grandpa."

Joe nodded. "Yes, I know that, Max."

Max picked up a small stone and threw it into the center of the pond, then he picked up another, and threw it so it hit near the edge. He enjoyed watching the ripples intersect without canceling each other. It gave him a strange feeling that he was seeing something very important.

After several failed attempts to get closer to the island, Ben sat for a long while without moving. He decided that he was waiting it out. "It" was the island and it was keeping him away; it was spitting him out, throwing him to the fish.

At last, he gave the outboard another try. It sputtered, as if on the verge of starting. He took the spark plug tap off, studied it closely, decided it was clean, put it back, tried the motor again. It sputtered once more, but did not start. He tried it again, and then again. It started. Within minutes, he was home.

TWELVE
Evening

Jean Ward opened her cottage door and found Arnaut on her porch. "Oh," she said, clearly startled, "hello."

He gave her an embarrassed smile. "I was about to knock. I was going to knock."

"Yes?" Jean said tentatively.

"I stood here a time."

"You did?"

"I did. And as you appeared my hand dreamt of being raised up and knocking."

"It did?"

"May we talk?" he asked.

"I was going out," she answered. "To dinner."

He looked confused. "You're not going to eat at the inn?"

"Yes. I was. That's where I was going."

"We can go together?"

She hesitated.

"Of course, if not—" Arnaut began.

She cut in, "Yes. Together. I'd like the company." She stepped out onto the porch. Arnaut got a whiff of her perfume—a slight, pleasant smell, evocative of nothing.

"I like your perfume," he said.

"Thank you."

"Chicken piccata."

"Sorry?"

"The special at the inn."

"Oh."

They went down the porch steps and turned left to walk the lighted path to the inn. After a few steps, Arnaut stopped and turned his gaze toward Dog Island, visible as a narrow, cream-colored line in the moonlight. Jean kept walking for a dozen feet, then looked back. Arnaut didn't notice at once that she was looking.

She thought that in the yellow glow of the plastic lanterns he looked very large against the darkness, and yet very fragile, too, like a huge candle burning. She had no idea why such an image would come to her. She did not believe that she knew him at all well, certainly not well enough for such images to mean anything.

She called to him, "Is there a problem?"

He shook his head a little but did not turn to look at her.

"Arnaut?" she called again.

He gave her a quick and expressionless look, then turned his gaze once again on Dog Island. He gestured at it. "It's like a living thing," he said.

"What is?"

"The island."

She looked. She saw what he saw—a narrow cream-colored sliver of light. There were stars above it and they were reflected in the black surface of the lake. The island moved as she watched it. It shivered, arched, settled back.

Arnaut said, "The earth promises life."

Jean said nothing.

Arnaut said, "Martha used to say that. I believe it."

"Martha is your wife?"

"Yes. Was." He paused. "The earth promises life," he repeated, as if to himself. "All we *have* is life."

"And memory," Jean said, wondering at once where the observation had come from.

But Arnaut had no response to that, and they finished their short walk to the inn in silence.

He had gone to Jean's cottage with the idea that something more than a friendship might develop. So, over dinner, he let go of thoughts of his wife as much as possible, and he spoke with Jean as he would any woman he found interesting.

After a while, the subject of Jean's brother was broached. She said that he was "stable, doing well." Then she smiled feebly and admitted that he was "simply holding on, I think. Just holding on."

"I'm sorry," Arnaut said.

Surprising him, Jean asked, "Do you ever wish that you were immortal?"

And, surprising her, Arnaut smiled and answered, "I am."

"Oh?" she said. She cut a slice of her chicken piccata, said, "It smells good, Arnaut."

"Thank you," he said. He buttered a roll, then set it on his plate. He had no appetite tonight; he wasn't sure why. He shrugged. "No matter. This body, that one, Joe Schmoe. It's no matter. Something *is,* something comes after, and it knows itself."

"We're talking about . . ."

"Immortality."

"Oh." She sipped her glass of Chablis. "Something 'comes after,' Arnaut? And it knows itself? I don't understand that."

"I do. In here." He touched his forehead. "In here I know what the tooth I'm saying."

"The tooth?"

"What the *tooth.* Yes. Tooth."

"Deuce?"

"Deuce?"

"Do you mean 'what the deuce'?"

He cocked his head at her. "Is that like 'what the tooth'?"

"Yes," she said. "It's like 'what the tooth.'"

He nodded. He said, "Life happens. It springs up and falls down and springs up again."

"I don't understand," she said again.

His brow furrowed. "Are you . . . making yourself uneasy for me?"

"Uneasy for you?"

"Sure. Are you making yourself *uneasy* for me? It is simplicity inside itself."

"I'm sorry, Arnaut, but that sounds a lot like a proposition."

"I'm not propositioning you." He paused. "I *know* what that means." He paused again, then continued, "I have it, I have it; you're giving me hardness."

"Hardness?" A pause, then, "Do you mean I'm giving you a *hard time?"*

"That's like making yourself uneasy?"

"Is it what you were trying to say?"

"I don't know. What do I know? I only know what my head tells me to know."

She grinned. "No, I wasn't trying to give you a hard time." She paused, took a bite of her chicken piccata, proclaimed that it was good. She said, "Tell me about your wife, Arnaut."

"About Martha?"

"Yes."

"She is," he said, and shrugged. "She is. It's simplicity inside itself. She is. You are. I am."

"And are you playing some kind of game with me, Arnaut?"

"I don't think so." He grinned. "Maybe a little. I don't know. A little. I'm sorry, Miss Ward."

"Jean."

"Jean."

Arnaut smiled. "Parameciums."

"Sorry."

He drew an oblong oval with his finger in the air. "Little, small one-celled creatures of the water. They come apart, they resurrect from the stuff in the water, from the . . . stuff of the water, and then there they are again. But they are something new."

Jean gave him a weary smile. "I don't understand . . . any of this, Arnaut. I'm sorry."

Much of the rest of the dinner was eaten in silence. At last, Jean stood. "I'm tired," she said. "Could you walk me back to my cottage, please?"

"Yes, certainly," he said, and walked her to her cottage.

She turned after opening her door, smiled at him. "Come inside, please."

He looked at her a moment, confused. Then he said, "No. Thank you. Perhaps there is another night." And he turned, went down the steps, and walked back to the inn.

When he got there, he felt good. He felt clean.

January 19

Harry Stans told Lynette, "That John Kennedy fella, the one they was lookin' for out on Dog Island, well they never found him, Lynette. You remember I was telling you about him?"

She nodded. They were in Harry's pickup truck, on the way to Many Pines. Pete Jr. was sitting between them, sullen because he did not want to be sitting next to Harry after Harry had threatened him several evenings before ("You ain't gonna tell her no damn thing, Pete"). Pete was thinking, over and over, *Dammit, I don't wanta be here!*

Lynette said, "Ain't what I heard. I heard they found him. I heard he drowned and they found him."

"Who'djoo hear that from? Sounds like crap to me."

"I heard it at the Many Pines," she answered, eyes straight ahead.

Pete glanced at her, stopped his mental incantation of *Dammit what am I doing here* long enough to wonder what was wrong with her, then looked away.

Harry slowed the truck around a long, snow-slick curve, picked up speed, smiled, and said, "Those people there are addlepated, you know?"

"They're not no more addlepated than you are, or me, and it's what I heard. I heard they found this man's body and he was drowned and it was the same man you was talking about." She glanced at him. "This John Kennedy."

Harry harrumphed. Pete looked at him. Harry scowled at Pete, then looked at Lynette as if to check whether she'd seen him scowl. Pete looked at her, saw that her eyes were still on the road ahead.

Harry said, "Well, *I* heard it from Tom Lord and he knows one of the deputy sheriffs."

"No, he don't," Pete said and looked at him.

Harry scowled at him again. Pete looked away.

"Well, we're almost there," Lynette said, nodding. "It's around that bend and it's on the right, real quick, too, Harry, so you slow down or we're gonna slide right on past it."

"Shit, woman, I know where in hell the damn Many Pines Inn is at." He put the truck in a lower gear. The engine growled; the truck slowed. "Didn't my uncle work there once? I told you that."

Many Pines came into view on the right, its parking lots and lawns covered by a blanket of fresh snow that had begun to melt now under a bright midmorning sun.

Lynette pointed at a small, rectangular sign that read, MANY PINES ENTRANCE. "It's there, Harry," she declared. "Slow down."

But when Harry applied the brake, the truck skidded on the wet road and stopped a dozen feet beyond the entrance.

Lynette looked back. "Dammit, Harry, dammit, I told you."

"Shit!" Harry grumbled, put the truck in reverse, backed it up to the entrance, and pulled in.

Arnaut was writing a letter to his daughter, Mary:

". . . I do not like it, I think," he wrote. "Perhaps it is the cold of the winter, and perhaps I am being a forty-nine-year-old man who does not want to be a fifty-year-old-man alone and it is very alone here—" He was interrupted by a knock at his office door. He looked up from his letter, waited for another knock. He did not want to be interrupted, and he thought that if he didn't answer at once then whoever was at his door would go away. But there was another knock and he called, "Yes?"

The door opened. The caretaker, Francis Carden, stuck his head in. Carden was a tall, thin, congenial man of sixty who had a long face and lively gray eyes. He'd been at Many Pines for nearly two years. "Arnaut," he said, his voice was very low pitched, nearly sepulchral, "we have got to talk, we have really got to talk."

Arnaut said, "Yes, okay, come in."

Carden came in and sat on a small gray loveseat at right angles to Arnaut's desk, with his long arms draped on the back of the loveseat so his big hands dangled over the front. He smiled. It was a broad smile, very toothy, and it crinkled the folds of skin his eyes. "We have a problem, Arnaut."

"A problem?"

"We're going to have snow deep enough to hide elephants in within the next few days, if the scuttlebutt I hear is true."

"I have often seen the snow fall, but never so much as that."

Francis grinned. "It was a joke, Arnaut."

"I am complacent of that." He smiled. "I have a little Armenian in my accent, true, but I'm not quite so stupid as a place mat."

Francis' grin became a smile. "We've never talked much, have we?"

"We have dissimilar duties here at this place."

Francis shook his head. "No. We don't. We have just never talked much." He paused very briefly. "Let's talk sometime, okay?"

Arnaut nodded. He'd never been sure how to react to Francis Carden; he had often thought that the man was trifling with him. "Yes," he said now, "we'll talk sometime. I view ahead of me about it."

"You look forward to it?"

"I'm sorry, but I don't run with this language as well as almost anybody. Now, please Francis, what is it about the snowfall deep as elephants?"

Francis nodded. "Yes, I'm sorry. We were straying, weren't we? I wanted to tell you that we're going to have to move the snow around once it gets here."

"There are shovels," Arnaut said. "And the snow thrower."

"They won't do shit with the kind of snow we're going to get, Arnaut. I'm sorry. We need something bigger. We need a tractor. A snowcat—" A knock at the door interrupted him. He answered it.

Lynette Meyer had arrived and she was ready to start work.

HISTORY—NOVEMBER 14, 1976

Anita Mosiman said, "We're out of wood, Ben."

He looked at her from his chair across the living room. "What do you mean, we're out of wood? How could we be out of wood? I just bought half a cord."

"No, dear." She gave him a flat, long-suffering smile. "You didn't *just* buy it. You bought it a month ago. It's been awfully cold since then and we've used it up."

Ben sighed. "What are you telling me?"

"Only that when we're out of something we usually go and get *more* of whatever it is we're out of. We're out of firewood, so what I'm telling you is that we should go and get more."

"What you're telling me is that *I* should go and get more."

She came across the room, leaned over, kissed him on the forehead. "One of the advantages of being married so long," she told him, straightening, "is that we don't have to say what we mean. Thank you. I'll have lunch ready when you get back."

He sighed once more, stood, shoved his hands into his pockets, pulled them out again. "Do you have the keys to the boat?"

"No, Dad does. I'll go and wake him."

Joe Archer had gone to his room for what he'd explained was "A morning nap."

Ben shook his head. "No, don't wake him. He'll want to go with me."

"What's wrong with that?"

Ben shrugged. "Nothing, I guess." He looked away, as if embarrassed. "We haven't been getting along lately."

"Oh?"

He looked at her, shrugged again. "It's no big thing. He believes that I . . . patronize him. I don't, of course. I treat him as an equal. He's got to realize, Anita, that his age and his . . . condition impose certain limitations on him."

"What limitations?"

He scowled. "What do you mean, 'what limitations'? He's an old man. And he's not well, besides. So, as a consequence, he's not able to do the things that he used to do—"

She cut in, "He fixed the refrigerator yesterday."

Ben shook his head. "Goddammit, Anita, I told him not to touch it. Those damn things can be dangerous . . ."

"Well, it's working again, Ben, and, as the saying goes, the proof is in the pudding."

"That's catchy, Anita. I'll jot it down and put it in my wallet."

She gave him an exasperated look. "Get some aspirin while you're in town, too, okay? I've got a headache. Hell, I've had it since I got up."

"Join the club," he said. He crossed the room, looked back. "I'll wake him. If he wants to come with me, fine."

"Thanks, Ben." She smiled. "Every day it becomes clearer to me why I love you so much."

THIRTEEN
Evening

Jean Ward said to Arnaut, over dinner, "This is the first time you've reopened the inn this late?"

He nodded. She seemed tense, he thought. "It is," he said. "Repairs aplenty abound, and so . . ." He nodded to indicate her plate of swordfish steak and the green salad next to it. "You are vacuous?"

"Vacuous?"

"A vacuum. Yes. Nothing inside."

"I'm sorry?"

"It's okay. We have a cat."

"Oh," she said, understanding him at last. A small, clearly false smile played on her lips, then vanished. "No. I'm not hungry," she said. "I'm sorry."

Arnaut looked distressed. "There's something . . . fishy with it?" He grinned, aware of the unintentional joke he'd made.

She shook her head. He thought, in so many words, that she was good to look at. "There's nothing wrong with it, Arnaut. I'm sure it's delicious—"

"No," he cut in, "it's tough and chewy and you're right to keep it away from your stomach. I think that my cook wants to beat a hasty retrieval before the cold snaps."

Jean said, "My brother died this morning."

Arnaut looked fixedly at her. There was nothing he could say, and he knew it; he waited for her to continue. After a moment, she did. "Complications of pneumonia. They said he died of complications of pneumonia."

Arnaut put his fork down.

Jean went on, "I thought only old people died of that, Arnaut." She had been looking at him. Now she looked down, at her plate.

He wanted to reach across the small table and take her hand, but there was a basket of bread in his way, and a carafe of red wine, two tall silver candlesticks, and he knew that he'd have to move all these things, or move his chair, or reach wide around the edges of the table to take her hand. So he said, "I'm sorry," and thought it was not enough, how could it be, how could it even nudge the grief she was feeling? He added, "You seem a woman with strength," because he thought she was; hadn't she accepted his dinner invitation very graciously, without a hint that there was something wrong? Hadn't she carried on light conversation for a few minutes when he'd picked her up at her cabin? "I'm sorry," he said again.

She shook her head. "It's not right that I'm here, Arnaut. Forgive me. I think I've misled you in accepting your invitation."

Arnaut shook his head quickly. "No. No. You need to adhere with someone these moments, in these griefs."

"I didn't like him," she said flatly. She closed her eyes a moment, opened them, repeated, "I didn't like him. No one did, really."

Arnaut wanted again to say something, knew again there was nothing he could say.

Jean went on, with a wan smile, "He was unlikable, that's all. I can't defend it. Anything. Him." She closed her eyes again, opened them. "I'm making no sense." She shook her head. "I don't need to, though. There are times in life when we don't *need* to make sense. This is one of those times."

"I understand that," Arnaut said.

"I know you do." She nodded once. "Can you help me with the arrangements, Arnaut? Sending him back home. I would simply like you to be with me when I do that. I'll take up an hour or two of your time."

"I'll do that," Arnaut said, his voice husky from the sorrow he was feeling for her. "It is my needs."

She stood. "I'll go back to my cottage now."

Arnaut said, also standing, "I understand. I understand. I'll walk you back. I understand."

She looked at him a moment. "You're a nice man, Arnaut. I like you."

"Yes, thank you," he said, feeling suddenly foolish and not knowing why. "Thank you," he repeated, and looked quickly about the dining room—the Romans were chatting over dessert at a table at the other end of the room. Muriel Fox was dining alone close to the kitchen. Jeff and Amy Glynn were just then coming in, their daughter Samantha in her portable bassinet. Arnaut said, "Of course, of course, such feelings as that swim together. Yes. I like you, too."

Jean nodded a little, said, "I'll find my way back, Arnaut. Thanks, anyway."

Arnaut was disappointed by this. "Of course," he said. "I understand. If you incubate passions or chitchat . . ."

She came around the table, touched his hand gently, stood on her tiptoes and kissed him on the cheek. She whispered, "Thank you, Arnaut, but I have someone to talk to."

HISTORY

The Mosimans stored firewood in a large shed near the back of the house. The shed had a tarpaper roof and chicken wire walls; this gave the wood protection from rain and snow, but still allowed it to dry easily.

Ben despised getting a load of firewood because it was a hell of a lot of work. Half a cord took up most of the interior of the family's old Buick wagon, and loading the wood safely into the powerboat for transporting nearly a mile across Seventh Lake to the house on the island required three trips back and forth. And today, because Anita's father had complained of chest pains, it was a job that Ben was doing alone.

He was carrying an armload of wood from the dock to the shed when he noticed that the crack in the stilt at the back of the house had lengthened and widened, as if the stilt itself had bent slightly. He put the firewood in the shed and went back for a closer inspection. He bent over and fingered the crack. It was horizontal and extended nearly one hundred eighty degrees around the stilt. He sniffed his finger; faintly, he smelled the tangy odor of sap.

He thought it was odd that the crack seemed to have widened, that he could nearly get his little finger into it; if it really had widened, he realized, it meant that the house itself was shimmying forward—a prospect he found disturbing. He stepped back and sideways so he could get a view of the stilt that would allow him to judge whether it had bent forward, toward the lake. He cocked his head, closed one eye. "Hell," he whispered, found a thin branch that had fallen from a tree and held it up like a plumb line several yards from the house so the stilt was behind it. Yes, he decided at last, the stilt was clearly leaning forward, toward the lake, and that meant that he had to check the stilts at the front of the house as well for the same kind of misalignment. He'd need to walk in the water to do that, and now, in mid-November, the lake was very cold.

Anita opened the back door and stuck her head out, "Did you get the aspirin, Ben?" she asked.

He nodded. "Yes. It's in the boat."

"I could use it."

She looked tired, Ben thought. He said. "Sure, when I'm done here." His own headache had gone away.

"What are you doing?"

He shook his head. He did not want to tell her what he was doing for fear that he would alarm her. "Nothing," he said. "Playing." He smiled a little.

"Playing?"

He nodded. "Checking this." He indicated the cracked stilt. "It seems okay. No worse than it was."

She nodded as if in acknowledgment. "Could you go and get the aspirin, Ben? I'm afraid that Max and Catherine don't feel well, either."

He gave her a concerned look. "Jesus, I hope it's not something we ate. How's your father?"

She shook her head quickly. "I haven't checked on him."

"Maybe you'd better." He considered a moment then told her, "I'm okay. My headache's gone. I think the fresh air helped."

"Uh-huh," she said, as if unconvinced. "Fresh air." She closed her eyes. Ben thought again that she looked very tired. She added, "Please, Ben. The aspirin," and she went inside.

When Ben was halfway down the dock to the boat, he heard Anita call, "Ben, hurry, Ben, please—it's Dad!"

After Jean had gone back to her cabin, Arnaut had gone to sit with Muriel Fox. He found her pleasant and amusing, and he often enjoyed the stories she told about herself and her life. She had been talking for a few minutes about her husband.

"Yes," she said, "as you can see, Arnaut, I have good

memories of him. Fond memories. They're mundane but I enjoy them."

"Continue," Arnaut coaxed. He liked watching her remember. He liked the gleam that came into her dark eyes, the way she smiled to herself. He thought that he was looking into her soul, seeing far more than what her words alone were telling him.

"We used to bake bread together," she went on. "Actually, I did most of the baking and most of the preparation. His part was usually in watching the yeast become active." Her smile increased. "I know, that sounds like 'watching the grass grow' and the 'rocks age,' doesn't it? It wasn't. I made whole wheat bread. I put warm water and honey into a big silver bowl and then I added some dry yeast and usually it started foaming up almost at once. Sometimes it didn't, and Earl insisted on stirring the mixture. He told me that that stimulated the yeast. Maybe it did. He was an adventurer in the kitchen. I'm not." She paused, went on, "What was most endearing about those times was the fact that we would both have our heads over the bowl at the same moment, and when I look back on it, now, it makes me smile."

FOURTEEN

Walt Roman wondered if he should apologize. He was the one who'd wanted to make love, after all, and look at him now—limp as a shoelace.

"Sorry," he grumbled. "It's the cold. The cold makes me limp, I guess. I don't know."

It was dark in the little bedroom. Mitzi much preferred making love in the dark. She preferred even more not making love at all. It was a chore and it hurt and Walt had what she considered "perverse fixations," and my God, she had often wondered, why in hell couldn't he simply go masturbate and leave her and her body openings alone? Her first husband had. *He* had been sensitive. Not like Walt, who sometimes seemed to have no more sensitivity than a rubber boot.

"Did you hear me, Mitzi?" Walt asked. "I said I was sorry."

"No need," she said. "I'm tired, anyway. Let's go to sleep."

Walt shook his head against the pillow. "I can't do that, Mitzi. I'm still horny."

"Walt, please, I've asked you before not to use that word. I don't like it. It's animalistic."

"Well, it fits, dammit. I'm horny as a hoot owl and I can't get it up. Don't ask me *why* I can't get it up."

"I wasn't about to."

Walt said, "I'll bet Arnaut doesn't have no trouble getting it up."

Mitzi said nothing. She rolled over so her back was to Walt and pulled the blanket and heavy quilt up to her neck. The faintly spicy odor of Walt's perspiration drifted over to her and she grimaced.

Walt pressed on, "Do you think Arnaut has any trouble getting it up, Mitzi? I don't. These foreign types never do. They always got sex on their minds."

"I'm not listening to you, Walt." She had her eyes open; they had long since adjusted to the darkness. There was a large round mirror on top of a dresser a few feet away and she could see most of the room reflected in it—pictures against one wall, a tall, dark metal chifforobe, because the room had no closet, and, at one edge of the mirror, the gray oblong of the doorway. Walt had said they should leave the door open; that way, heat from the fireplace in the front room could augment the oil heat and maybe, he said, "we won't freeze our asses off."

Mitzi stared at the reflection of the doorway as Walt rattled on. She had never liked looking into mirrors, especially in the dark, but she had always been unable to tear her gaze from them. She thought it was her way of challenging her fears and her imagination, her way of standing ground against whatever it was that might appear there. In the mirror.

Arnaut wrote palindromes—sentences which read the same backward as forward, such as "Madam, I'm Adam." His quirky and undependable way with the language, he thought, was enhanced and refined when he wrote palindromes. On one of her visits to the inn from Cornell University, his daughter Mary had gotten a look at some palindromes he'd jotted down that day:

SOME PALINDROMES

Tab a bat.
Now I won.
Sleep on no peels.

Rats on keep peek no star.
Repel a ton, not a leper.
Live on room, moor no evil.
Ha, tug at a gut, ah.
Name no one man.
Warsaw was raw.
Stop, pals lap pots.
Toot, otto, toot.
Nat 'as a tan.

She said to him, "Some of these don't make sense, Dad."

"No need," he said. "But they do."

"For instance, what does 'Rats on keep peek no star' mean?"

"Again," he said, smiling coyly, "no need for sense. But there is. Think about it, okay?"

She smiled back. "And how about, 'Live on room, moor no evil'?"

His smile increased. "Don't think about that one. It will make you crazy." He paused. "How's school?"

She sighed, grinned. "Mother used to tell me to make the best of a bad situation." She nodded at the list of palindromes. "'Sleep on no peels'? I'm afraid that one slips past me, Dad. Anyway, why do you do them?"

"I think that it's like coming down at a maze from above," he said.

"A maze?"

"The language. Yes. To me it's a maze and my mind . . . skitters about in it like a . . . a ball in a pinball machine. Doing these things makes it seem less confusing."

She shook her head. "I don't understand that at all. I've tried to do them and I couldn't get anywhere."

He smiled. "Ah, talent," he said.

She smiled back. "I'll remember that." She turned

her head to look out the window that faced Seventh Lake. She said, almost at a whisper, "This is the anniversary of mother's accident, you know."

"It was not an accident."

She leveled a hard gaze at him. "Meaning?"

"Meaning, yes, it was, but no—it was not so gentle as an accident, it was a drowning, and we should so look at it."

She sighed, said, "Oh," looked out the window again. "It took her," she said.

"What took her?"

"That lake. It takes everyone."

"That's dumb."

She turned her head and gave him a stunned look. "It's something *you* said."

He shook his head. "No such thing."

"It is too. It is too." She sounded petulant. "After she died. After the accident. Don't you remember? You said to me, 'The lake has taken her.' I thought you were being . . . philosophical. But you weren't." Her brow furrowed. "Were you?"

"It's beyond me. I've stored it away."

The conversation had ended there.

Walt said, "Have I ever had trouble getting it up before, Mitzi? No, 'course not. Some men do, but I don't. Not usually. Except for tonight. And it's only temporary, you realize." A very brief pause; Mitzi kept her gaze on the mirror, on the gray oblong of the doorway reflected in it. She saw a dull orange glow appear there and she thought, *Yes, that is the fireplace glow.* Walt continued, "It's the cold. The cold makes me limp." He paused. "I *am* sorry, Mitzi, I really *am* sorry," he added, as if he had not merely failed at lovemaking, but had instead denied her food and warmth.

"There's no need, Walt." She saw the white high-gloss enamel of the doorframe then and she wondered if she had just that moment noticed it, or if her eyes had merely needed more time to adjust. She closed them a moment. *Don't open them!* she told herself, *Don't open them! You won't like what you see if you do.* It was a kind of grim game she'd played practically all her life, but, as she had always done before, she opened her eyes. She saw the gray oblong of the doorway reflected in the mirror, the white enamel of the doorframe; she saw a soft red glow—*Yes,* she told herself again, *that's the fireplace glow.*

"Fire's out," Walt told her.

"No," she said, then realized he was telling her that he was no longer horny. "Good," she said. "Let's go to sleep."

"Can't sleep," he said.

The dark shape of a man appeared in the doorway.

"Can't sleep," Walt repeated. "I gotta pee."

Mitzi took a quick, deep breath. She could make out the man's face just faintly, as if she were seeing the face of an owl at night, and she could see, too, that his arms hung limply at his sides and that his fingers were extended. "Walt, someone's there," she said, though not loudly enough, she realized, because Walt said,

"Huh?"

"There's a man in the—" she began, no more loudly.

And Walt cut in, "Who in the *hell* are you?"

"Warm," said the figure in the doorway.

Walt launched himself from the bed, into the doorway; Mitzi watched openmouthed in the mirror; she saw the figure reflected there step aside, saw Walt crash into the wall beyond, saw the figure reappear, watched it come into the bedroom.

"Warm," it said. "Warm."

* * *

Arnaut blinked at Lynette Meyer, who had knocked at his bedroom door and awakened him. "Yes? Hello," he said.

She was dressed as if for a day's work, he noticed, in a pair of brown pants and an oversized white blouse and sneakers. She said, nodding to her right, "I thought you should know there's trouble in one of the cabins. I heard it. People fighting."

He had been in a very deep sleep and now was having difficulty pulling reality back to him. "Yes?" he said. "Trouble in one of the cabins." He only mouthed the words; he did not assimilate what she had said.

"A fight," she said. "Some kind of fight, Mr. Berge."

He was dressed in a pair of blue pajamas. He looked down at himself. "I am not dressed. Fight? What fight?"

"In one of the cabins. Those people had a fight in one of the cabins."

He was coming around, now. "Which cabin?"

"And how the hell should I know that?"

He stared at her.

"How the hell should I know *which* cabin, Mr. Berge? I think it's your duty to go down there and find *out* which cabin, don't you?"

"Please," he said, smiling flatly, "I am not customized—"

"And right quick, too, I'd say," she snapped. "Now you'll excuse me, I got my work, Mr. Berge. We all of us got our work." Then she turned to her left, marched down the hall and disappeared down a north-south corridor.

"Fight?" whispered Arnaut. "Fight?" He heard a door being opened down the corridor where Lynette had gone. A second later he heard the door close. *Odd,* he thought, because the room he'd given her and Pete Jr. was in the other half of the inn.

He went back into his dark room, to a window that

overlooked the cabins one hundred yards away. He looked out. He saw that the bright yellow porch spotlight was on over the center cabin, where Walt and Mitzi Roman were staying. Its glow illuminated new snow on the cabin's porch roof and much of the area in front of the cabin, including the beach and ten feet or so of thin ice. He could see, as well, the small, moving shadows of a snowfall just starting. The shadows were cast upon his window by the spotlight on the Roman's cabin and gave what he was seeing an exaggerated three-dimensional effect, as if he were looking through a tunnel—and the falling snow, the cabin, and the bright yellow spotlight were somewhere beyond it.

His phone rang. "Good Lord," he whispered, startled. He quickly crossed the room and snatched the phone up on the second ring. "Hello."

"Hi, Dad. Have you got room in the inn for a long-lost daughter?"

"Mary?"

"The same. Can you come get me?"

"Where are you?"

"In Eagle Bay. I could walk if you'd like."

"You're joking."

A chuckle. "Yes, dad, I'm joking. I need a ride. Do you still drive like a madman?"

"I don't drive like a madman. Mary, you didn't call, you didn't write—it's so advantageous to be hearing you."

"It's good to hear your voice, too, Dad."

"Where are you?"

"I'm at the firehouse. You know where that is, right?"

Arnaut nodded. "Yes, Mary."

"Dad, I would have hitchhiked the rest of the way but it's late. You understand."

"Don't hitchhike, Mary. The car is available to me and I am all but dressed—"

"I'll wait for you, Dad." Another chuckle. "Thanks. I can't wait to see you, I've got lots to talk about. Bye." She hung up.

Arnaut had not yet turned on the light in the room. It was an oversight. He had always told himself that he did not like dark rooms at the inn, but he had found that he often forgot to turn lights on and that he made his way around well enough in the dark. When he realized his oversight he usually corrected it almost at once. Sometimes he didn't. Sometimes he stood quietly in the darkness and let it do what it had always done to him—wrap him up and make him feel cold and warm at the same time, as if he were sliding into a sweet and welcome and temporary death. There were times when he thought that it was like drinking something that shocked the tongue at first, but which, once swallowed, left a wonderful aftertaste. Hard cider did that to him. He had, in fact, once written to Mary, "The darkness here at the inn is like apple cider." That is where he left it, and when Mary wrote back, "What does that mean, Dad?" He had not answered her because he thought it had been a silly observation.

Tonight he stood quietly for a minute, even though the urgencies of the moment—the disturbance in one of the cabins below, Mary's unexpected phone call —were nudging him. And as he stood in his room, the darkness did again what it had always done, ever since he had been a child: it wrapped him up and hugged him tight and made his skin cold and his insides warm and his spirit comfortable. He thought then that it was not so much the darkness that did this to him, but, simply, the absence of light and the presence only of shadows to represent the paraphernalia of his life—his desk, his couch, his bed, the lamps, the telephone, all became simply rough-edged shadows that undulated softly, as if there were small insects on them. It made him shudder, it made him warm, it made him smile. And he had thought more than once that, if he wished hard enough, his dead wife, Martha, could be among those shadows.

He switched on the lamp near the telephone.

FIFTEEN

Change occurs quickly in the Adirondacks. Temperatures rise and fall as if on a whim. The darkness happens all at once, with only a nod to twilight. Autumn ends like the closing of a door.

It is a place of contrasts, a place where the colors of the land do not bleed together but are as sharply delineated, as exquisite and mundane as the words of a lover. It is a place that does not embrace, but holds and keeps. A place that does not need its people, but tolerates them and gives them life, pain, exhilaration.

The cabin, where the Romans were staying, was the largest of Many Pines' cabins. It had three bedrooms —each large enough for two twin beds, a dresser and an end table—a good-sized kitchen with table and chairs at the back of the cabin, and, in front, a living room with fireplace, armless, green vinyl couch, two brown vinyl loungers, and two pine end tables. The bathroom was between two of the bedrooms. All the rooms were accessible from a long, narrow hallway. There was a small window halfway down this hallway; it was the only window on the cabin's south side, the side facing away from the main inn.

The cabin's attic had been converted years before for use as a fourth bedroom, and access to it was by a stairway built onto the outside back wall. This stairway, as well as the attic bedroom, had not seen regular use or maintenance for over a decade, and the wood was succumbing to rot. It was from this stairway that Walt Roman had fallen while in pursuit of the man who'd come into his bedroom.

Walt was seated in the kitchen when Arnaut arrived.
He had his right leg up on a chair, a cup of black coffee
in front of him, and he was wearing only a red-checked
robe and blue corduroy slippers. The robe covered him
to midthigh and was open down to his navel. His legs
and chest bore a thick mat of coarse, dark hair and
Arnaut stared a moment when he came into the
kitchen because he had never before seen so much hair
on a man's body.

"Hirsute," Walt Roman said.

Mitzi Roman was seated across from him at the
small enamel-topped table. She had a cup of cocoa in
front of her; there was a marshmallow, half melted,
floating in it. "He means hairy," she said.

Arnaut, embarrassed, said, "What transcendence is
this, Mr. Roman? Lynette Meyer"—he gestured a little
with his hand toward the main inn—"said there was a
problem." He noticed that Walt's leg was swollen
around the knee. He went on, "A bulbous thing there,
Mr. Roman. My car is in waiting and I was anyway just
now going with it out to Eagle Bay. Ride with me and I
will afford you the hospital."

Walt Roman said, eyes fixed on his coffee cup,
"There was a man here, Arnaut. He scared the holy
bejesus out of my wife and he knocked me off the
stairs, and what I got to ask you, Arnaut, is what the
hell you're going to do about it."

Arnaut gestured at the chair between Mitzi and
Walt. "May I sit?"

"Help yourself," Walt said.

Arnaut sat, folded his hands on the tabletop. "You
have gone in search of this man?"

Mitzi said, "That's how he fell, dammit. Off your
rotten stairs."

"Yes," said Arnaut; only a week before he had made
a mental note to have Francis Carden repair those

stairs. He looked at Mitzi. She fished the half-melted marshmallow from the cocoa with her spoon and ate it. Arnaut went on, "I understand and my apologies are residing in you."

"Yeah, sure," Mitzi said, clearly skeptical.

Arnaut looked at Walt. "You think this person went into the attic?"

"How could he?" Walt asked. "If I couldn't get up those stairs without falling through, he couldn't have either."

"But you visualized him there."

"Sorry?"

"He means," Mitzi said, "did you see the guy go up there, into the attic?"

Walt nodded, grumbled, "Uh-huh, I did," sipped his coffee, set the cup down and pulled his robe closed around him. "It's fuckin' cold, Arnaut. You oughta have some fuckin' heat that fuckin' *works* in these damn places!"

"Again, my apologies dwell within you. And my invitation still exists to ride with me to the hospital in Eagle Bay."

Walt shook his head. "I'm okay." A short pause, then, "I'm gonna sue ya, Arnaut, you realize that, don'tcha?"

"You're going to sue me, Mr. Roman?" Arnaut was flabbergasted.

Walt nodded. He smiled again. "It's a clear case of negligence. Mitzi thinks so, too. We both think we've got a litigious situation here."

Mitzi said, smiling, "Damn sure of it, in fact!"

Arnaut said quietly, "I have no money, Mr. Roman. Whatever I have, though, I am delirious to share with you in the prospects of further good health."

Walt shook his head. "That won't work, Mr. Berge. I know it's an act, Mitzi knows it's an act, the fuckin' *walls* know it's an act. You've got yourself a gold mine here and you figure as long as you pretend to be some dumb foreign type—"

Arnaut stood at once. "Pardon me, please. I am going to visualize into the attic space and then I'll be gone."

Walt shrugged, then winced and grabbed his knee.

Mitzi said, "Are you all right, Walt?"

He shook his head. "No. I'm not. I have a lot of pain." He looked at Arnaut. "I'll take that ride, Mr. Berge."

Arnaut hesitated only a moment. "Certainly," he said. "Give me some moments up there." He pointed at the attic.

HISTORY

"*This* is why it was a mistake to come here," Ben Mosiman hissed.

Anita, who had her father's ankles in hand—Ben was carrying him under his arms—said, without looking up at her husband, "Shut up. Please shut up."

"It's simply not *right* for people to live without a telephone, Anita. It's not *right.*" They were at the boat dock, now, alongside the boat. The children, Max and Catherine, were watching quietly, openmouthed, from not far away. Ben went on, nodding at the boat, "We've got to do this together, Anita."

"Together?"

"Yes. We'll each put a foot in at the same time, then we'll lower him carefully into the boat. Okay?"

Joe Archer was semiconscious, his breathing labored, his skin color a light blue.

"We'll tip the boat if we do that, Ben."

He shook his head. "No. It'll be okay."

"Ben, I'm telling you, we'll tip the goddamned boat!"

He closed his eyes briefly, took a deep breath, and said slowly, "We will *not* tip the boat, Anita. Now, on three—"

"He's going to die, isn't he?" Anita said.

"No," Ben said. "He'll be fine. Now, one, two, three . . ."

They stepped into the boat at the same time. It tilted precariously; water flowed over the gunwale. Ben snapped, "Quick. Put him down, now. In the center."

Joe Archer was not a heavy man, but Anita's muscles were tired from carrying him so far, and when she swung his body over the edge of the dock toward the center of the boat, her left hand slipped first, then her right, and Joe's feet hit the side of the aluminum boat. He groaned. Ben leaned forward, to balance the shifting weight, and set Joe's upper body down in the center. The boat righted. Water flowed around Joe's head, reaching to his ears. Joe whispered, "My God, my God!"

Ben motioned to Anita, "Put his feet in." Anita did it. He looked at Max and Catherine. "We'll be back before long. You'll be all right. Your grandfather will be all right." He was aware that he sounded like he was babbling. He pointed at a seat cushion near Anita. "Give me that." She did it; he propped Joe's head up on it, and moments later, they were on their way to shore.

The half-hour ride to Eagle Bay had so far been made in silence. Walt Roman had positioned himself catty-corner in the cab of Arnaut's Jeep Cherokee, with his swollen right leg propped up so his foot was on top of the dashboard only inches from the steering wheel. It was an awkward position, and he had been doing a lot of shifting about trying to make himself comfortable.

Halfway to Eagle Bay, Arnaut said, "I'm sorry."

"Uh-huh," Walt said. Except for his right foot, which had only an argyle sock on it because the foot had begun to swell, he was dressed warmly. When he wasn't shifting about, he kept his gaze straight ahead as if to help Arnaut see through the dense snowfall that had started shortly before they'd left the inn.

Arnaut said, "It was my real and benevolent inclination to persevere in the matter of the stairs rotting and so I intended, truthfully, to accost Mr. Carden—"

"Can it," Walt Roman said.

Arnaut fell silent.

Walt Roman said, "I gotta sue ya, you know that, right? If I don't sue ya, then I'm an asshole."

"I don't understand that."

Roman shifted around; his foot moved an inch or so closer to the steering wheel. He was seated, now, with his back against the passenger door. "What I'm saying, Mr. Berge, is that we have to recognize opportunity when we see it. And this here is a fucking great opportunity. It's nothing personal. As a matter of fact, I like you. You're okay. You got your con game and I got mine. We're businessmen."

"Con game?" Arnaut asked.

"Yeah, your act."

"I have no con game," Arnaut said, and slowed the Jeep. The snowfall had increased; now there were whiteouts every few seconds, and though he had driven this stretch of road a thousand times in the last ten years, it still held its surprises. Many of its twists and turns were marked, but some were not, and tonight, anyway, the road signs he could see were covered by snow and unreadable. Even the feel of the tires against the road was far different than he was used to; normally, the Jeep's tires gave him a harsh, gritty ride that transferred itself to the wheel. Tonight, the road felt gentle and sloshy, as if he were driving on balloons. The whole aura of the ride—the whiteouts, the sloshy feel of the road, the silence—gave him a sense of separation, as if the hands he was seeing on the steering wheel were someone else's hands, as if the voices he was hearing were not his and Walt Roman's, but the voices of another conversation over which he had no control.

"Uh-huh," said Walt Roman, "you got your con game, Arnaut. We all of us do. Maybe you're not even aware of it." He paused, then, "Christ, this is like driving through cotton candy."

"It is damn thick," said Arnaut, pleased that he had made such a direct statement, "and I am not in love with maneuvering in it."

"Sure," said Walt Roman. "Anyway, that's why I gotta sue ya, because if I don't, then I'm an asshole and everyone will know it. Hell, you got insurance, right?"

"That is at right angles to this discussion, sir."

The road was bordered on both sides by thick stands of pine trees; if there was a wind, Arnaut knew, then visibility would be much better—the trees would act as a barrier. But there was no wind, and so the snow fell straight down, thick, and wet, and though he kept the windshield wipers on high, the snow piled up almost at once and made him all-but-blind.

Walt Roman said, "That bastard did go up there. Into the attic. I saw him."

"I saw no one," Arnaut said. Instead of risking the stairs that Walt Roman had fallen through—he was thinner than Roman, but considerably taller, and so weighed nearly the same—he had brought a ladder over from the inn and had climbed it to the attic entrance, gone inside, looked about, found nothing but twin beds made years before and never slept in, and doilies placed just so on a big mahogany dresser. There was also a black plastic ashtray on a pine end table near the bed; the words *Fourth Lake* were printed on it in rustic, stylized gold letters. Overhead, the wallboard nailed to the ceiling joists had warped badly and Arnaut supposed, seeing it, that the insulation had been installed with the moisture barrier facing the wrong way, thus trapping humidity between the wallboard and the roof. He found a bird's nest, too, under the room's one window, which faced the lake, and an empty Hellman's Mayonnaise jar just under the bed.

Roman said, "I can't help what you say you found, Mr. Berge. I *know* what I saw." The loose cloth on the elbow of his coat caught on the door handle, and, several moments later, when he maneuvered himself around because the window crank was sticking into his back, he accidentally pulled the door open. Arnaut looked over, suddenly aware that the white noise of the tires on the snow was louder and aware, also, of the change of pressure inside the truck. He saw a look of surprise on Roman's big, square face, and he saw amusement, too, as if the man were saying to himself that he had done something very stupid, but that it was all right because he'd fix it quickly enough. Arnaut saw, also, that Roman's left hand was rapidly slipping from the grip it had on the door frame. Roman's look of amusement changed at once. Now there was only panic. Arnaut hit the brake. The truck began to slide. He let off on the brake, touched it, let off on it, touched it again. Roman lost his grip on the door frame and silently tumbled backward into the night. The truck came to a stop. Roman's door swung back, nearly closed, then fell open once more.

Arnaut threw his door open and ran around the front of the truck to where he guessed Roman should be. The snowfall was very thick now, and as he stood near the open passenger door he supposed that he could see, in the light from inside the cab, the impression that Roman's body had made when it hit the shoulder. "Mr. Roman?" he called, and started off the road. "Mr.

Roman?" He heard nothing, only the low whine of the Jeep's engine. He peered past the rough circle of weak orange light cast by the overhead light in the cab. He saw only a flat and featureless darkness, as if he were looking at a child's drawing of night done in black crayon. "Mr. Roman?" he called, and took a couple of steps into that darkness; he felt the shoulder drop off sharply, imagined himself tumbling into a gulley which might or might not be there; he backed away. "Mr. Roman? Please, please, call to me!" There was no response. He glanced around at the truck. The cab's interior was only a pinpoint of square orange light and warmth in the cold darkness, the bluish glow of the truck's headlamps flattened and diffused by the snowfall. Arnaut whispered, "Goddammit to hell!" If only he knew exactly *where* he was, if he was just around the fourth wide turn on the road to Eagle Bay, or if he was near the little fruit stand where an old woman, whose name he could not recall, sold apples in the fall, or if he was near the sign which read Deer Crossing/Next 2 Miles. If he knew exactly *where* he was he'd be able to mentally picture what lay in front of him, and picture, as well, where poor Walt Roman might be. But he knew only that he was partway to Eagle Bay, and that the snow was as dense as it had ever been— "As deep as elephants," he whispered—and that unless Walt Roman called to him there would be nothing he'd be able to do at that moment but get help from somewhere. If he maneuvered the Jeep around so its headlights pointed where Roman had fallen, he knew that they would show him only the snowfall.

"Goddammit, goddammit," he whispered. He had rarely felt as helpless in the face of another person's need. "Mr. Roman!" he called. He waited. He got no reply. He called again, and again. Finally, he turned, went back to the truck, closed the driver's door, maneuvered around, tried first the high beams, then the low, and drove into Eagle Bay.

HISTORY

Anita and Ben dropped Joe into the water at the shore when they docked the boat. He slipped first from Ben's grip, and then from Anita's, and he went sideways into a foot and a half of water. It stunned him, made him gasp, and when he gasped he took in a cup of water and then began to cough it up. The coughing helped. It dislodged the clot that had begun to take root in his aorta; the clot began to move again. Joe came around a bit. He became aware of where he was exactly.

In the water.

He panicked. He screeched; high, wheezing noises. He tried desperately to push himself up, out of the water, but his muscles had no energy. "Help me, help me," he whispered.

But Anita and Ben had already gotten him by the shoulders and ankles and were carrying him out of the water.

He saw Dog Island in those few seconds before his daughter and son-in-law turned toward where they kept the Buick parked. And when he saw the island, he made a feeble reach for it.

And knew, deep inside him, that he would be reaching for it for a very long time. But that he would never go back to it. That death and the lake would prevent it.

The clot that had been dislodged from his aorta found a new home.

The young doctor on call in Intensive Cardiac Care at St. Jerome's Hospital, in Eagle Bay, said, "Yes, it is a heart attack, Mrs. Mosiman, and I'm afraid it's quite serious."

"How serious?"

The doctor hesitated. Clearly, he was inexperienced at giving people bad news. He said at last, "I would like to tell you, Mrs. Mosiman, that there is hope. But I'm afraid that that would be . . . misleading—"

Ben Mosiman cut in, "Be straight with us, please. Is my wife's father going to die?"

The doctor hesitated only a moment, then nodded. "Yes, sir. That's my judgment. I'm sorry. His heart has sustained far too much damage."

Anita Mosiman broke into tears.

The doctor said. "Excuse me, please," and left the room.

Beneath the numbness that overwhelmed him, Joe Archer could feel that his lips were moving but he could not be sure that any sounds were coming out, or, indeed, that there was anyone in the room to hear him.

Above him, the paraphernalia necessary to keep him alive were like the shapes and shadows of a dream. He knew that he was closer now to death than he was to life. But it was okay. He had expected it for quite a while. He had even thought that he would welcome it (though he realized now that that had been fanciful, had been designed to prepare himself for it; he no more welcomed death than he welcomed pain or discomfort). His life was done. On balance it had been good and productive and pleasurable, but now it was done and it was foolish to deny it or to fight it.

But, goddammit, *their* lives weren't done. *Their* lives had barely started!

A nurse standing near the bed saw that Joe's eyes were wide and that his mouth was moving slightly, as if his lips were dry. She bent over, kissed him lightly on the cheek, straightened. She supposed that she was being kind, that she was ushering him out of this world with tenderness, and if circumstances had been different, if an awful turmoil had not been gripping him at that moment, she would have been right. But when she straightened she saw his eyes crinkle up and his mouth go into an O, and she misinterpreted what she was seeing. She supposed that he was panicking at the inevitability of his death and she became ashamed. "I'm sorry," she told him. "I'm so sorry." And she realized, not for the first time, that dying was a process to which she hated being witness.

"Propane!" Joe Archer cried.

The nurse cocked her head at him. *Propane?* That was certainly a very odd thing for a dying man to say.

"Propane!" Joe Archer cried again.

The nurse smiled a flat, sad smile of recognition. Of course. The words of the dying were nonsense words. They spilled out of a memory in release—names of loved ones long dead themselves, much-used obscenities, even words screamed during orgasm. They were the products of a memory in release, of floodgates opening. They were the sounds of a fire going out.

She leaned over again so her face was close to Joe Archer's. "I understand!" she whispered at him. "I understand, I care. And I want you to know that you are not alone."

"Propane!" screamed Joe Archer.

She backed away because his breath smelled of his insides, of blood. She opened her mouth as if to speak, but she said nothing. She stared at him; at his agony, she told herself—at the agony of pain she knew was churning inside him, and the agony, too, of being forced to leave a place where he had lived for so long, of leaving the earth forever. "I understand," she said again. "And I am sorry."

Then she slipped from the room.

Seconds later, Joe Archer rose from his bed and fixed his gaze on the closed door. "Propane!" he screamed, and lurched toward the door like a drunk.

The young doctor looked very gloomy. "I have bad news," he said.

Ben Mosiman stood from his seat in the waiting room. "Mr. Archer is dead?"

The doctor nodded. "Yes, sir."

Anita Mosiman, still seated, wide-eyed, voice trembling, asked, "When? When did my father die?"

"Several minutes ago, Mrs. Mosiman." He paused, continued uneasily, "There were unusual . . . circumstances." He shook his head. "I'm sorry, Mr. and Mrs. Mosiman . . ." He pronounced it *Moseman,* and Ben corrected him. "It's Mosey-man."

"Yes, sir."

Anita asked, her voice steady now, "What circumstances, Doctor?"

He shook his head again. "I shouldn't have mentioned it. I'm sorry." A pause. "He got out of his bed. For some . . . reason Mr. Archer got *out* of his bed and he went to the door,"—another pause—"and that's where we found him. Behind the door."

"Christ," Ben whispered.

"Yes, I'm sorry, but apparently, Mr. Archer was trying to leave his room. This is only conjecture, of course. But he was trying to get out of his room and he . . . couldn't do it, he was leaning against the door, against the bottom of the door and he . . . I'm sorry, forgive me, I shouldn't be sharing this with you, it is not germane to the fact that your father is dead, Mrs. Mosiman, Mr. Mosiman, but I think that perhaps it is germane, really—the last few moments of any man's life are germane . . ."

"Please," said Anita Mosiman, but the doctor, misinterpreting her, went on.

"Yes, I'm sorry—Mr. Archer had his hand around the bottom of the door, which was open partway, and I would say that if he was trying to open it then . . . his own body prevented it—"

"Please!" Anita demanded.

The doctor fell silent.

Anita said, "Can I see him?"

The doctor cocked his head. "See him? I don't understand. Mrs. Mosiman, as I just explained . . ."

"I know what you just explained, dammit, and I would like to see him." She emphasized each word, as if the doctor were slow-witted. "I would like to say good-bye to my father. May I please do that?"

The doctor nodded. "Of course. Forgive me."

SIXTEEN

When Arnaut got to the firehouse in Eagle Bay, there were four men playing cards. His daughter, Mary, was there, too. She was tall, lithe, blond, with a strong, square face. He hugged her, said, "Hello, daughter," then turned to the men playing cards. "I need your help," he said. "I have lost a man in the snow."

Two of the men—Tom Lord and Manny Kent—had had dealings with Arnaut and were accustomed to his way of speaking. The other two men looked at each other and smiled.

Arnaut said to Tom Lord, "A man fell from my jeep into the snow and I have lost him."

Tom Lord, a big, bearish man of forty-five with a full beard and long dark hair, nodded and stood. "I'll get my coat," he said, and went into a side room of the firehouse. Manny Kent placed his cards flat on the table. "We gotta call in the sheriff, I guess," he said, went to the wall phone nearby and dialed the operator. He waited. He got nothing. He pressed the shutoff with his finger, dialed the operator again. He cursed, hung up. "I'm gonna use the phone across the street," he said, and left the firehouse.

One of the two men still playing cards said to Arnaut, "Where'd you lose this guy?"

Mary said, "You really lost someone out there, Dad?"

Arnaut nodded. "Yes, a man staying at the inn. His name is Walt Roman and he fell through the door of the jeep into the snow and is lost."

"Christ," said one of the men playing cards, "didn't you go looking for him?"

"Yes, I did quite naturally, but his escape was into the densest of darkness and there is more snow now than elephants—"

Manny Kent reappeared. "Sheriff says he'll follow us."

"Yes, of course," said Arnaut.

Amy Glynn, in her room at Many Pines, gently nudged her husband. "Wake up, there's someone at the door."

He grumbled something she couldn't understand, then pulled the blanket over his head. She nudged him again, less gently. "Wake up, dammit!"

He sighed. "*What* do you want?"

"There's someone at the door."

He listened a few moments. "I don't hear anything."

"They haven't knocked yet, Jeff. Whoever it is hasn't knocked yet."

Jeff stuck his head out from under the blanket and looked toward the door. There was a long sliver of white light showing beneath it. "What the hell are you talking about, Amy? There's no one there."

"Jeff—"

Samantha, in the bassinet near the bed, let out two short cries. Amy looked at her, though she could see little in the darkness.

Jeff said, "Is she all right?"

"Yes," Amy answered. "She does that. All babies do. If you took any real interest in her—"

"Quiet," Jeff said. He saw that the sliver of white light at the bottom of the door was broken at the center now and he called, "Who's there, please?"

There was a knock.

"Who's there?"

Another knock. "It's Lynette Meyer. I gotta talk to ya; you gotta listen."

"Do you know what time it is?" Jeff called. He checked the alarm clock on the end table. "It's 10:30, dammit!"

"You let me in, we'll talk!"

"Is it important?"

"You let me in, we'll talk."

Jeff threw the blanket off, got his robe on, went to the door, opened it. Lynette Meyer nodded, attempted a smile as if in greeting, which came out cockeyed, and said, "I gotta tell you folks that you gotta leave, and if you don't then I guess you're gonna die, and so is your baby there."

Jeff looked around at Amy. She was sitting up in the bed, had gathered Samantha into her arms, and was nursing her. She shrugged. Jeff looked back. Lynette was walking toward the registration area. He called after her, "You're a sicko. You're a fucking sicko, and don't think that Mr. Berge won't hear about this. Who *are* you, anyway?"

She opened a door and went out into the night.

HISTORY—NOVEMBER 15, 1976

"I don't feel . . . what I thought I'd feel," Anita said. She was standing at the house's front window; it overlooked the lake. The curtains were drawn and she was holding one side open slightly. She went on, "I thought I'd be heartbroken. I thought I'd cry." A brief pause. "I did cry, of course. But not much. Not as much as I thought I would."

"It hasn't sunk in yet," Ben told her. He was seated nearby in a big green armchair. He was letting his head rest on the back of the chair. "You don't believe it, yet." His tone was casual, designed to comfort her.

"Of course I believe it, Ben."

"Something inside you doesn't. The part that controls you doesn't."

She sighed. "I don't know."

"Yes, you do," he said.

"Maybe I'm simply . . . a cold woman." She glanced back at him. "That's possible. Maybe I never really loved my father. Maybe I'm glad he's dead."

"No, you aren't."

She looked out the window again. "The lake is very rough this afternoon, Ben."

"Yes," he said. "Storm coming."

"Oh," she said.

"You loved your father, Anita."

She nodded. "Yes. I loved him. You didn't."

He shook his head, though she was still looking out the window. "That has no real bearing on anything, Anita. No real bearing at all."

"He was trying to tell us something."

Ben looked at her. She looked at him. She repeated, "He was trying to tell us something. I know it. I can feel it." She looked out the window. "I could feel it when I . . . saw him. When I saw him and said good-bye. I could feel that he was trying to tell us something."

Ben sighed and let his head rest on the back of the chair again. "I won't tell you that it's fanciful, darling."

"It isn't," she said calmly.

There was a short pause, then he said, "Headache."

"Oh?"

"Yes. Bad one."

"Me, too," she said. A pause, then, "The sky's as black as a frying pan."

Ben pushed himself to his feet, sighed again. "I'm going to go lie down, darling."

"Yes," she said. "I'll join you."

He glanced about. "Where are the children?"

"In bed. It's been a long two days for them, too."

He went over to her, put his arms around her, kissed her forehead. "I love you. And in my own way, I loved your father, too."

"That would be nice to believe, Ben." She kissed him. "Let's go upstairs."

SEVENTEEN

The snow had stopped and Arnaut had parked his Jeep sideways in the road, its headlights pointing at the shoulder. Manny Kent pulled his old Chevy Impala up next to Arnaut's Jeep, headlights also pointing at the shoulder. The deputy sheriff parked his car next to the Impala, flashers on and roof lights bathing the area intermittently in a harsh red glow.

Arnaut stared into the dense snow-covered pine forest that pushed nearly up to the road. He said to Mary, seated next to him, "I don't know. Maybe this is the spot and maybe it isn't."

Mary gave him a sympathetic look, but said nothing.

There was a knock at Arnaut's window. He turned. The deputy sheriff was there; he was a stocky, blond man in his early twenties. He smiled often —apparently, Arnaut thought, in an effort to put people at ease. Arnaut rolled his window down. "Yes, sir?"

"You're certain this is where Mr. Roman fell from the car, Mr. Berge?"

"No," Arnaut answered.

"You're not certain?" He smiled.

"What's certain?" Arnaut said. "But of the possibilities rising up tonight, this one is best."

"Yes, sir," said the deputy, still smiling, opened Arnaut's door, and continued, "Could you show me, please?"

HISTORY—NOVEMBER 20, 1976

Lucius Kellogg kept his eyes on the sky as he piloted his mail boat to the house on the island. As happened two or three times a month, he had a package to deliver to the Mosimans along with the regular mail and he looked upon that as a chance to set a spell, have a beer, chat with Mr. Mosiman (as contrary as the man could be; he was young, though, and he'd outgrow it), and watch Mrs. Mosiman simply because she was real nice to watch.

Kellogg hoped the weather held long enough for that. The sky had been threatening to repeat the awful storm it had unleashed several days earlier, and if it did, then the middle of Seventh Lake in his twelve-foot mail boat was precisely the wrong place to be.

He was a quarter mile from the house on the island when he said to himself that it looked odd today, that it seemed to be tilting slightly forward. He allowed immediately that this could not be, that what he was seeing was merely an illusion created by the choppy lake and the black sky that was the backdrop of the island and by his new route to get there, necessitated by the fact of a new customer south of the Many Pines Inn, to whom he delivered first. It did not take him long to realize that the house was indeed tilting forward, toward the lake, and when he realized this he felt a sense of satisfaction—hadn't he warned Ben Mosiman more than once about the dangers of staying at that house?

His view of the house showed him four windows in front, facing the lake, a door between the two bottom windows—it opened onto the dock—and the house's north wall. There were five tall, narrow windows in this wall—three on the first floor, two on the second.

When he was five hundred feet out, he saw a face appear at one of the second-floor windows. He waved.

He could not tell for sure at that distance if he was seeing the face of a child, but he assumed that it was because it was close to the bottom of the window frame. He got no reaction to his wave. The face stayed put; he guessed that its eyes were on him. He waved again, then held up the package he was delivering, a sizable Book-of-the-Month Club shipment. Those people sure did a hell of a lot of reading, but that was okay; what else did they have to do out here? TV reception was awful because of the mountains, and they had no telephone, either. So they read books. Hell, it could have been worse. They could have been axe murderers!

The face in the window on the north side of the house slipped away. A minute later, Kellogg docked his boat, collected the Mosiman's mail, and climbed onto the dock. He glanced into their mailbox. Yes, the mail was still piling up in it. Odd that they hadn't collected it.

Walt Roman was in no mood to thank his rescuers. He yelled at Arnaut—who, with the deputy, was helping him back to the road—"You bastard, you bastard, now I'm going to sue you twice, you realize that, don't you? Once for those lousy stairs and once for letting me ride in your damned defective truck. I've been thinking about this, I've been thinking about this, and I'm duty bound to warn you that your ass is in a sling . . ." He moaned from pain and exhaustion and the first effects of hypothermia. Arnaut, who had Roman's right arm around his shoulders, while the deputy had Roman's left around his—they were carrying him under his legs—said nothing. The man was right, of course, Arnaut decided. The Jeep was clearly defective, otherwise Roman wouldn't have fallen out into the dark and been breathless and in pain from the fall and therefore unable to call to him. Roman was right and he—Arnaut—had much explaining to do.

Roman regained some strength and started in on another harangue: "And I'll tell you this, too, you foreign nincompoop, after I'm done suing you for the damn stairs and the damn defective truck, then I'm going to sue you for leaving me here in these damn woods with the damn bears and the damn bobcats, and . . . and the other damn wild animals, what do you think of that?"

"I'm sorry," said Arnaut.

But Roman didn't hear him. "I'm going to start at ten million dollars and work my way up from there, do you understand what I'm saying? Have you got ten million dollars, buddy? I'll bet you don't. I'll bet you don't even have any goddamn insurance, am I right, am I right?"

"I'm sorry," Arnaut repeated, struggling to keep the grip he had on the deputy's wrists under Roman's thighs. "Forgive me. After you fell how could I hear you in this snow deep as elephants? Forgive me."

The deputy smiled at Arnaut. *"Do* you have insurance, Mr. Berge?"

Arnaut answered, smiling back, still straining to keep a grip on the deputy's wrists, "I have insurance. Oodles."

"Oodles?"

"Ten millions bucks worth?" Roman barked.

"Your misfortune is unworthy of a sum so magnificent," Arnaut said.

"What was that?" Roman was flabbergasted.

"He means your injuries aren't worth that much money," the deputy said, smiling.

"I under*stood* what the hell the man was saying, sheriff; I've had practice—"

Arnaut lost his grip on the deputy's wrist. The deputy caught Roman's left leg—the one with the bad knee—and Arnaut let go of his right leg altogether, so for several seconds it trailed backward on the snowy ground. Roman cursed. Arnaut grabbed the leg, hoisted it, got a grip again on the deputy's wrist. "I'm sorry," he said. "My hand became misdirected."

Roman gave him a vicious smile. "I'm wondering just what exactly I'm going to do once I've bulldozed that hotel of yours, Mr. Berge."

Arnaut said nothing. They were at the police car.

When Francis Carden was deep in thought he liked to walk around Many Pines with his Swiss army knife in hand, the slotted screwdriver and Phillips head open—they opened at opposite ends of the knife and therefore were always at the ready—and unscrew whatever screws he could find. In the wing of the hotel that held his three-room apartment, he had unscrewed practically everything and put it back together: doors, cupboards, latches, table legs (though these only rarely; the rule was that a screw should be easy to get at). This simple physical activity helped him to think, gave him a point of focus, and tonight—the night that Arnaut was busy carrying Walt Roman around, the night that Amy and Jeff Glynn were still puzzling over Lynette Meyer's puzzling visit—Francis Carden was very troubled. He sensed something alien in the hotel, and around it, something cloying and breathless and desperate. It gave him a sense of foreboding he disliked because he *liked* to believe he had been in intellectual control of his emotions for all of his sixty years, that any *sense of foreboding* he had ever felt was in the same basket with devils and angels and people who claimed to know the future. This particular sense of foreboding, he was beginning to feel, amounted to no more than the side effects of indigestion or loneliness.

He stuck the Phillips head end of his Swiss army knife into a screw in one of the hinges of a display case set into a wall not far from the hotel's registration office. The display case held tennis trophies won in the early sixties, when Many Pines had boasted its own tennis team. All the trophies were for first place, except one, which was for Sportsman of the Year—the award had gone to a man named Leland Foster Wood.

As he unscrewed the Phillips screw—one of three in the hinge—Carden kept his eye on that trophy. It was made of very highly polished brass—he polished the trophies once a month—and he could see his face and much of the hallway behind him reflected in it. He thought about his face. He thought that it looked rounded and bizarre reflected from the belly of the trophy, that his eyebrows were too thick, and that his chin was growing weak with age, that his eyes were the eyes of a man possessed, or obsessed, or acting under compulsion. Then he thought that it had probably once been a good and kind and handsome face, that it would be nice if he could remember such a face, though he couldn't. The photographs he had saved from his tour of duty in the Navy showed him a young man he was reluctant to admit had been himself; a young man who was beautiful and naive and vulnerable looking, like an Irish setter.

"Old Irish setter," he whispered as he bent over and unscrewed the screw and studied his reflection in the polished brass belly of the tennis trophy. He watched his lips move as he whispered. Their movements, too, were exaggerated by the roundness of the trophy and it amused him. He stopped unscrewing the screw a moment, kept the screwdriver's tip in the slot, and said aloud to his reflection in the trophy, "What are you doing here, what are you doing here?" He enjoyed the exaggerated movements of his lips, as if he were watching two caterpillars crawling on the pink and brass mask of his face. "Shit," he said, "I've got to grow a beard again. I'm good with a beard, it hides my chin, I don't like my chin." He said all this very slowly, his lips moving dramatically. He did not like looking into mirrors—for different reasons than Mitzi Roman didn't like looking into mirrors—but this, he decided, was not really a mirror; this was a movie he was watching, a movie of himself. He was watching his face become fat and his eyes become obsessed and he was watching his lips move like two caterpillars.

"You're an old fart," he said, and he remembered that years and years before he had realized he'd someday become an old fart, and he remembered thinking at the time that he hoped he would recognize it, and cure it, and as he was remembering this another reflection appeared in the polished brass belly of the trophy, and he didn't see it at first because he was studying himself, making love to his own bizarre reflection; then he did see it and it frightened him and he jerked erect.

Jean Ward said to him, "It's very cold in my cabin, Mr. Carden." She looked confusedly at him. "What are you doing?"

He shook his head, folded up his Swiss army knife and put it in his pocket. He was embarrassed. He didn't like being embarrassed—he saw it as an invasion of his privacy. "I'm unscrewing screws," he said. "I unscrew screws, then I screw them back in. Do you mind?"

She shrugged. She was dressed in a blue pea coat that was too large for her, and black rubber buckle boots that still had some snow clinging to them. "I don't mind," she said. "Where is Mr. Berge?"

"I don't know," Carden answered.

"Is he out?"

"It's possible. It's possible he's out. You say your cabin's too cold?"

She nodded. "Awfully cold. That fireplace heats up the area around it and that's about all, and I think I'm out of fuel oil, besides."

"You want to switch?"

"Switch rooms?"

He nodded. "You can have any one you want, except the north wing isn't heated because the furnace is down."

"Then how does the rest of the inn get heated?" she asked.

He gave her a stiff, impatient smile. "We've got four furnaces. One for each wing. A place this big has got to have more than one furnace, right? If you have only one furnace, then the rooms that are furthest from it are going to be cold, anyway, because the heated air cools off on its way down the heating duct. Do you understand that?"

"Yes, I do."

"Good. I thought you would."

Jean raised an eyebrow. "Thanks. You said I could have any room I wanted?"

"I said that."

"Can I have one now?"

"You can have one now, yes."

"Are you always this brusque?"

"No."

"Oh. When are you not so brusque?"

"I'm always brusque," he said. "Do you want another room or not?"

She sighed. "Yes. I do. Can you get me a key?" She looked up and down the hallway. "Any one of these rooms is fine. I'm not fussy. I think the man in the cabin next to mine will be wanting a new room, too."

"Oh? Who's that?"

"I don't know. I don't know his name, anyway. We've talked. He's very nice, but he complains quite a lot about the cold."

Carden nodded. "Don't we all?"

EIGHTEEN

HISTORY

Lucius Kellogg remembered Catherine Mosiman as a mischievous, bright little girl, and as she looked up at him now from the back doorway of the house he thought that it had been she who had been watching him from the second-floor window moments earlier.

He said to her, "Are you all right, child?" because she looked ghastly pale, and her expression was oddly flat.

She did not answer. She held the door open—if unattended, it swung shut on a heavy spring—and she stared wide-eyed at him, as if, he supposed, he were someone she should be leary of.

He indicated the big package he held under his arm, and the fistful of mail he'd collected from the Mosiman's mailbox. "I got this stuff for your ma and your pa," he said. "They at home?"

Still she said nothing. She continued holding the door open, continued staring at him.

"Can I come in?" he asked and thought, looking closely at her, that her skin was so very pale that it was nearly translucent and that her gray eyes were as expressionless as the eyes of a toad. He repeated, "Can I come in?" She moved out of the way; her long yellow Sesame Street robe—it had a Kermit the Frog decal on it—hid the movements of her feet and gave him the uncomfortable feeling that her feet did not move at all.

He stepped into the house, said "Thanks," heard the door close behind him, and looked back. He saw that Catherine was still looking up at him and he wondered, since she had not yet said anything, if she were able to speak. He remembered meeting her—three months ago, he thought, perhaps four—and she had been chasing her brother Max around the dock then, had nearly knocked him into the water a couple of times, in fact. He remembered Ben Mosiman hollering at her to "slow down," and he remembered that Catherine had barely acknowledged him. Kellogg said again, "Are you all right, do you feel all right, Catherine?"

She said nothing.

He noticed an odd stuffiness in the house, as if the air were heavy and moist. He knew that lake houses often held such an atmosphere, but he thought that this was different, though he couldn't pinpoint why or how.

Catherine moved past him then, past the refrigerator, toward the door to the hallway which led to the stairs. Again, as he watched her, Kellogg supposed that her Kermit the Frog robe was hiding the movements of her legs and feet.

"You're going to go and get your folks?" he called to her, but she did not answer or look back, and in a moment had disappeared up the stairs to the second floor.

Kellogg assumed that she was indeed going to get her parents, so he sat in a chair in the kitchen and he waited. Eventually, he saw that the sky visible through the kitchen windows had darkened considerably and he remembered his concern about the storm. He got up from his chair, went to a window, peered out. "Dammit," he murmured. He'd have to give up the idea of having some coffee with Mr. Mosiman —the storm was almost here. He'd be lucky if he made it back to shore before it hit.

He went into the living room, hesitated: Odd, he thought, but it had been some time since he'd heard any movement in the house. If Catherine had gone up to get her parents, then he would have heard them moving about, even if she'd interrupted them in a nap or in lovemaking. He shrugged. If there had been anything wrong, Catherine would have told him.

"Mr. Mosiman," he called. "I left a package for you on your kitchen table." He waited. There was no answer. He went to the stairs, gazed up, saw the landing, a closed door beyond it. He listened. The house was very still, except for occasional shivers sent through it by a sudden wind.

"Mr. Mosiman, are you all right, sir?" He saw the suggestion of movement to the left of the landing, where a hallway led to the house's back bedrooms. A moment later, Catherine reappeared. She was still in her yellow robe. She came to the top of the stairs. She stopped, looked down at him, her gray eyes very wide, as if she were surprised, or as if, he thought, she were on the verge of a scream.

Kellogg said, "Good Lord, child, what in the name of heaven is wrong here?"

She did not answer. She stayed very still, her eyes wide, her arms hanging loosely at her sides.

"Answer me!" Kellogg demanded. "You speak when you're spoken to!"

Her mouth opened very slightly, as mouths sometimes do in sleep.

The house shook. A vicious tearing sound came from beneath it. Kellogg grabbed the newel post, felt himself going backward. The house steadied. "Child," he began, and looked up at the landing again.

Catherine was not there.

Kellogg was a tall, thin man, and strong, and he took the stairs quickly. He hesitated on the landing: *Jesus,* he said to himself, *I'm going to be a hero.*

He tried the door in front of him. It would not open. He tugged at it, certain there was someone behind it. He called, "Mr. and Mrs. Mosiman, you got trouble here, you got a shitload of trouble here!"

The house shook again and he realized that for the past few seconds he had been leaning slightly forward to keep his balance.

He started down the hallway to the back bedrooms. He moved slowly, as if uncertain of his footing. He saw that one of the bedroom doors was open. He went to it. He looked in.

Ben and Anita were on the bed. Ben was on his side with a heavy blue blanket midway up his bare chest. Anita was behind him, with her chest against his back, and her arm over his arm.

Lucius Kellogg did not attempt to speak. It was clear enough that Ben and Anita Mosiman were dead. They were pale blue, their mouths open slightly, as Catherine's had been; Anita's eyes—he could not see Ben's because her forearm hid them—were halfway open, as if they were going to flutter and she was going to wake.

And there was the smell, too—an awful, sickly sweet smell, like potted meat left out in the sun.

He backed away from the room, hand covering his nose and mouth. The house shook yet again. He realized that he was bending even farther forward to keep his balance. He saw movement out of the corner of his eye. He looked. Catherine was there, at the end of the hallway, in front of the closed far door. He took his hand briefly from his mouth and called to her, "Catherine, come here, child, come here!" He covered his mouth again.

Catherine did not move.

He started for her slowly, smiling through his hand. He nodded as he smiled; he supposed that his nodding and smiling would take the place of soothing words.

She smiled. The red bow of her lips, which had before been slightly parted, broke into a broad and open-mouthed smile that he could not take his eyes off because it was a mouth that opened onto incredible darkness. He stopped moving toward her and realized that the same awful, sickly sweet smell that had swept out of the room where Ben and Anita lay was also coming from within her.

He knew what he was seeing, but he did not believe it. He thought that desperation and creeping panic had invented it; he thought that his brain was capable of any invention, that the child standing before him in her yellow Sesame Street robe with the Kermit the Frog decal was only a child in trouble; that the smell coming from her was merely the smell of the house, the smell of death that had gotten into her because she had lain down with her poor parents for a while or had merely sat in the room with them, weeping, confused. And now that smell pushed out of her pores, the way garlic did, so he said to her in pity and compassion, "Catherine, I'm sorry, your mother and your father . . ." *are dead,* he was about to say, but he did not say it because surely it was something she knew, and because it was something he did not want to tell her, if she didn't (he was too kind). He went on, "Where's your brother, child? Where's Max?" But she continued smiling at him, the red bow of her lips in a nearly perfect and impossible O, and her eyes as expressionless as a toad's, and her skin so translucent that he could see the hard knot of bone beneath.

Then she screamed.

And Ben and Anita screamed on their bed of death, and got up together, and came out into the hallway.

And Max got out of his bed. And came out into the hallway, too. And stood in his Big Bird pajamas beside Catherine.

And Anita stood beside Ben, naked and blue and reeking of death.

And they screamed.

As the house began its long, slow slide into the lake, as Lucius Kellogg threw himself weeping out of that hallway and down the stairs and into the cold arms of the storm.

They screamed.

NINETEEN

The thing waiting just inside the door of the cabin thought, *A stitch in time saves nine.* It was a phrase that floated about with a million other phrases in the dark water of its memory. Now that phrase caught what little light there was and the thing clutched at it. *A stitch in time saves nine.* The thing had no idea what the phrase meant. It was simply a memory and it came and went with a million other memories, like a mosquito.

The entity knew about cold and about warmth. It knew that it was constantly cold and that there was a time when it had been warm. But that was in another place, in another life—*this* life had everything to do with cold and nothing to do with warmth, and that was the payment that had been exacted.

By someone.

For some sin or crime.

But the entity knew very little about sin or crime, either, nor did it care.

It cared about cold.

It whispered into the still air of the cabin, "I am cold. I am cold, I am cold."

Jean Ward said, "This looks fine. It's warmer. Thanks."

Mr. Carden said, "I doubt that Arnaut will object. Better than having you catch pneumonia."

Jean nodded. The room Carden had given her was spacious. There were two twin beds, a large dark blue oriental rug, and a small oak desk and chair. It was also the only room in the hotel with a window seat, a fact which Carden noted; "It's the only bay window in the whole damn place, so you got yourself a window seat," he said.

She nodded again. She was not sure how she felt about Mr. Carden, but for the moment he was making her feel ill at ease. "I'll get the rest of my stuff in the morning," she said.

He nodded. "Uh-huh."

"Perhaps you could go and offer the man in the cabin next to mine a room here."

Carden shook his head. "It's a long walk on a night like this," he said. "You need anything else?"

"No. Thank you."

"Good night, then."

"Good night," she said, and Carden left the room.

Jean Ward sat on the edge of one of the twin beds and thought about her brother. She thought she should miss him and grieve over his death and that she should wonder about it—about his dying, about the fact of it and the way he might have proceeded with it. After all, it's what she'd done, painful as it had been, when her father died. But she was not doing that now. She had accepted the news of her brother's death as calmly as if it had merely been the death of a neighbor—with regret, and with pause for reflection. But nothing more.

Because there was something else on her mind. Or in it. She had no idea what. She caught glimpses of it now and again, but they were quick and useless and told her nothing, as if she were in the lobby at a theater and saw the movie playing only when the door was opened.

And it was that which had nudged her brother's death away and had made it something of only passing interest—that thing she caught only swift and meaningless glimpses of, that terror, that insanity, that desperation, happiness, pleasure. That incredible *need*.

And she glimpsed it as if from a distance, as if she were looking up out of a very deep hole.

She whispered her brother's name. "Dave," she said. It came out hollow and unrecognizable.

Amy Glynn was thinking about her cousin Alex, who had committed suicide five years before. She had been close to him, had known him as a very sensitive, caring, and exquisitely gentle person—the kind who catches flies in his hands and puts them outside rather than kill them. Ultimately, that sort of exquisite gentleness and caring had made him painfully lonely —people simply did not notice him, he was so good at becoming an almost inanimate part of the backdrop of their lives. Amy had thought for a time that he was gay, but he told her, without being asked, or the subject mentioned, "I'm not gay, Amy. I'm just very tuned in to other people." He gave her a flat smile. "It's hell sometimes. It really is. It's like I'm burying myself in my own kindness."

No one could ever say for sure why he committed suicide. He had left no note, had made no complaints. He carried on with his job as a high school guidance counselor up until the day of his death.

Amy was thinking about the method of his suicide. She was thinking that he had designed it to be a very caring suicide, very loving, very much an Alex sort of suicide, because he made sure that his death left people with even less trouble than if he had not committed suicide, if, instead, he'd been run over by a truck. He got a few deadly pills and a can of root beer, his favorite drink, went to the emergency room of the hospital in the small town where he lived, went up to the desk, asked the nurse, "Is there a gurney free?"

And she said, "A gurney, sir?"

"Yes. Is there one free?"

"I don't understand. Are you employed here, sir?"

"No. I need to lie down."

"Oh," she said, and she was so taken with him and with his need that she pointed to a corridor to her right and said, "There's one down there, sir. A doctor will be with you shortly."

And he went there, to the gurney, got his wallet out, took his medical insurance card from it, set it down at the head of the gurney, near the edge, put the pills in his mouth, took a long slug of the root beer, and set the can down at the foot of the gurney. Then he lay on his back with his hands folded on his stomach and he died.

Amy was thinking about this and she wasn't sure why. She had always supposed that she hated to think about it. It was probably the most disturbing thing that had ever touched her life—people did not commit rational, neat, caring suicide. They did it with guns or knives or in bathtubs full of warm water with razor blades at their wrists; and even if they used pills, they invariably made a mess for other people to clean up. That was the normal way to do it, the natural way to do it. So what in the hell had been wrong with Alex? She realized then that that was why she was thinking about him and his suicide—for the same reason that she had always thought about it, because she enjoyed making judgments of him and, as she had said once, of "his unnatural act." But then she realized that she didn't feel the same sort of grim-and-smirking sense of superiority—*"I* would never do it that way; it leaves people flabbergasted"—that she always had. She was thinking about it because it was the closest that death had come to touching her life and she was grabbing hold of it, tasting it, savoring it as if it were a glass of peach schnapps. She shook her husband, Jeff, to wake him. He grumbled. She said, "Jeff, I'm thinking about my cousin Alex."

"Uh?" he murmured.

"The one who committed suicide," she said. "Alex

Foxworth. My mother's sister's son. The guidance counselor. You remember him. The one who went to the hospital and got on a gurney and took pills with root beer and died. I'm thinking about *him,* Jeff." A pause. She took a deep breath, went on, "And I *like* thinking about him. About his suicide." Another pause, another deep breath. She whispered tightly. "And that *scares* me. I never *liked* thinking about it before." She listened. "Jeff?" she said. He was snoring lightly. She snapped, "Wake up, dammit. Talk."

"Uh?" he said again from the shallows of sleep.

She sighed, lay back, smiled. She continued thinking about her cousin Alex.

HISTORY

Lucius Kellogg scrambled up the muddy slope behind the house just moments before it let go under the onslaught of the storm. It hit the stilts holding the house up; they buckled forward, the house settled back onto the plane of mud, and over the space of several minutes, it slid very slowly into the lake.

Then it floated.

Lucius Kellogg thought, watching it openmouthed, *It looks like the top of Noah's Ark.*

BOOK TWO

A MATTER OF
WARMTH

HISTORY

Lucius Kellogg's mind went numbly from one possibility to another, because surely he should be able to do *something;* he wasn't powerless, but all he could really do was watch the Mosiman's house, pushed by the storm, float out on the lake. God, there were *people* in that house. People who screamed.

And so he thought that he could run to his mail boat and fire it up and pilot it to the house and . . . And peer into the top of one of the second-floor windows. And call to the Mosimans that help had arrived and they weren't doomed to go down with their house. And as he thought this scenario through, as he saw himself doing it, he revised it continuously, made minor corrections for errors in judgment— pulled the boat up *parallel* to the house instead of straight on because that would make it easier, of course, for the Mosiman's to climb in; headed directly into the waves so he wouldn't be swamped, and covered his mail with the tarp, first, because an emergency was an emergency, certainly, but the U.S. mail was the U.S. mail. And when he thought that, he wondered just what kind of man he was—the lives of those people in the house were certainly a hell of a lot more important than someone's Sears catalogs, or a letter from their Uncle Herman, or even the long-awaited Social Security check. All those things could be replaced, *anything* could be replaced, except a person's life, especially the life of a young girl and her big brother, poor innocent things, swept up in that . . . misery, swept away by a freak storm, swept away by mud and water and filth, and by disease and by death, poor screaming things, poor miserable things screaming at their own deaths, being grabbed at by death and screaming at it to go away. And he'd have to check his fuel level first, that was important, be damned foolhardy to go out on that lake the way it was with no fuel and not be able to power up into the waves, and be swamped. And drowned. Like them. Water filling their lungs up instead of air.

Hang on! he decided to yell. *Hang on, it's floating!* he decided to yell, and realized at the same time that the storm was letting up, that it was dying, like they were, in the house. *Hang on, the storm's dying!* he decided to yell. Then the water was over the top of the second-floor windows, then, as quick as sound, and with a great gurgle from within the attic, the water was over the roof and the house was gone.

Lucius Kellogg smiled. The house and its people were gone. Thank the Lord.

ONE

January 20

Mary Berge said to her father, as they watched Mitzi Roman drive Walt Roman away from the inn, "He won't sue you, Dad. He's all mouth."

Arnaut said, "I am impacted with sympathies vis-à-vis Mr. Walt Roman. I rained on his vacation."

Mary looked up at her father and smiled because he was smiling. She said, "Why are you smiling?"

"Because that sentence was incredibly no good."

She shrugged. "I understood it, which is all that's important. No one expects you to be the great communicator, Dad."

Arnaut sighed. They were in his office, standing at one of the tall windows that overlooked the parking lots and tennis courts. He thought the midmorning sunlight was warm and pleasant through the glass. He said, "I'm glad you're here, Mary," paused and continued, "I just don't understand *why* you're here."

She answered, "Because I got thrown out of school," she went to Arnaut's liquor cabinet, opened it, and looked inside. "There's no booze in here, Dad." She bent over for a closer look. "Just diet pop." She made a face.

"How did you accomplish becoming thrown from school, Mary?" Arnaut asked.

She gave him the kind of coy and charming smile which, in the past, had always put him at ease. "Because I called one of the professors an asshole."

Arnaut asked, nonplussed, "Who?"

Mary's pixieish smile vanished, as if the question had surprised her. "Who? Does it matter? Dr. Gerenscher. He teaches theology."

"And this Dr. Gerenscher is in a position of such magnificence that he can cause you a quick exit? Crap!"

She grinned. *"Crap,* Dad? That's a new one." She got a diet soda from the liquor cabinet.

Arnaut went to the phone, lifted the receiver. "The number, Mary."

"What number?" She twisted the cap off the bottle; there was a *whoosh* as the carbon dioxide escaped.

Arnaut said, "Your school number. I am going to accost this asshole Gerenscher, Professor of Theology."

"I deserved being tossed out, Dad."

"Of course you did." He paused, grinned at her. "The shorter the better," he said.

"The shorter the better?"

He nodded. "Sentences. The shorter the better. The school number, please."

She came over, took the receiver from him, put it back on the cradle. "Dad, thanks, but no thanks. It's just a temporary suspension. Besides, I've applied at another school, so it's no problem."

He nodded. "Yes. It's a problem. I have no money to send you to another school." She had been going to Cornell on a scholarship.

"No money?" she said. "Since when?"

"Since it becomes of necessity that the inn reopen in snow as deep as the elephants."

She chuckled. It was a pleasant and mature sound, and Arnaut found that it had more of a calming effect on him than did her pert, childish smile. He decided that they were both growing up. And he realized, not for the first time, that ever since Mary had reached puberty she had scared him, he wasn't sure why—he was afraid to *ask* himself why. Now he thought he was dealing with her as much as if she were an adult, a young woman, as simply his daughter. "'Deep as the elephants,' Dad?" she said, smiling.

"It is a phrase," he said.

"Whose?"

"Mr. Carden's. I have . . . apocalypsed it."

"Appropriated it?"

"Yes."

She gave him a confused look. "Dad, are you really glad I'm here?"

"Yes," he answered quickly—too quickly, he realized. "Yes," he said again. "And no. I don't know. I'm befuddled. Things are happening."

"What things?"

"No things. No things in particular, nothing I can stab my finger in."

"You're being cryptic."

"What is that? Is it like *crypt,* meaning *grim?"*

She shook her head, took a drink of the diet soda, grimaced. "No, it means you're not communicating with me."

He said nothing for a moment. He patted his shirt pocket, glanced about. "I want a cigarette," he said.

"You don't smoke."

"I did once. In the medieval past. Before there were dinosaurs."

"Want one of mine?"

He gave her a shocked look. "You smoke, Mary?"

"Yes. And I'm trying to quit. I don't like it, I don't like it at all. I know—then why did I start?" She shrugged. "Why does anyone start?" She paused. "What things, Dad?"

Arnaut shook his head, looked out the window again, let the sunlight bathe his face in warmth. "Peo-

ple," he said. "People are happening. People I don't
know."

In the house under the lake, the refrigerator that
killed the Mosiman's was still upright in the kitchen. It
had changed position, however, when the house sank.
Now it was near the entrance to the living room. Its
door was closed, and there were foodstuffs inside: a jar
of Mrs. Filbert's Sandwich Spread, a quart of plain
yogurt, the remains of a dozen oranges in a plastic bag,
two quarts of solidified low-fat milk, both unopened.
These items were floating in the refrigerator; over the
span of years, lake water had filled it up.

The kitchen table floated as well. The Book-of-the
Month Club shipment that Lucius Kellogg had
brought to the house eleven years before lay waterlogged and unrecognizable, like a lump of pudding,
near the stove next to the screen door. The brown
teapot-shaped kitchen clock still hung on the wall over
the stove and still was plugged in. It read 3:45.

Early Evening

Muriel Fox came to Arnaut's office and asked him if
she could stay at the inn for a few days. The furnace at
her house was being worked on, she explained. He
said, "Yes, of course," then, digging into his memory,
went on, "And Mr. Heinz?" meaning Leo Heinz, the
seventy-five-year-old man with whom she had kept
company for several years.

"Dead," she answered, and smiled wistfully.

Arnaut said he was sorry.

Muriel nodded. "So am I. For my sake. Not that he
would have been much good on a holiday." She was
going to explain the remark, was going to tell Arnaut
that Leo had liked to undress at odd times and wander

into her bedroom and, in his low, gurgling whisper, beckon to her, "Let's do it, Muriel." But she decided that that was Leo's business, not Arnaut's. She said, instead, "There's never really been anybody since Earl." She was on Arnaut's gray loveseat. He was sitting behind his desk. She decided to change the subject. "How are things here at the inn, Arnaut?"

"Work." He smiled. "Much like work. It seems that once a day some repair grows up and knocks me on the knee." He paused. "But this gets us off on byways." He sensed that Muriel had something on her mind and he was trying to coax her into talking.

"Meaning?"

"We weren't talking about the inn."

"Oh? What were we talking about?"

"You're being sly," he said.

"Coy," she corrected.

"Coy? What is that? Is that like sly?"

"In a way."

"Then you're being coy, now?"

"No. I'm being sly." She paused, glanced away, glanced back. "I have lots of memories, Arnaut. Good and bad. It's all I have, really. All any of us have." She gave him a flat, expressionless smile. "We've known each other for quite some time, haven't we?"

"Yes." He nodded. "Ten years. More, maybe."

"And I've been coming here and enjoying this place that long—longer, really—and you and I have never really talked, have we?"

"We are now."

"Yes. But it doesn't mean much." Another pause. "You're an enigma, my friend."

"As in enigmatic?"

She nodded. "Yes. A kind of mystery. You seem so open and accessible, and yet you really aren't." She could see clearly that this distressed him. "It's nothing personal, Arnaut," she hurried on, thought a moment and continued, "Yes, of course it is. Of course it's personal. How can it not be?"

"I want people to talk to me," Arnaut said. "I like it when they do. Just now, for instance . . ."

"Yes. I came here to talk. I need to talk to someone. But being here with you, I realize that I can't talk to you, Arnaut. I'm sorry. When I talk to you, when I get past the mundane with you, I get the clear idea that you're somewhere else." A pause. "I think you're *always* somewhere else. *With* someone else."

"No," Arnaut protested. "You're wrong." *Martha.* "Very wrong."

"Yes. Perhaps." A pause. "At any rate, Arnaut," —she stood—"thanks for letting me stay here. I brought my things. I'll pay the going rate."

He shook his head. "No. Please." *Martha,* he thought. *She is, she exists. Everywhere. In my dreams.* "You are welcome. Needed. We'll talk." *Everywhere.*

TWO
Evening

Jean Ward answered the knock at her door and found Mary Berge there, smiling. Mary stuck her hand out. "Hi," she said, "I'm Arnaut's daughter. Can we talk?"

Jean shook Mary's hand, forced herself to smile back. She did not like the disturbance, had been resting. "Arnaut's daughter?" she said, trying to sound friendly and realizing she sounded false. "How nice."

Mary's smile faded a bit. She gestured to indicate the room. "May I?"

"Yes," Jean answered at once. "Please, come in."

Mary went into the room, glanced about, nodded at a wooden chair near a white kneehole desk close by. "Can I sit there?"

"Certainly," Jean answered.

Mary sat in the chair, crossed her legs, put an elbow on her knee and clasped her hands. She was dressed in blue jeans, a white blouse, white sneakers. "It's cold in here," she said, and did a mock shiver.

Jean sat on the edge of the bed. She nodded. "Yes. I've been meaning to speak to your father—"

"Do you like him?" Mary cut in.

Jean smiled thinly. "Are you his dating service?"

Mary smiled back. "I'm sorry. That was forward. But *I'm* forward. I get it from my mother."

"Your mother?"

"Sure. You certainly can't say my father's very forward, or *he'd* be here instead of me."

Jean's thin smile flattened. "What exactly did you want to talk about, please?"

Mary lowered her head as if in apology. "That was a little too forward wasn't it? I'm sorry. It's just that . . . there's so little time in life, you know, so why fart around playing games? Do you follow me?"

Jean nodded. "You came here to be philosophical?"

"I'm disturbing you, aren't I?"

Jean sighed. "No. Forgive me. I was resting. I've been tired. Perhaps your father told you that my brother . . . died here recently."

"Yes. He told me. I'm sorry."

Jean nodded dully. "So that's been . . . wearing me out. It's very wearying to lose someone so quickly."

"Yes," Mary said. "My mother went the same way." She paused, then continued, her tone brighter, "Dad says you're going to be staying with us a while."

"I am, yes. There are . . . problems. So I have to stay."

"Oh?"

"Yes."

"What sort of problems?"

Jean sighed. "Complications."

"You don't want to talk about it, do you?"

Jean shook her head. "No. It's personal. It has to do with Dave. My brother. I want to take him . . . I want to take his body home . . ." She gave a deep and weary sigh. "I want to take him home and they won't release his body to me until the autopsy is completed." She paused, then hurried on, as if her mind were racing, "The authorities are trying to claim it could have been suicide—it wasn't, of course—and so there has to be an autopsy they say, and it's scheduled for tomorrow, the next day; they're not sure. Who is? Who's sure of anything?" She looked away, closed her eyes. "Who?" she whispered.

Mary said, standing, "I *am* disturbing you. Forgive me. I'll go."

Jean looked at her as if surprised. "No. Please. Sit down. You're here. There's no need for you to go."

Mary sat down. There were a few moments of uneasy silence, then Mary said, "It's that lake. It takes a lot of people."

"Yes," Jean said, without inflection.

"Yes," Mary said. She ran her hand nervously through her long hair. As she spoke, she looked away. "It took my mother." She glanced at Jean again, then looked away once more. "She went out in a boat one morning and fell overboard and that was it. No more Mom. I remember she was going to go somewhere later and she had her suitcase open on the bed when I went to her room afterward." She smiled quiveringly, eyes still averted. "And I remember when they pulled her out . . . when they pulled her out of the lake, I could see that she'd painted her fingernails mauve. She had always used red. I remember that the evening before they were red. So when I saw them . . . after they pulled her out, I said to myself, 'She must have painted her fingernails this morning. She was looking forward to the day, to people noticing.' That's strange, isn't it? That's a strange way to think?"

"It's not strange. We survive. We have to."

Mary went on, as if mindless of what Jean had said, "And she didn't know when she painted her fingernails mauve that someone would see them, sure, but that she'd be dead when they did."

Jean gave her a studied look. She said, "That's a morbid way to think."

Mary shook her head. "No. I don't dwell on it. On my mother's death. I think about it from time to time. And when I think about it, when I play it out in my memory, I try to see it through everyone's eyes.

Hers—I mean my mother's—and my father's, even the people who pulled her out."

Jean gave her a confused smile. "I don't understand why you would do that. Wasn't your own sorrow . . . sufficient?"

Again Mary shook her head. "No. I was eleven years old, and I was selfish." She thought a moment. "Maybe not selfish. Maybe that's too critical. I was self-serving. Most eleven-year-olds have to be, don't you think? And I didn't love her. I had fun with her, of course. We were pals. We went shopping together, we went to movies, she took me to the Philharmonic in Utica a couple of times. And I liked her. I really did." A pause for thought. "What wasn't to like? She was smart and friendly and nice to look at. That's important. I think it's important for a kid to like looking at her parents and to think that maybe she's as good-looking as they are. I think that's important. But I didn't love her." Another brief pause. "I love her now."

"Of course you do."

"It's true, Miss Ward."

"Jean."

"It is true. I love her now. I cherish her. If you think about it, we don't love anyone because of the person they are at the moment we're looking at them, at the moment that they're standing in front of us. How can we love someone because they're sleeping or watching TV or eating a hamburger? We love them for what they were to us in the *past,* what they were to us yesterday, how they made us feel last week, for the eggs they cooked for us five minutes ago, even though they hate the smell of eggs. It's all in the head, Jean. It's all in the memory. That's where we get love from."

Jean said, "That's quite a speech."

"It is, isn't it? But it's not original. It's one my father gave me a couple years ago. I told him that I loved my mother at last, after she'd been dead for so long, and I thought it was strange. So he gave me that . . . speech. Except it sounded different coming from him."

Jean smiled. "I'm sure it did."

Mary shook her head again. A look of annoyance creased her mouth. "I don't mean because he louses his words up. I mean it sounded . . . real. It sounded like something that was true." She furrowed her brow. "And it was true, of course. It wasn't blindingly profound, on the face of it. What is? But, coming from him, it sounded like . . . I don't know. Food. It sounded like nourishment. That's his talent, I think. The things he says are like food, they're so real. *He's* so real." She cocked her head. "That's pretty close to father worship, isn't it?" She smiled prettily. "And maybe that's precisely what it is."

Muriel Fox had company.

Her room was in the inn's west wing. It faced the beach and looked obliquely out on the cabins lining the lakeshore. She had unpacked, had been on her way to dinner, on her way out the door with her head down, had been humming a tune from *The Sound of Music,* when she smelled anesthetic. She looked up. The face looking down at her was very old, the skin heavy with lines and liver spots, the eyes soft blue, gentle, imploring. Muriel saw need and desperation in them. So, without a word, she pushed her door open.

Now she was talking, her eyes rising every few moments to meet the soft blue eyes that were unblinkingly on her. "I am an Adirondacks person," she said. "An ice child." It was the continuation of a monologue she had begun minutes before. She added, "Not, perhaps, the typical Adirondacks person." She was thinking, as she talked, about what she was saying —though this required very little thought; she was a wonderful talker, words came easily from her, and she was engaging and vivacious, as well; since early adulthood she had realized that people liked to hear her talk, liked to watch her face animate and her eyes sparkle. Encroaching age had done little to dim that sparkle. Indeed, she thought that people saw something special in it from a person like her, as if they were looking into a fountain of eternal youth whose outsides were slowly weathering. And she was thinking about the eyes that were on her. She continued, "The typical Adirondacks person is . . . gritty and poor and sincere. I'm not poor." She smiled. "I'm well-to-do, in fact." She thought they were the eyes of a man possessed. "Have you ever examined that phrase? It doesn't make any sense, does it? It doesn't need to." Possessed by himself and his memories, by his needs and desperation. This made her uncomfortable. This made her want to touch him, made her want to hold him, to caress his age, his humanity, his mortality. He was temporary. He was proof of his own temporariness. He was coming apart before her eyes. If she looked very closely, she'd be able to see his skin fold up and the color leave it.

And yet there were the eyes. Soft blue. The color of pond water. Eyes without sparkle. Eyes that had life in them nonetheless, like eyes in a photograph. She continued talking, did not hear herself directly, did not feel the words echoing in her throat and then forming on her tongue, and did not feel her lips move in the final revision of speech. Someone else was saying what she was hearing. It had been so before, she thought, standing back and looking at it. It was a good way to communicate—to talk, to let the words come out, and to think at the same time about things that were very important. It was a wild talent, really.

But this was different somehow.

And there were those eyes. The soft blue eyes of a man possessed and coming apart. She said, "I was married once. And I've had many lovers. I'm an expert at loving. And you?"

"There are things we do not understand." That voice, *his* voice, she decided, matched nothing about him. Not his eyes, not his age, not his purpose here. It was a voice that matched nothing at all, a voice that could have been a thousand voices wedded into one. The voice of air.

"I appreciate that," she said. She was becoming uncomfortable. She was becoming warm and cold and confused and very, very tired.

Suddenly she wanted to talk about dreams. She said, "I dream every night. I have good dreams and bad dreams."

"A stitch in time . . ."

"Saves nine." She smiled.

"A stitch in time saves nine."

"A stitch in time saves nine," she said.

"A stitch in time saves chickens before they hatch."

And so she was becoming uncomfortable, but it was okay, because this man understood her, knew her, was inside her—it had happened before, it had happened often. "I am an Adirondacks person. Not the typical Adirondacks person. The typical Adirondacks person is poor and sincere. I am not sincere."

"Most men live lives of quiet desperation."

"I'm sorry?"

The soft blue eyes, eyes the color of pond water, eyes that did not sparkle, but which had life in them. The eyes of a photograph. The eyes of times passed. The eyes of memory. Eyes that could tell only truth. "I'm sorry?" Muriel said.

"Most men live lives of quiet desperation, don't count your chickens, count your chickens, a stitch in time saves nine. Help me. Help me." The eyes turned briefly from her, toward the lake, then back to her.

"I'm sorry?" Blue eyes inside her.

"I'm sorry?"

Blue eyes searching out her insides, knowing her, being her.

"I am cold."

"It's a cold day. Not as cold as we've yet to see, of course."

"I am cold."

"Here, hold my hand."

"I am cold. Help me."

But they were not eyes. They were meat. Something from the earth. Pond water sloshing about inside her, washing her up. "Here, hold my hand."

"Hold my hand."

"Hold my hand."

"I am cold."

"When I see birches bending to the left and right, I know some boy's been swinging them."

"A stitch in time saves nine . . ."

"Boys been swinging them."

"Here. Hold my hand. I am cold."

"I am cold."

January 21: Morning

Mary Berge said to her father, across the breakfast table in the inn's second-floor dining room—all-but-empty because some of his guests had gone, "You like her, don't you, Dad?"

"Who," he said, and took a spoonful of Rice Krispies. "Like who?"

"Mrs. Ward."

"It's not Mrs."

"But you like her, right?"

He nodded. "Yes."

"She's very pretty."

He shrugged. "Pretty is okay."

"Meaning what? That you're beyond being attracted to an attractive woman? I don't think I believe that, Dad." She nodded at his plate of toast. "Are you going to eat that?"

"Yes. You can have some."

She reached across the table, took a slice of toast, set it on the napkin beside her bowl of cornflakes, pursed her lips. "I didn't get any milk for my cornflakes. Or sugar, either."

Arnaut said, "Sugar rots you up."

Mary grinned.

Arnaut asked, "That was not so precise?"

She nodded. "That was very precise. And you're right. Who needs sugar?" She paused, added, "And who needs cornflakes?" She pushed the bowl away.

"No," Arnaut said, "I am not beyond being attracted to an attractive woman whatsoever." He didn't like having such conversations with his daughter. Dealing with her as an adult was one thing, but discussing his love life with her—or she discussing her love life with him, which she had done since she was fifteen—made him uncomfortable. Some things were private between father and daughter, after all. "What I am beyond, I live and breathe, is being carried out from under my feet by such attractions."

She took a bite of toast. "The old passion bug is gone, huh?"

"Passion bug?"

"Do you know, Dad, that a woman reaches her sexual prime at forty? Of course, men reach theirs at eighteen or nineteen, which I'm finding out,"—she raised an eyebrow, looked exasperated; Arnaut began to squirm—"but that wasn't what we were talking about, was it?"

"I am capable and joyous, Mary, at discussing with you the . . . machinations of your—" He took a bite of cereal.

"Love life?"

"Certainly." He smiled. A Rice Krispie appeared on his upper lip. Mary nodded at it, said, "Napkin," and Arnaut wiped it away.

Mary said, "How come you don't eat adult food, dad?"

"This is not adult food?"

She shook her head, took another bite of toast. "No. It's kid food. Like Sugar Pops."

"I don't eat Sugar Pops. They rot you up." He said as he smiled, "I have your mother," then lowered his head to take in another spoonful of Rice Krispies.

Mary said nothing.

Arnaut chewed, swallowed, said, "In here," and touched his temple. "So what else do I need? A raftful of Jean Wards? No."

Mary sighed. "Dad, your *memories* reach only to the top of your neck. And you're not simply a . . . a talking head. You're a *whole person.*"

"Huh?"

"Think about it, Dad."

He did. After a moment, he said, "Oh. I see."

"Good," said Mary, "then you'll talk to her?"

"I talk to her all the time."

"I don't mean just talk about the weather, I mean *talk.*"

"Yes," he said at once.

"Good," Mary said.

In the house under the lake, the refrigerator that killed the Mosimans was still upright in the kitchen. It had changed positions, however, when the house sank.

The kitchen table floated as well. The Book-of-the-Month Club shipment that Lucius Kellogg had brought eleven years ago lay like a lump of pudding, near the stove next to the screen door. The brown teapot-shaped kitchen clock read 3:45.

The house leaned at a slight downward angle.

The front door stood open. Gravity kept it open. Just as it kept the screen door in the kitchen closed.

The only movements in the house were the movements of catfish and bullhead.

THREE
January 21: Evening

Jeff Glynn said to his wife, Amy, "Do you remember her, Amy? She was so . . . offensive. Do you remember? She was always crinkling her nose up like something smelled bad."

"And?" said Amy.

Jeff shrugged. "And it made me very uncomfortable. It made *every*one uncomfortable. It was like she was telling us that someone in the office smelled bad, but she was too kind or diplomatic to say exactly *who,* but, of course, not too kind or diplomatic to let us know about it."

"What was her name?"

"Susan. It was Susan. And she looked like a Susan, too. You know the kind I mean, right? The *Susan* kind. Sort of thin and dark haired and mousy looking and . . . sexless." He paused. "Not sexless, exactly. She had sex—I mean, it was clear that she was a woman."

"What in the hell are you talking about, Jeff?"

"Just talking. You don't mind. Do you mind?"

"No."

"It was her ass. She had a nice ass. You know the kind of ass I mean, right? The kind that . . . moves."

"You're saying she had a wiggle? *Every* woman has a wiggle. We can't help it."

"Really?"

"You're joking, right?"

"Right. I'm joking. I know every woman wiggles.

But Susan didn't just wiggle. She *moved*. Do you know what I mean? She made a *point* of *moving* her ass."

"And you made a point of watching her move it?"

"Damn right. It was interesting. There she was, this mousy . . . woman, this mousy *person*—I couldn't really think of her as a woman; no one could—and she had such a great ass. A really classic ass."

Amy sighed her annoyance. "Jeff, I'm getting sick of hearing about Susan's ass."

He looked surprised. "Why? It wasn't like she was another woman. She wasn't."

Amy pursed her lips. "Perhaps what I'm saying, *dear,* is that I don't view asses, *per se,* as wonderful topics for conversation."

"You don't? Why not? What's better? Your damn cousin's suicide?"

"There's nothing quite so real as suicide."

"Huh?"

"If you're going to psychoanalyze me, don't. I was only making a . . . metaphysical statement."

"So am I? Who's to say there's nothing metaphysical about asses? Or about sex, for that matter. Who's to say that . . . that sex itself doesn't . . . survive."

"Survive?"

"Beyond death."

"What kind of talk is this around Samantha? Look at her." She nodded at the baby, asleep in the bassinet, little puckered bow mouth sucking at the air. "She looks disturbed. She's probably having . . . dreams."

"Disturbed? Probably having dreams? For God's sake, the kid is only six months old. If she's having dreams, it's about your damn tits." He pursed his lips. "Sorry, that didn't come out right. There's nothing damned about your tits."

"They are not *tits. Cows* have tits."

"No, they don't, they have 'teats.'"

"Tits, teats—"

"Let's call the whole thing off." He smiled.

"Very funny."

"Thanks." He nodded at Samantha. "Look, she's stopped sucking."

Amy looked at the baby a moment. She cocked her head, said, "Jeff?" went over to the bassinet, leaned over, put her hand on Samantha's chest. She smiled a nervous smile, looked back at Jeff, shook her head. "I don't know," she said, "but I don't think she's breathing." She paused, then went on, her voice rising in alarm, "I don't think Samantha's breathing, Jeff!"

In his office, Arnaut said to Mary, "I'm uncomfortable this winter at the inn, Mary. Last year, two men came to be drowned in the lake. One was a man named Meyer whose wife works here from now and again. And I don't know anything about these men except that they drowned." He paused. He gazed out the window that overlooked the dark, snow-covered parking lots and tennis courts. He went on, "I don't much love this lake any more. I have always loved it, even when Martha was killed by it. I did not blame the lake, then. I blamed God. And still do. Why not? He could have stopped her death, but He didn't and so He is no longer on my *Hit Parade.*" He grinned. "I like that phrase, but it is a grisly use I've made of it."

"No," Mary said, "I understand."

"I don't," Arnaut said, turning to look at her. "I don't understand this place. I think that something unkind has been brought to it, something unloved, or cold . . ." He paused. He looked away again; tears came to him suddenly. "I can't expostulate why I'm doing this, Mary." A flood of embarrassment pushed through him. "Crying because something has made me see devils." A brief pause, then, "No. Not devils. I do not see devils anywhere but in books for children. I see something else. I see it in my dreams. I see it in the faces around me. I see it in the air. Something cold. And alone." He paused.

Mary said, "I feel what you feel here. Not as strongly as you, I think." She paused, then, "How do you characterize it?" It was a question she was asking herself, but Arnaut answered, "I feel it like a shrunken suit."

She looked at him. He looked back. "Like a shrunken suit," he said and looked away. "It pinches. It makes me feel . . . closed inside myself."

"Claustrophobic?"

"That is?"

"Closed in. Like being in a dark closet."

"I don't know. Who knows? No. Not claustrophobic. Inside myself. Locked inside myself."

There was a knock at the door. It was pushed opened; Francis Carden stuck his head into the room. "We've got some trouble, Arnaut," he said.

FOUR

The house under the lake leaned at a slight downward angle.

The front door stood open. Gravity kept it open. Just as it kept the screen door in the kitchen closed.

The only movements in the house were the movements of catfish and bullhead.

Cold existed in the house. But it was cold far deeper and far more chilling than the cold of the lake in winter.

With that cold there was desperation.

And there was need.

The need for warmth.

"Sleep apnea," the doctor announced. He was tall, chunky, red-faced; he sputtered when he talked. His name was Linden.

"I know," said Amy Glynn. "SIDS. Sudden Infant Death Syndrome."

"No," said Jeff Glynn.

"Your child is going to be fine." Dr. Linden said. He leaned over, put a fat, pink hand on Samantha's cheek. The child was sleeping and sucking at the air again. "She's six months old?"

Amy nodded. "Almost seven. Her birthday's in June." She paused. "It's going to happen again, isn't it?" Her tone was casual, almost offhand.

Dr. Linden nodded gravely. "Yes. The chances are good that it will happen again. But the chances are also good that when it happens, your daughter will snap out of it herself. Sleep apnea is a common disorder. All of us stop breathing for a moment or two, then our bodies

tell us what's going on and we begin to breathe again."
He gave them a wide, reassuring smile. "Your child is
fine. She looks very healthy. I don't think you've got
anything to worry about unduly. Simply take a few
precautions—"

Jeff pounced on that. "'Unduly'? Why would you
qualify it, Doctor Linden? What you're saying is that
we *do* have something to worry about, that our daughter could simply stop breathing one night—"

"There are monitors available," Linden said. "I'm
not a pediatrician, so I can't give you the kind of
advice you need. But there are monitors available
that can alert you if this should happen again. And
if it should happen again, simply *handling* the child
should be enough to rouse her, as it was this
time."

Jeff was not satisfied. He shook his head vehemently,
his normally pixieish face became severe. "Where the
hell are we going to get *monitors* up here?"

"If you're concerned," Linden said, "my suggestion
would be to go home and consult your daughter's
pediatrician."

Jeff hesitated, clearly on the verge of speech, but
uncertain what he wanted to say.

Amy said, "No. I don't think so. We've been looking
forward to staying here. It's a return trip, Doctor. We
were here on our honeymoon, five years ago." She
shook her head. "No. I think if we simply keep a close
watch on her—"

"You've got to be kidding!" Jeff cut in.

Amy looked annoyed. "Why would I be kidding,
Jeff? We could set the alarm clock. We could wake
up . . . every hour, every half hour, and check her. I
think the chances are good that if there were a problem, we'd spot it."

Dr. Linden said, "That would be a terrible burden
on both of you. My advice would simply be to leave

and seek professional care for your daughter. As I pointed out, I'm a G.P., not a pediatrician."

"Yes," said Jeff Glynn. "I think you're right. A pediatrician is the person we should be talking to. We can come back again next year, Amy——"

Amy shook her head. "It's simply not necessary to leave, Jeff. I am perfectly willing to keep an eye on Samantha."

"This is our daughter's *life* we're talking about," Jeff snapped.

Amy gave him a cold look. "Whatever problem she has is without a doubt a problem she'll *always* have. Are we supposed to restructure our lives around the vague possibility that she's going to stop breathing for a few moments?"

"Listen to yourself," Jeff said. "I've never heard you talk like this before."

"I'm being rational," she came back. "One of us has to."

"Rational? You're putting our daughter's life in jeopardy for the sake of a few week's worth of cross-country skiing. Is it really *you* I'm listening to, Amy?"

"Oh, for God's sake, who do you *think* it is? You're so damned used to my . . . overreacting to every situation that when I finally keep my cool——"

"*Cool* is not the word. It's not the word at all."

Dr. Linden, embarrassed, backed toward the door. "This is a family matter," he explained. "Please excuse me."

Neither Jeff nor Amy noticed when he left the room.

January 22

Harry Stans pleaded with Lynette, "But Lynette, honey, it's been a long, long time. Don't you think it's been a long time?"

She scowled at him. "You're talking dirty and I don't like it."

Harry had come to Many Pines to ask Lynette to a movie in Old Forge. It was midafternoon. The morning's blue sky had given way to a blanket of gray clouds that threatened snow.

Lynette was dressed very warmly. She had an axe in hand when Harry spotted her, and she was on her way toward the line of cottages.

"I ain't talking dirty," he protested. "What's so dirty about lovemaking, anyway?"

"You didn't say anything about *lovemaking*. I knew it. *That's* what I mean, Harry. You're a liar."

He shook his head. "You're confusing me, Lynette." He nodded at the axe. "Where you goin' with that?"

"To chop wood," she said.

"Why you gotta chop wood?"

"For the cabins."

"People staying in those cabins this time-a the year?"

"No."

"Course they aren't."

"But I gotta keep 'em warm."

Harry sighed. "Lynette, I thought we was something . . . special. From the sound of it, we ain't nothin' in your eyes."

She said nothing for a moment and Harry thought he saw confusion on her face. It vanished. She said, "You hear whatever you want to hear, Harry. And you see whatever you want to see, too. I ain't sayin' nothin' about nothin'. And anyway, how can I say something about what never was?"

"What never was? I ain't followin' you one bit. You're 'bout as understandable as rain on a clear day." He waited. Again he saw what he thought was confusion on Lynette's square, handsome face, and again it vanished quickly.

She told him, "I ain't sayin' nothin' about nothin',

like I told you. Now unless you got a mind to help me, I got to get to choppin' some wood so these stupid people don't freeze their asses off tonight." She turned away from him, walked a few feet, looked back silently.

"Lynette?" Harry said.

She said nothing. Once more, Harry saw confusion about her. And something else, too. Fear.

"Lynette?" he said again. "You okay, darlin'?"

She said, smirking suddenly, *"Darlin'* is what Pete used to call me. He used to say, 'Ain't no sense my havin' to look at you at a time like that, darlin'.' You know what he was talking about Harry?"

Harry said, regretting it immediately, "Well, I guess I do, Lynette."

Her smirk disappeared. "He was talkin' about when he was screwin' me. So don't you call me *darlin'*. I ain't your darlin'. I ain't nobody's darlin', 'cept Pete Jr.'s."

Harry didn't like her tone. It was a tone he hadn't heard from her before. It was pleading and angry at the same time.

He said, "You still miss Pete, don'tchoo?"

"I don't miss Pete." Now she was simply angry. "I don't miss Pete. I never missed Pete!" The muscles of her face grew taut. "Pete was a goddamn waste of oxygen in this world. Pete was lazy and he screwed other women besides and he didn't love me, so hell, no, I don't miss him. And I don't need you neither. And I don't want to go to no movie in Old Forge just so's you can grope me in the dark." She turned and started down the line of cottages.

Harry called after her, "I'm comin' back later. We're gawna thrash this out, you and me." She did not look back, and he watched as she disappeared around the corner of the far cabin, on her way to the path that led up the high hill there, the axe swinging slightly, its head down, in time with her quick walk.

FIVE
January 23

Muriel Fox thought she had been sleeping. She had no recollection of it, could remember no dreams. She remembered the man who had been with her in the room, who had come there on her first night; she remembered his eyes, soft blue and lifeless, and his skin, translucent as paper. She remembered that he sat on the bed with her.

But now it was morning and there was no man in the room with her. Only the smell of anesthetic.

She stood. She was hungry and she was cold. She glanced at herself in a mirror over the bed. It showed her reflection from the waist up. She was wearing a black silk blouse and a light green scarf tied at the neck with the long end hanging over the right side of her chest. She thought that she looked good.

She wondered once more, why she had let a man into her room, and why she couldn't remember his name. She decided he had not told her his name, decided that he had merely looked at her and had sat with her, and she had felt comfortable and cold.

She studied her face in the mirror. She whispered, "I am Muriel Fox," and as she spoke, she watched her lips move. She concentrated on them, became interested in them, in their movements. "I am Muriel Fox." And then her eyes caught her. They were soft blue, like his, she thought. They were like his. They *were* his. But what were the reflections of eyes? They were like photographs of eyes. They were no one's eyes. They were everyone's eyes. They were what they were. Eyes collected the light, if there was any.

If there was any.

There was none here.

She turned from her reflection and went to a window. The curtains were drawn. She held them open with her hand and looked out. She saw her image in the window, cast there by the morning sunlight on her. She saw herself and was warm. "I am Muriel Fox," she said.

In the house under the lake, more than catfish and bullhead moved. In a second-floor bedroom there was a fluttering of sheets and blankets and a twitching of arms. Foot bones flexed. Fingers widened, closed, widened again, curled up so tips touched palms, then relaxed.

Sound did not exist in the house. The walls would not conduct it, nor would the water that filled the house up. Sound reached from above and was stilled close to the roof of the house. The sound of a seaplane going over. The sound of Canada geese wheeling in to rest near the island. The screeching of cats.

Sound existed for others.

And so did light.

Memory existed in the house under the lake. Cold existed there, too. And need.

On the surface of the lake, a patina of ice formed and broke up, formed, broke up. At the shoreline near the inn, in the frigid, still shallows, the ice built quickly to finger thickness.

And in the house under the lake, a figure made its way through the cold darkness to the top of the stairs and went down, feet touching each step in turn, its rhythm the rhythm of water, of cold, of memory.

Above, in one of the second-floor bedrooms, sheets fluttered. Feet flexed. Fingers curled.

Night

Change occurs quickly in the Adirondacks. Temperatures rise and fall as if on a whim. The darkness happens all at once, with only a nod to twilight. Autumn ends like the closing of a door.

It is a place of contrasts, a place where the colors of the land do not bleed together but are as sharply delineated, as exquisite and mundane as the words of a lover. It is a place that does not embrace, but holds and keeps. A place that does not need its people, but tolerates them, and gives them life, pain, exhilaration.

Early in the evening on January 23, a snowfall came to Seventh Lake. It came all at once, carried in on a strong wind. It did not settle immediately, it scattered and drifted, sought out corners and hidden areas and rested there, then was pushed on again by the wind. A low front plunging out of Canada brought the snowfall and the wind, and it brought a numbing Artic cold with it, too, the kind that stops the breath and makes the earth crunch underfoot. Quickly enough, the snow and the wind stopped. Then the cold settled into Many Pines like the news of a death.

Francis Carden was standing inside the gazebo at the tip of the peninsula. He was dressed as if for summer, in a green short-sleeved shirt and jeans. He was thinking that he had never before been so god-awful cold, but that it was all right because cold was forever, cold was eternal, cold was the way of things in the universe (if it was really true that the stars and planets accounted for only a very, very small part of it, and of course it was true, any fool could see that it was true). And he was thinking also that he wanted desperately to get warm, that all he had to do to get warm was go back to the inn, and that was simple enough; and he was thinking that there was something very wrong with him for doing what he was doing, for standing inside the gazebo at night in January. Alone. Dressed as if for summer.

He was shivering. He knew what shivering was for—it was to keep the blood warm with movement —and he decided that the body possessed comically ineffective defenses against cold. It put hair on the head because most body heat was lost there, and then, with age, made that hair disappear. It put itself to sleep in the cold, and so made itself comfortable, and death easy. But it was clear enough why these defenses were so ineffective, so much as if they were an afterthought. It was because the body was mortal and cold was eternal; cold was the way of things—life and warmth were like tiny artificial bits of color on the still, flat, dead face of the universe.

He was seeing lights on the dark opposite shore of the lake. They were the lights of year-round cottages, and there were only a few of them. One of the lights winked intermittently, as if someone were walking back and forth in front of it.

He realized at once that there was something wonderful and comforting about standing in the gazebo in the cold. He was giving himself up to the universe, to eternity, giving up his long fight with it, giving up his stupid and futile humanness.

Because cold was forever.

Then he realized that there was something standing with him in the still, cold dark in the gazebo.

And he screamed.

Pete Meyer Jr. heard him, rose from his bed, and went to his window. He saw the roof of the gazebo, a cream-colored splotch in the darkness. He said, eyes on it, "Mama, there's a man down there screamin'," though he saw no one. He turned his head. Lynette had been in the room with him, resting. "Mama?" He padded over to her bed, leaned down, felt it. The bed was empty. He went to the door, opened it, stepped into the hallway. "Mama?" he called, but got no reply. He had his hand on the doorknob. He hesitated, uncertain. He shivered, stepped back into the room, returned to the window. He thought about Harry Stans, about Harry and his mother in bed together, and he hoped that it was Harry who was screaming outside, that the devil itself was gouging out Harry's eyes, or pulling his arms off.

From below, Francis Carden's screams continued.

<u>SIX</u>

And continued, and the thing standing beside him —its soft blue eyes turned his way, its skin as translucent as paper, its mouth lipless and flat—withdrew.

And Francis Carden ran from the gazebo.

Pete Jr. said to himself, "That man is damn stupid."

January 24: Morning

Arnaut had laid out an alternate route for cross-country skiing. It led through flat country north of the inn, then, circled back, onto some high hills, and finally turned west, to an area not far from the little group of cottages where Lynette Meyer made her home. From there, he planned to follow the lakeshore back to the inn.

Today, there were six inches of powdery snow on a base of four inches of packed snow, and the morning sky was overcast, the air frigid.

Arnaut said to Jean Ward, standing with him in her skis near the southern edge of the line of cabins, "You're going to perspirate to kingdom come in that, as I said," and nodded to indicate the several layers of sweaters she was wearing; she had borrowed them from Arnaut.

She gave him an embarrassed grin. "I got up feeling cold this morning, Arnaut. I'm still cold."

Arnaut smiled back. "Take my words in it, Jean, the manner of skiing this is will enlarge your sweat."

She nodded. "I'll chance it." She glanced back, toward the main inn. "How many others are coming along on this excursion, Arnaut?"

"The Glynns," he answered, "and Muriel Fox. And Francis."

"That's it?"

Arnaut shrugged. "There is Mary, not a skier—"

"Mary can't ski?"

Arnaut shook his head. "No ambition in it. And that is fomented by a hatred of snow and of dire cold, as she would pronounce this morning."

"I had no idea. I thought that, being your daughter—"

"And so is like her mother, also not a skier, and not a swimmer, either. Mary swims. I impositioned it on her."

A hawk soared over, heading north, toward Dog Island. Jean watched it. "Wonderful creature," she said.

"Yes," said Arnaut. "My agreements. It goes there." He pointed at Dog Island. Its outline was obscured against the backdrop of the north shore of the lake so it was little more than a dark gray lump sticking out of the water. He continued, "It makes its nest—" and was interrupted by Jeff Glynn, who called to them from just outside the inn's south entrance, "Good morning. We're ready?" and began skiing over, a distance of one hundred fifty feet.

Arnaut called back, "All ready, Mr. Glynn. And your wife?"

Jeff shook his head. "Not coming. Watching the baby." He pushed himself expertly forward on his skis and a few moments later was standing alongside Jean. "Good morning, Miss Ward. How are you feeling?"

"Good morning," she said, and smiled. "Call me Jean."

"Okay. And I'm Jeff."

Arnaut said, "Your wife's not coming?"

"No. She says she's not in the mood for skiing. She's watching Samantha. I guess she decided it wouldn't be smart to bring her along, after all." Jeff was dressed in his loose-fitting dark blue ski jacket, matching dark blue ski mittens, and brown corduroy pants. He wore no hat, and his midlength blonde hair shot off in many directions, as if he had washed it the night before and then had slept on it. He patted the pocket of his jacket and scowled. "Would one of you have a cigarette?"

"Sorry," Jean told him.

"No such habit for me," said Arnaut, and added, "Wasn't it your wife's thought to linger here at the inn in order that she might ski?"

"Yes," he said. "She changed her mind. It wouldn't be the first time. She says she's very comfortable just where she is."

Muriel Fox and Francis Carden came out of the inn. They were both carrying their skis, Muriel at the horizontal, Francis at the vertical. Muriel waved, and Jean, Arnaut, and Jeff waved back simultaneously, ski poles dangling from their wrists and wagging in the gray early morning light. Muriel and Francis stopped to put their skis on before coming over.

Jeff again asked if either Jean or Arnaut had a cigarette, again was told that neither of them smoked, and by this time, Francis and Muriel had come over to join the group and begin the morning.

From a second-floor window of the inn, the entity saw nothing recognizable. It saw snow and people and cabins beyond, trees and color and ski poles wagging, and it saw the lake shore, the tennis courts, cars passing now and then on Route 43. But all of these things were props from a past that was far behind it, a past that was part and substance of another world, and the entity saw them the way a lizard might watch a TV game show, with its eyes on the movement and its attention fixed forever on itself.

Only this had survived intact from the world of its past to the world of anarchy it now inhabited. The entity said, with its pale blue eyes on the movement below, "Tell them, tell them, tell them!" and as it said these words, other words came from it, as if the entity had a dozen sets of vocal chords, although, in fact, it had none: These words were, "A stitch in time saves nine," and "Don't count your chickens," and "I love you, Charlene," and "Propane," and "I'm not stupid"; anyone listening would have guessed that there was a crowd in the room, although it was empty. Except for the entity. Which was the length of galaxies, the breadth of air, the weight of dust.

"Tell them," it whispered.

Jean Ward said to Arnaut, "I wonder if he would like to come with us." She nodded toward the window at which the entity stood. She went on, smiling as if in apology, "No, perhaps not."

Arnaut said, "And he is purported?"

"Sorry?" Jean said.

Francis Carden said, "He means to ask—"

Arnaut interrupted, clearly miffed, "It was translucent. I want to know who the man in the window is."

"He's another guest," Jean said.

"And his name?" said Arnaut.

"I know his name," said Jeff Glynn. "He told me." He cocked his head. "I'm sure he told me."

"I've spoken with him at length," said Muriel Fox. "He's very comforting. He talks about inconsequentials. He doesn't like the cold." A look of contentment gathered on her small, square face. Her heavy-lidded, dark eyes crinkled up a little, as if she were remembering something that gave her pleasure. "I believe that his name is . . ." She paused. "He never told me his name," she went on, and her look of contentment became a look of confusion. "We talked for a very long time and he never told me his name, nor did he ask mine."

Arnaut said, "I have little consequence of this manifestation."

"Sorry?" Jeff said.

Arnaut said, "This man is unknown to me. He's an interloper."

"Oh," Jeff said.

"He was in the cabin next to mine," Jean said. "We talked quite a lot. He came over and we talked. He was always very cold, he always complained of the cold." She nodded at the window. "See there—he's gone now."

The entity stood by the closed door and waited. It had experienced a lifetime of waiting. It had waited for love and it had waited for money and it had waited for death. Now it waited in the cold room for the door to be opened. And once the door was opened, the entity would go to the next door and it would wait there. It accepted as unquestionable fact that unopened doors were barriers. It went through only when doors were opened. It went through only when it was invited through. It existed in a world of confusion, where switches opened and closed at random, where tears fell into mouths caught in the climax of a laugh, where need was left over from the world that had gone before, but was mixed with lust, and with memory, longing, pain—and pain was mixed with pleasure, and pleasure with guilt, hatred, love, and love with confusion.

And in the house under the lake, a figure in Big Bird pajamas stood at the bottom of the stairway. The figure's small mouth was opened very wide, as if to scream. The figure remembered screams. It remembered the screams that the sting of hornets caused, and it remembered the screams that nightmares caused. It screamed now, and no sound came from it. The water in the house would not conduct it, nor would the walls. Sound was stilled somewhere above the roof.

"Maybe he's like a stowaway," said Jeff Glynn. "Maybe he's a hotel stowaway." Jeff smiled at the little group listening to him. "I like that," he said. "I think that's pretty creative. He finds himself a room in a hotel that, for all intents and purposes, is empty, and he stays there. A hotel stowaway."

Francis Carden grumbled, "Let's get this show on the road." He looked at Arnaut. "What do you say, Arnaut? Can we get this show on the road?"

"Yes," Arnaut answered. He pointed toward the parking lot. "Today, we'll go there first," he said, as a way of describing the route he'd laid out for them.

"Across the parking lot?" asked Muriel Fox.

"Alongside it," Arnaut said. "It's a five-mile distance." He pointed south and swung his arm east as he talked. "A mile and a half there, a mile there, by the lodges owned by Mr. Oakland, from whom I have permission on which to trespass, then there,"—he was pointing east—"up to the high hill you see tipping the air, and so back around to the cabins here,"—he was pointing at them—"alongside the lakeshore to our point of emergence."

"Sounds like more than five miles to me," said Francis Carden.

Muriel said, "It's a good warm-up."

"Warm-up?" said Carden and smiled.

"You haven't been cross-country skiing before, have you, Mr. Carden?"

He shrugged. "I've been skiing."

She shook her head. "It's not the same."

He said, "What is?"

And Arnaut jumped in, sensing animosity between them, "So in respect of the morning's decay, the departure of us all should speedily enmasse."

"I agree," Jean said.

"With what?" Francis Carden asked.

And Arnaut said—using a phrase he used often, one that he thought was a lifesaver—"You know what I mean."

Lynette Meyer felt as if she were going to burst, as if she had eaten heavily and was bloated and could do nothing but sit and rest. There were things inside her and they were eating her up. That is what she thought and how she saw herself. It was not the first time she had felt that way: She had felt that way a hundred times before, sometimes when her period was due and sometimes when she had actually eaten too much —Thanksgiving and Christmas dinners especially, which she took, along with Pete Jr. and Jolene (and, in years past, with her husband) at her Aunt Carol's house in Syracuse. Carol was an eater. She was a talker and an eater. And she was poor. But she put together a hell of a Thanksgiving dinner and a hell of a Christmas dinner. She explained that she was thanking herself for still being alive, giving herself the "gift of gluttony" because she was still alive. And Lynette had always joined with gusto in her celebration. So had Pete Jr., and so had Pete Sr., whom she was missing now, in her room at the Many Pines Inn. Her eyes were on her own eyes reflected from the mirror and her mind was on the idea that she was fat and that there were things inside her that were eating her up. She was thinking that she missed Pete and that Harry Stans could not possibly take his place, no matter how hard he tried, and Lord knew that he tried very hard; Lord knew that the hardest stabs he made at taking Pete's place were in bed, where, he had told her, Pete had been wanting. "An' where'djoo hear that from?" she'd asked. "From you," he'd answered. "Ever' time you talk about Pete you tell ever'one how bad and lousy he was in bed an' what a terrible lover he was." And she'd come back, "He wasn't no terrible lover, he was just selfish is all." Then Harry would grin and say that lovemaking shouldn't be selfish, that it should be a "shared thing, like eatin' garlic, you know," and he'd laugh because he had always laughed at his own bad jokes. But he wasn't a replacement for Pete. Not in any way, not in bed and not in conversation and not in the way he treated Pete Jr.—for sure not in the way he treated Pete Jr.

But still there was something eating her up from the inside, something had gotten into her belly and was devouring her, she could feel it. And because it was inside her it was making her feel bloated, as if she were going to burst.

"Mama," said Pete Jr. from the bed. "It's awful cold."

She looked at him and nodded; she said, "Yes, it certainly is," then looked again in the mirror, at her own eyes, and liked them, and felt the cold that Pete Jr. felt, and felt the things inside her that were eating her up, the things in her gut and in her heart that were eating her up. They all had to do with Pete, of course. And nothing to do with Harry Stans who only wanted someone to screw now and again, who didn't have Myrna any more and so wanted someone willing to screw, and that was her, that was Lynette Meyer, someone willing to screw. Damn him, damn Harry Stans for saying that—"Well, I reckon that I do, Lynette." She wasn't so bad to look at. She was even almost pretty. If she squinted into the mirror, she *was* pretty. Squinting was like looking into the past, into her past, seeing herself the way she had been fifteen years ago when men had been tripping over themselves to get at her, Pete Sr. especially, God bless him.

"Mama," Pete Jr. said again. "It's awful damn cold in this room and I think we oughta go home. Mama?"

This time she added a smile to her nod, and she said, "We're gonna go home sooner or later, Pete."

"I ain't feelin' so damn good, Mama. I feel awful funny. I feel funny inside."

She nodded. She knew what he meant. She could feel her insides wanting to get out, wanting to spray the walls. It was very comfortable here. The cold was comfortable, it felt right, it felt the way her memory of Pete's kisses felt, and that was good. Pete's kisses had been good once, had been wet and slurpy, the way kisses were meant to be. The cold felt like her memory of those kisses and it warmed her everywhere but where her nerves touched the surface of her skin. She said, "I feel good here, Pete."

"I feel like shit," said Pete Jr.

She continued looking at her eyes reflected in the mirror. She thought they were good eyes, her own eyes, someone else's eyes. Pete's. They were Pete's eyes, and that was all right. They had the coolness of his eyes, puffy lids and stumpy eyelashes. He had invaded her, she was sure of it. He had come down the hillside and followed the lakeshore past the cabins and had come into her body. It was him there. Him making her feel bloated and filled up, and him eating her guts.

Pete Jr. said, "I'm scared, Mama. This ain't no place for us and I don't feel good."

But Lynette felt good.

She kept the axe in the closet of her room. She went to the closet now, opened the door, took the axe out.

Pete sat up in bed, wide-eyed. "Where you goin' with that, Mama?"

"There's ice on the lake, son," she said. "I'm gonna go and chop it."

SEVEN

"It's like ice skating," Arnaut called. "It's like ice skating. Pretend you're ice skating." He glanced back, arms swinging in a close, wide arc near his body, legs pushing powerfully. He had once considered that cross-country skiing on flat terrain was an awkward-looking pastime, unnatural to the normal rhythms of the body, like running a three-legged race. Now he thought it was similar to the movements in a dream —fluid, graceful, capable of much more in distance than could be accounted for by the energy expended.

Francis Carden called, from the rear of the little group, "We've all done this before, Arnaut. We don't need your instruction."

"Pretend you are ice skating," Arnaut repeated. "It's like ice skating." He noted a tinge of anger in his voice, and he had no idea where it came from.

Jean Ward was a couple of feet behind and to his right. Muriel Fox, giggling as if at some private joke, was behind Jean. Jeff Glynn and Francis Carden were ten yards back and had been talking together since leaving the inn twenty minutes before.

The group was at the center of a wide, flat field. The snow here was shallower than near the inn because the wind the previous evening—unfettered by buildings and trees—had pushed it into narrow, sharp-edged drifts, and occasionally Arnaut had had to detour past spots where the brown earth showed through. He wondered if the wooded area they were approaching would also be bare of snow in spots and he thought he should have paced the route out first before bringing the others. But now they were here, they were moving, and that was all that was important—bare spots could be detoured around, the route restructured to the demands of the lay of the land. Now they were moving, *he* was moving, putting time behind him, working himself into exhaustion, centering his mind and his energies on the movements of his arms and his legs, on keeping them fluid and graceful and efficient.

Not thinking about Martha, or about the inn, about the cold, or the memories, about the tragedies that had visited themselves upon Seventh Lake again and again over the years, as if the lake were the focus of bad news.

Here, nothing haunted him.

"It's like ice skating," he called. "Pretend you are ice skating."

"We've heard that," said Jean Ward.

Muriel Fox giggled again.

Arnaut looked back at Muriel. She had her eyes straight ahead. She was moving with much skill and grace and efficiency. He nodded at her and turned his head back.

He decided that he was covering the distance across the field to the stand of woods a half mile off very quickly. As quickly as in a dream, that was certain. As quickly as sound. The stand of trees was sweeping toward him as if he had taken flight; what had only seconds before been a muddle of brown and green, like woods modeled from a lump of clay, was rapidly taking definition—there, a knot was visible, and there a black squirrel chased another black squirrel up the trunk of an oak, and there a clump of leaves, still green, clung to the lower branches of a young maple tree, and there . . .

Were people.

But no.

"This is taking forever," called Francis Carden.

Muriel Fox giggled again.

"This is quick," said Arnaut. "Like ice skating."

"Arnaut?" said Jean Ward; he did not hear the concern in her voice.

No people. Only the spaces between trees, the undulations of branches, the change in perspective as his body moved right and left, the overcast sky, the sweat flowing into his eyes from exertion, the memories.

The tragedy.

As if Seventh Lake were the focus of bad news.

"You're going awfully slow," said Jean.

"I am as quick as sound," said Arnaut.

"You're barely moving," said Jean.

Like movement in a dream. Molasses movement in a dream. Feet stuck, mind numb, memories pushing hard.

"We're going to get there sometime tomorrow, for Chrissakes!" yelled Francis Carden.

Muriel Fox giggled.

Jean said, "Arnaut? Are you all right?"

He did not answer.

Jean said, "Let's stop. I think we need to stop. Arnaut?"

He said nothing.

They sat him down in the snow. The woods a half mile off swept toward him and past and he was on the hillside, then down, at the lakeshore, struggling over mounds of ice pushed up by a storm, jabbing his ski poles in hard to keep his balance.

"Arnaut? Can you answer me, please. Can you see my fingers?"

They stood him up.

"We should take his skis off," said Jeff Glynn. "I think it would be easier if we took his skis off, don't you?"

"We could slide him," Jean Ward suggested. "We

could slide him along on his skis back to the inn. It would be easier than trying to walk him."

"That's a good idea," said Jeff Glynn.

Jean said, "Arnaut? You're making me feel very concerned."

Jeff said, "It's like an epileptic seizure, I think."

Pushing himself along over the ice on the lake to the spot where Martha had gone in and hammering the ice with his hands, breaking it and crawling in through the hole and going down into that immense cold, finding her, holding her, holding her, and laughing, kissing her, and laughing.

"I think we'd better get him back to the inn," Jean said.

"It's damn cold," said Francis Carden.

"I like the cold," said Muriel Fox.

"I am fine," said Arnaut.

"Arnaut?"

"Fine," he said.

"You had us worried."

"We'll continue now. It's like ice skating. Remember. Like ice skating." He pushed himself to his feet.

Jean took his arm, shook her head. "No. We're going back to the inn."

He thought a moment. Reflected. Considered. "Yes," he said. "The inn."

At the house under the lake, nails holding the staircase intact had begun to rust, but the wood was waterlogged and swollen, so the staircase, like the house, held itself together. And though the thing that moved with aching slowness down the staircase, through the frigid dark water, possessed the weight of need and desperation, the weight of memory, and the crushing pressure of eternity, that pressure was on everything in the house—on every fiber and cell—so it was equal here to there, from floor to ceiling, staircase to archway to hall, and the staircase held the weight of it, and the thing moved down the staircase and stood silently with its mouth wide as if to scream, because the scream of its own dying was still in it, just as the groan and pleasure of living had been in it.

It stood naked and apparently female in the cold dark water at the bottom of the staircase. It opened its mouth impossibly wide as if to accept some huge mouthful of food. Its eyes, which were green and sightless, shed tears, and the tears floated off like droplets of oil.

"On some mornings," Arnaut said to Mary, "in summer, in late summer, in the early morning, in the heat . . ." He smiled up at her from the loveseat in his office. She was seated on the arm of the loveseat. She smiled back.

"Yes?" she said, and he was instantly uncomfortable with her tone—it was too adult, too mature, too much the tone of a woman offering her understanding and good will.

He went on, "In the early morning, if it is warm —and there's nothing quite so enchanting as early morning warmth here, at the inn—I have seen a mist rising from this lake"—he nodded at Seventh Lake, visible out the big window in his office, though he couldn't see it from where he was sitting—"and I see her in the mist, in the movements of the mist." He smiled to himself. "Of course."

"Of course?"

He nodded. "How could I not see her, Mary? I see her everywhere."

Mary put her hand on his shoulder. He put his hand on her hand and said, "I have trouble."

"Yes?" she said; it was a question.

"Yes. She is here."

Mary took her hand away. "I'm sorry for what

happened today. I wish I'd been there. I think I would have known what to do."

He smiled at her again, a smile of thanks. "They knew what to do. Jean did, and the others."

"What do you think caused it, Dad? Was it something like . . . epilepsy?" He noticed that her tone had changed. It was a tone he liked, now—the tone of a daughter worried about the father she loved.

He shook his head. "I wish I knew. I don't."

Mary leaned over, kissed him on the forehead. He felt her breasts against his shoulder and he squirmed away. She straightened, smiled, had apparently not noticed. "I'm glad you still love her."

"I don't." He shook his head, repeated, "I don't," added. "How can I love a dead woman?"

Mary's smile faded. She cleared her throat nervously and stared at him a moment in what he knew was miserable incomprehension.

He said, "It was a mistake opening the inn this winter."

Mary would not be gotten off the subject. "I love her, Dad. You know I love her."

"You love what you see in your memory. You love a ghost."

She took her hand from his shoulder and went to the window that looked out on Seventh Lake. She said, back turned, eyes on the lake, "Ghosts are all we *can* love, Dad. You told me that, and you were right."

"Then we can love nothing," he said. "Life is all we have. And if you love a ghost, then you love nothing."

EIGHT
January 25

"There's nothing keeping us here," Jeff Glynn said. "And you know it's going to end up costing us an arm and a leg."

From the bed, as she nursed Samantha—Jeff disliked the squishy sucking noises the child made when she nursed—Amy answered, "I don't think we should leave just now. I think it would be bad for Samantha to travel, don't you?" She gave him a quizzical smile and Jeff thought how very comfortable she looked, how motherly and how soft. She even looked plumper, somehow, though she was far from overweight. She looked, he decided, like a child's picture-book representation of a mother with child: dark, soft hair fluffed around her head, red rosy cheeks denoting the glow of health, and plump, inane smile.

"I don't believe," Jeff began, and took his eyes off her because she was making him nervous, "that it's in Samantha's best interests to *stay*. And besides, I'm not sure that I like it here."

"I love it here," Amy said without hesitation. "It's comfortable. It's like being home."

"How could *that* be?" Jeff looked at her again, mystified. *Home* for both of them was a tract house in a Syracuse suburb—just the kind of place that she'd been raised in.

"It is," she declared, still smiling. "It simply is, Jeff." She studied Samantha a moment, then pulled her gently away from her breast and turned her around to start on the other. "Home is where the heart is, Jeff."

He grinned. "I think you're losing it, babe."

"I've lost nothing," she said softly, still smiling. "I've found something. I've found peace, I've found it here, and so I'm going to stay."

"As simple as that?"

"You can go if you want."

Jeff grinned nervously. "You're joking."

"Who's joking? I don't need you to stay with me. Besides, don't you have work to do at home? Why don't you go, Jeff. It'll be easier for us all."

"I don't believe I'm hearing what I'm hearing."

She ignored the remark. She said, "I took her to the lake yesterday, while you were skiing."

"Sorry? Took who?"

"Took who? Who do you think? Samantha. I took her to the lake and I stood at the shore with her. She loved it. She was very comfortable with it, as I was."

Jeff's nervous smile wavered, came back, wavered again, came back. "I don't understand that," he said. "Comfortable with what?"

"You see," she said. "That's why I say you should go back to Syracuse. You don't belong here. I do. So does Samantha." She tweeked Samantha's little nose with her finger. "Don't you, darling—don't you *love* it here?" The child made a quick cooing noise, like the sound of a pigeon. "You see, Jeff—she agrees. She's comfortable here, too, and she wants to stay. But you don't. You aren't comfortable and you don't want to stay. I can understand that. This is not your element. You're more . . . artificial—no, I don't mean that. Yes, I do. I mean it." She paused, adjusted Samantha's hold on her nipple, stroked the child's cheek. She continued, "I know what it is we have here, Jeff. What Samantha and I have here. We have eternity."

*   *   *

These stolen moments of warmth were delicious and brief, like the tang of apples taken from a private orchard. They were moments when time came back, and with it pain, and longing, and desperation. So the warmth was returned, and the cold allowed to clamp down hard, which was the way of things in the universe.

The entity understood the reasons for none of this. It passed from here to there like dust. It paused, it possessed for warmth, it moved on.

And the entity did it all as blindly as a photograph which captures color but does not see it.

Mary was remembering a letter that her father had written to her several years earlier, but had sent only recently. The letter had read, in part; "The reason we do not like to be alone is simple. We do not like to be alone because when we are alone, and there are no distractions, then we must look inward, and when we do, we experience there, inside us, a sea of stars, cold, infinity. And that is when we seek out the artificial around us, when we must go to a movie by ourselves or call a friend or dig out the cards and play solitaire."

She remembered thinking that it had been merely the meanderings of a mind still obsessed with the loss of love, because his wife, Mary's mother, had died only a month earlier. But he had added, "So I wonder how the dead react to that, to looking constantly inward and experiencing only what there is to experience there. It is what I see for Martha. It is doubtless what hell is about."

He had touched a bit of that hell himself the day before, Mary thought. She had felt it in him later, had *glimpsed* it *with* him. Infinity. Eternity. Power and powerlessness all at once—like the wonder and ease of flight through the realms of a dream, over landscapes that had no more substance than the landscapes of a dream.

She shivered. The inn was very cold, she thought. She fancied that she could see her breath, though she couldn't. She was dressed in brown corduroy pants, a white cotton blouse, and a brown bulky knit sweater; she'd fastened the blouse at the neck with a green porcelain brooch she'd had since childhood. And still she was cold.

It was 7:30 and darkness had settled over Seventh Lake hours earlier. She thought she should regret having to leave the inn before long, but she looked forward to leaving as much as if it amounted to an escape, as if there were something that was bent on holding her here against her will. And perhaps even without its own knowledge.

Because it already had the rest of them, she thought: Arnaut, Jean Ward, Muriel Fox, the Glynns, Francis Carden. It had them and it was going to keep them.

She smiled. These were fanciful, romantic notions, and she enjoyed playing with them.

It was the heft of the axe that was comforting, the feel of it, the weight of it.

"Mama," said Pete Jr. from the bed, "where you goin' with that?"

"I ain't goin' nowhere, Pete. I'm goin' out. And it's none-a your business, so you go back to sleep."

He was propped up on his elbows as he watched her. She was warmly dressed, in clothes he had grown accustomed to seeing his father in—several bulky dark sweaters, an old brown leather jacket, faded jeans; her large body made the clothes look as if they were tight fitting—and she had the axe in a kind of backward grip, as if she were going to use it to pound a peg into the ground from overhead. As he watched, she changed her grip and held the axe as if she were going to chop wood, which was her normal way of carrying it.

Pete said, "You gonna chop wood, Mama?"

"No," she answered at once. "I ain't gonna chop no wood, I'm gonna go out and it's none-a your business so you go back to sleep." She did not look at him as she said this. She kept her gaze on the window over his bed. There was nothing visible through it but a few lights across Seventh Lake; if the room were dark, she could have seen the black mound of Dog Island a mile off. But she was looking at nothing beyond herself. She was looking inward. Remembering. Obeying.

"Don't go out, Mama," Pete Jr. pleaded.

"Got to go out," she told him, and lowered her head as if to look at him. "If I don't go out, then there's creatures gonna be awful cold tonight. You want that, Pete Jr.?"

"I don't want no one to be cold, Mama. Why you ask me that?"

"Wasn't askin' nothin'. I was tellin' you. I'm goin' out." She raised her head.

Pete lay down and pulled the blanket up to his neck. "It's awful cold, Mama. This place is awful cold."

"Always been so, darlin'," she said. "Always been so long as I can remember, or anyone. It's the way of things. The lake is cold. And people want to live here, well, they'll be cold, too."

"Can I listen to the radio while you're gone, Mama? Can I watch the T.V.?"

"Watch what? Some crap? You do whatchoo want, Pete." And with that, she left the room.

In the house under the lake, the entity which had once been Benjamin Mosiman rose from the remains of its bed on the second floor—the same bed the entity that had once been Anita Mosiman had shared with him for many years—and made its way very slowly to the door and then down the hallway to the top of the stairs. It stopped there.

* * *

"I'm leaving soon," Mary said. She was sitting in a chair in front of her father's desk.

Arnaut said, "Where will you go? This is your home."

"There are people I can stay with, Dad. I'm uncomfortable here. I'm sorry."

"I want you to stay, daughter."

"Why?"

"Because I love you."

She could not be deceptive with him. She said, "I love you, too. But I *have* to leave. I want to."

He gave a few moments to silence. Then he said, nodding, "I know that. And I know why."

This surprised her. She said, "What do you know?"

"Only that we are in trouble."

"We?"

"Us. All of us here at the inn." He nodded to indicate his office. "I stand alone here in the dark often. It encompasses me. I feel it as if it were . . . real, as if there were stars in it and I could touch them. But they are cold, daughter. The darkness is cold and I'm touched by it. I think it is your mother touching me."

"Oh, daddy . . ." She was distressed, wanted to reach out to him. But she sensed that he was making himself unreachable.

He said, "I look at you and I wonder, *Can there be anybody so young?* But there is, and it is you." He patted his shirt pocket. "I want a cigarette."

"You don't smoke."

"I did once. In the medieval past. Before dinosaurs."

"Daddy, come with me. Come away from here."

He shook his head. "No. Martha is here. She is dead. But she exists here. I can't alter what is here."

"But you can join her, Daddy?"

Again he shook his head. "I don't understand that. I have no need to join her. I have all I need of her here."

He touched his temple. "All I will ever need of her is here."

"I don't think you know what's happening, Daddy. I don't know. I don't think you know what's happening here at the inn, or what's happening to you."

Arnaut's face reddened with anger. After several long moments, he said, "You are telling me, daughter, that this is an evil place, and I do not credence such things. I have never. If this is an evil place, then there are things here which are evil, things I do not understand. And they killed her."

Mary said, reaching across the desk to touch him, although the distance was too far, "If you believe that, Daddy—"

"I'm not stupid," he cut in. "I may talk . . . strange, but I'm not stupid."

Mary withdrew her hand. "I'm sorry. I thought we could talk. But we've never been able to talk, have we? Not really."

He said nothing. Mary stood. He turned away. There was more than petulance in him; there was something about him that she had never before encountered, something cold and unapproachable, as if he were a winter ghost. It made her suddenly fearful. "We'll talk in the morning," she said, turned and left the room.

She did not look back before closing the door behind her, and so did not see that Arnaut had turned and was watching her, that there was pleading in his eyes.

NINE

Evening

"Do you see it?" asked Muriel Fox, and nodded at her window. She expected no answer. She got none. She went on excitedly, "The Christmas tree on the other side of the lake. It's a big one. They keep it lit right up until February. Where do they get the electricity?"

"Propane!"

She had served tea. Her cup was half empty. The other was full, untouched. She picked up her cup, lifted it to her lips, hesitated. "Propane?" she asked. "Do you mean some kind of propane-powered generator?"

There was no answer.

She sipped her tea, eyes on the other soft blue eyes. She smiled. "I'm glad you've come back. I'm comfortable with you."

"A stitch in time . . ."

"You're easy to talk to." She sipped her tea, found it tepid, set the cup down. "I've had many lovers." She smiled as if embarrassed, though she wasn't. "That's quite a confession, isn't it—I mean, from someone you've known . . . what?—a few days? But I've always believed that it's best to get all the cards on the table, to put our . . . selves, to put our *souls* out front where we can be seen for who we *really* are, not merely for what we want others to *believe* we are. Don't you agree?" She hurried on, not allowing time for an answer, "And so there I am. Someone who loves . . . to be loved, and loves to love. And I've had a lovely life, a lovely life. And that is the thing I most treasure, the people, the *men*"—another false smile—"who have filled it up. Like you." She paused, wanted an answer, wanted confirmation, got nothing. She hurried on, "Two of my lovers had the same name. It was Stuart Hawkins. And I think they had the same middle name. They weren't related, they were nothing at all alike . . . Ah, I know what you're going to say. You're going to say that they must have had *something* in common to qualify as my lovers. And you'd be right, of course. They were both dreamers."

"Propane!"

"They dreamed of rising from the obscurity of their pasts. One did it, the other didn't. The other married someone named Caroline and went to live in Binghamton, and sell appliances. That would be a hell of a way to live—to sell appliances. So much white. So much beige." She saw herself reflected in his eyes. She thought fleetingly that that was strange, as if his eyes were very, very large, mirror size, but that would be impossible, he would have to grow, would have to enlarge, to be the size of the room. "Tell me about yourself?"

"A stitch in time . . ."

"You're a man of few words." She studied her reflection in the soft blue of his eyes, where her skin was soft blue, and the room behind her was soft blue, and her dark red dress bore a soft blue tint. "Do you like my dress?" she said. "It's very old. A former lover gave it to me." It was a romantic lie. "Before going off to France. He was a writer and he liked to give women dresses." The eyes embraced her and made her cold. "He was a writer and he liked to give women dresses. He went off to France." She pulled her gaze from him and the room was soft blue, the night beyond the window was soft blue. "You've never told me your name. His name was Stuart Hawkins. He went to Binghamton. He sells appliances. White, beige, avocado appliances."

She saw her hand, like a photograph of her hand, and she watched it reach in fits and starts for her cup of tea. "Camomile tea," she said.

"Camomile tea."

"To sleep, to dream."

"I'm embraced by all of you."

"Nature abhors a vacuum."

"You make me cold." She brought the cup of tea to her lips, found it very hot, as if it were fire. She reached to set it down. She saw it leave her grasp, heard it clatter distantly to the floor. She leaned over, watched a dark soft blue stain spread and stop and crystallize. She thought, *It has changed to ice,* and as quickly as the thought came to her, it dissipated.

She rose. She crossed the room. She stood by the closed door.

She was remembering. The memories were real; she could touch them, listen to them, they spoke to her and wrapped themselves around her.

Then she was watching them and was part of them.

She was nine years old and the rough touch of gray barnwood was against her cheek, the sting of wind-driven snow on her forehead and on her small hands, her pleading whispers unheard, even by herself. Overhead, the sunlight was gray-blue behind the onrush of snow. To her left, down a slope, not far, not far, an opening to the barn, a way in, a place to huddle up against the cold, where there was the warmth and the living smell of animals.

She cried out. She heard nothing. And all at once she did not care.

She went to sleep.

And woke in bed. Cold. Forever cold.

* * *

Francis Carden saw her open her door. He put a smile on. He had his Swiss army knife in hand, had unscrewed some door hinges, screwed them back in, was looking for more.

When she appeared from within her room he said, "Hello, Muriel." He wondered as he said it about the onrush of cold air. She was a dozen feet away, her side to him and her head down slightly, as if her gaze were on the floor.

Francis repeated, "Hello, Muriel," added, "Cold night. Is your room cold? Is the heat working?"

She turned to look at him.

His breathing stopped when her eyes fell on him. They were eyes as cold and dead as marbles, in a face that was translucent, like ice, so the rigid thrust of bone showed through. She said, "I am cold. Forever cold," and her voice was without modulation, the voice of wind.

Amy Glynn had Samantha in her arms. Samantha was dressed as if for a summer walk, in a pink dress and bonnet and wrapped in a white receiving blanket. Amy said to Jeff, "I'm going to go out and look at the stars."

Jeff wanted to protest, to reason with her—"No, it's too cold, look how you've dressed her," he wanted to say. But he could say nothing reasonable, he knew that it would be futile. He said, "No, you're not," and Amy opened the door and stepped out of the room. Jeff threw himself from the chair and went after her. He caught her a short way from the door. He whirled her around. She clutched the baby to her bosom. "You are not taking Samantha from me!" she screamed.

"And you're not going outside, dammit! Not with my child!"

"My child!" she hissed. "We're going to look at the stars."

"No," Jeff insisted.

Amy said nothing.

"No," Jeff said again, more firmly.

Amy said nothing.

Jeff took her gently by the arm and coaxed her back into their room. She went to a chair with Samantha and rocked her. Then she slept and her child slept.

Harry Stans had gone directly to Lynette's room. He found Pete Jr. there, asleep. He found Pete Sr. there, too, smiling, flat-faced from time underwater, gray teeth prominent beneath lips as thin and white as string. He was standing very still near the bed where his son lay, gray-black hair scattered everywhere on his head. He was leaning against a wall, the wall was beige, and in the light from the hallway, Harry saw that clumps of his hair clung wetly to it where his head had turned left and right.

His head turned now. But it was not a motion that said *no.* It was simply a motion, ball and socket joints rolling out of control.

His shoulders rolled, too.

And his hands. As if he were getting ready to throw dice.

The sound these motions made in the bone was low and rough, like a baseball bat being dragged on cement.

Jean Ward stood at the lakeshore in front of the cabin she and her brother had shared. She remembered his walk into the lake and she said, "Dave, I'm so sorry." She wasn't able to tell herself what she was sorry for, other than his death—the fact that he was gone from her life—and that was enough of a reason. It was good to talk in the cold darkness to dead loved ones. It was reasonable to expect that they were there, listening. "Dave," she said, merely to mouth his name. She liked saying it. The mere fact of it, the sound of it, gave her comfort. "Dave?" She had not always called him Dave. She had once called him Davey, though he was older and it sounded strange for his younger sister to be calling him Davey. He'd told her that and had said that she could call him Davey if she did it in private. So she did, for a while, but it was not the same. Davey in private was stranger, somehow, than Davey in public. So she started calling him Dave, which he preferred. And they got along as well as any brother and sister can get along. He took her to dances when no one else would ask her, because she was too pretty in a time when that was intimidating, sometimes even to big brothers. He took her to movies, too, and to museums, and on shopping expeditions.

"Dave," she said. "I miss you." She realized that she meant it and she was glad. The pain was gone and she could miss him.

There was ice at the shore. It was finger thick, as wide as several sidewalks, and ragged at the edges because of a fitful breeze. Jean could see the ice because of a spotlamp on the main inn. All the spotlamps on the cottages had been turned off by Mr. Carden because no one was staying in the cottages anymore. The ice was blue-black and the water nearly the same deep, flat black as Dog Island a mile off.

She was aware of the cold moving off the lake. The breeze carried it and augmented it.

She looked up from the ice and saw the same Christmas tree, trimmed in a thousand lights, sixty feet tall, a ritual at the lake, that Muriel Fox had seen. She could see a few other lights near it. The lights of cottages, a pair of moving lights visible intermittently. A car, she decided. And then she looked at the ice again. She saw a shape moving beneath it. She told herself it was a fish, though she knew that it wasn't. The shape moved back, away from the light.

TEN

The Mosimans were like a dream of slow motion in Seventh Lake.

"Then you love nothing," her father had told her. "If you love a ghost then you love nothing." Mary repeated these words mentally again and again. They were reasonable. They made sense. She did not believe them, though she wanted to. She wanted to believe them very much because it was useless loving ghosts. Ghosts could not keep her warm in the night, they could not come into her little room and lean over and kiss her and pull the blanket up so it covered her neck, even when the night wasn't chilly; ghosts could not talk with her and give her a sense of her own life, they could not lead her this way or that, except to the extent that they once had, except to the extent that her mother had told her such things as, "Your decisions are ultimately your own. Blame no one else for their consequences," and, "We must try to give back to this life more than it gives us. I'm not sure why. Perhaps because *it* owes *us* nothing."

Because you loved the dead for such things. Such things lingered, like the final depression their bodies made in their deathbeds, or the blood stains left on their clothes by the grappling hooks that pulled them up.

Mary lit a cigarette. She coughed. She hated cigarettes, they made her throat itch, her hair smell, her breath foul at times. But habits were so much easier to keep than to break. Even the ones that hurt.

Her father knew that. Her father, who was so devoted to his own ghosts, so tied to the inn and to the ghosts that moved sullenly about inside it. The ghost of her mother, his wife. The ghost of himself, of his happiness before her death.

Mary studied her cigarette. Its tip was a cool orange glow in the darkness of her room. She said, "It's simple, Daddy, you go up to her and you say, 'I am attracted to you.' She knows it already. She's not stupid."

Mary took her eyes from the cigarette and looked out the window that overlooked the cabins lining the lakeshore. The cabins were like squat, dark lumps. She thought what great stillness and cold there was about them, and here, too, at the inn, and around the lake. She thought that that was good for her, now. She needed it.

Then she thought, all at once, that her father would love being a ghost, would love being the ghost of the person he once was.

She asked herself aloud, "Wouldn't anyone?"

The Mosimans moved through the cold darkness in the lake; they moved in the center between the surface and the stiff, rocky bottom.

"Wouldn't wanta have to look at your face at a time like that, darlin'," Pete Sr. said, and Lynette said, "I know. I'm sorry." And she was. Because her face was pretty, but it was pinched by jowls and layered with fat so the eyes were beginning to puff shut. In a few years she would have a constant fat squint and then he wouldn't want to make love to her at all.

"But I do love ya, darlin'," he said. She believed him. Why wouldn't he love her? She was a good person. She was a tireless worker and she rarely lied and she did harm to no one. He could love her as well as he could love any woman.

"I love you, too, Pete," she murmured in the cold dark near the lakeshore.

But he was gone, then. He was moving out onto the lake, over the expanse of black, paper-thin ice with his fishing pole in hand and sitting down to enjoy himself with his friends gathered around him, to make filthy jokes about women who weren't their wives or mothers. It was part of his existence. Part of what he loved.

She watched him begin his wait. His friends would not arrive for a very long time.

Harry Stans said behind her, startling her, "Gawd, woman, you're comin' with me away from this damn place and there ain't no two ways about it!"

She had the axe in her hand. She'd chopped the ice at the shore with it. She'd made a huge hole and there was water sloshing gently in it under the breeze. She swung around with the axe and caught Harry Stans with the side of it against his head. He fell over silently, left hand to his head. He did not move. He lay on his side with his hand to his head and he breathed raggedly, a gurgle erupting every now and then. At last, Lynette walked away from him and back to the inn.

HISTORY—JULY, 1979

"I'm sorry, Mr. Berge, but there was absolutely nothing anyone could have done. Believe me. You're blaming yourself without reason."

"I brought her here."

"Yes, sir. I'm sorry."

"I brought her here to this place. I knew it would . . . have her. I knew it would take her from me."

"Sir, my advice to you is this; you are stressed, sir, and under stress certain . . . aberrations may seem very, very real . . ."

"What is that? Aberration?"

"Sir, I would say, miscalculations of judgment. Do you understand?"

"My miscalculation of judgment was bringing her here. This place has killed her."

The Mosimans floated through the fluid cold darkness. Ben was naked, and Anita was naked, and the children were dressed in their pajamas, all as they had died. From above, the family might have looked like huge white fish moving just below the surface of thin ice at the center of the lake.

On Dog Island, the geese had moved on, and though there were owls in the stand of pines that lined the lakeshore, they did not hunt over ice.

Others did.

They sat with fishing poles ready and heads lowered, their shoulders hunched up against the cold.

While the Mosimans moved silently in the cold, fluid darkness below.

BOOK THREE

THE FOCUS OF BAD NEWS

ONE

Turmoil, Mary realized. There was turmoil happening inside her.

She stood. The room was very cold. She shivered, hugged herself for warmth, went to the closet, got her coat from it, put it on. She flicked on the overhead light to augment the light on the desk near her bed. She needed *light* in the room, she told herself. Light was warmth. She went into the bathroom, turned the light on, went back to the bedroom, gazed up at the overhead. It was very dim. Only one light working, she guessed. She brought the desk chair over, stood on it, unscrewed the globe from around the overhead, tossed the globe onto the bed. She looked at the light fixture. There were three bulbs. Two were working. She unscrewed the bad one, stepped down from the chair. She hesitated, stared confusedly at the bad bulb, set it down, went to the door, flicked the overhead light off, went to the bathroom, turned the light off, went to the desk, turned the light off.

She sat on the edge of her bed in the cold darkness. She felt herself being touched in the cold darkness.

"It was because I loved you," Arnaut said.

He got no answer.

"We do things . . . we live . . . in this life we do things and they have . . . pressure . . . effect on other people. Even when we love them. It was because I loved you that I did it."

Still he got no answer.

"I wanted to be with you." He took no notice of the

fact that words were coming easily to him, that he wasn't tripping over his tongue as he usually did. "So I brought you here and here you were. And then it took you." He nodded to indicate the lake beyond the window; he felt himself being touched in the darkness, felt a very cold hand on his back, felt it being taken away. He turned, looked. "You were always being taken away from me."

He saw Martha's face as if it were real, as if he could touch it, and he leaned over and kissed the air near him, felt the warmth of her cheek as if she had turned her head to meet him. Then he felt the cold of her lips on his; he hesitated, wanted desperately to enjoy it, wanted desperately to find in it what he had always found in her kisses.

Then he recoiled.

At the edges of Seventh Lake, the Mosimans moved very slowly, found the break in the ice that Lynette Meyer had made for them, and went up, through it, onto the land.

The memories swimming inside them were like scenes in a kaleidoscope.

The Mosimans stayed very still. Their eyes sought the light, because light was warmth.

And life was warmth.

The lights of the inn fell on them. They started toward it. Their feet moved as silently as air over the thick covering of snow on the lakeshore.

Muriel Fox felt the rough scrape of gray barn wood on her cheek; she felt the sting of wind-driven snow on her forehead, and when she dared to open her eyes against it, she saw the opening just below, where the animals were, and warmth, and survival.

But she could not move. Her limbs refused the commands of her brain. She wanted only to sleep. She could no longer feel the cold. She felt, instead, a strange, tingling coolness and comfort, as if she were very tired and under freshly washed sheets on a warm day.

She closed her eyes.

She heard, very distantly, as if she were hearing words she had once read being repeated in her memory, "I don't know, my God, I don't know, help me!"

And then, another voice, a man's voice, "I'm coming after you. Don't move from where you are. There's a drop-off. Do you understand me? There's a drop-off."

"No. My feet won't . . ."

The smell and the warmth of animals below, through the opening, into the darkness below.

"Muriel, for God's sake . . ."

"Help me, please help me!"

The sting of snow, the comfort of crisp sheets on a warm day.

"Please, help me, help me!"

"I'm coming after you. Muriel. I'm coming."

The smell of the animals in the opening below, the warmth of the animals, the refuge from the stinging cold in the opening below.

"You're moving away from me. Don't move away from me. I can't swim. Muriel, I can't swim!"

A tingling coolness and comfort, as if she were very tired and under crisp sheets on a warm day.

"Muriel, stay where you are. Stay there!"

She was enveloped by it.

"Muriel, for pity's sake."

It wrapped her up.

"I can't . . . I can't . . ."

And carried her off. And she was there, with the warmth of the animals, with the warmth and smell of the animals. Sleeping. At peace.

Francis Carden stood with his eyes on the spot where Muriel had gone into the lake. He glanced quickly, in confusion, back, at the inn, to his left, at the boat dock, to his right, at the squat dark cottages a hundred yards off.

He looked again at the spot where Muriel had gone into the lake. He whispered after her, at the black water moving sullenly about in the hole her body had made in the thin ice, "I can't swim, Muriel. I'm sorry. I'm so sorry." A quivering, self-incriminating grin spread across his mouth. He shook his head. "I just can't swim."

Lynette Meyer was on her way down the lakeshore toward her cottage with Pete Jr. and Jolene and Pete Sr.; they were going to have a picnic. Pete Sr. was grumbling that men didn't go on picnics, but she knew that he was putting on a show for his son.

"What good's a picnic, huh? Tell me that?" And he nodded at Pete Jr. "You listen now, boy." He looked at Lynette. "I asked you what good's a picnic except to get bitten by mosquitoes and bees and to get ants on your food. Tell me what good a damn picnic is, Lynette?"

"Well, I will tell you," she said. "It's so's you can be under the sunlight and in the warm air, that's what it's good for, so you won't be so damn pale—my Gawd, sometimes I think you're a sheet. And besides, food tastes real good on a picnic, don't you think so, Pete Jr.?"

But he was saying nothing, and Lynette guessed that he was being smart, being silently agreeable to his father, that he knew what side his bread was buttered on.

"And I say it's a crock," Pete Sr. protested. "It's a damn crock. Here gimme that, woman," and he reached out and took the picnic basket from her. She smiled at him and said, "Thanks, Pete, it was gettin' heavy," and he said, "'tain't the only thing," and gave her a quick once-over. Her smile flattened because she agreed but could not bring herself to admit it.

They came upon a recently dead carp on the shore. It was very large, the size of a dog, Pete Sr. said, and Pete Jr. readily agreed, having had fun poking sticks at such amazing creatures when he'd found them on lone walks along the lakeshore. "Big's a dog," he said. "Big's a dalmatian," which was a breed he knew well because the only book in his personal library was *101 Dalmatians*.

Lynette said, "It's disgustin' and we're gonna detour 'round it." She did. With Jolene in tow, she stepped wide around it so she had to walk in the water while her son and husband looked at her with wide, amused grins on their mouths.

She pointed at Dog Island. It was visible this spring afternoon as a green hump halfway across the lake on the horizon. "Very pretty, ain't it?" she said.

Pete Jr. said, "It's like a sea monster comin' up outa the water."

"What's a sea monster?" Jolene asked, looking first at him, then at the island, then back at him.

Lynette said, "It's only a island. Ain't a sea monster. Ain't no such things as sea monsters."

"Who says?" asked Pete Sr.

"You're gonna scare these two kids you keep that up," said Lynette.

"I'm gonna scare a lotta people," said Pete Sr.

The island started to move out of the water very slowly, like the round and moving belly of some sleeping giant. The water at its edges cascaded off in white fury; its rocky underside appeared. A great wave started and careened toward the little family out on their picnic walk.

Lynette screamed.

She looked, panic-stricken, at Pete Sr. She saw that

he was laughing, though she could not hear him above the fury of the mammoth wave sliding toward her.

She looked, open-mouthed, at Pete Jr. He was laughing, too.

She looked at Jolene, whose hand she held. She saw her evaporate like so much butter under the hot sun.

And the hot sun gave way at once to night.

The night gave way to cold.

The cold to stillness.

Her gaze fell on the island. It rested darkly in midlake, low and flat and barely visible except that the thin ice covering Seventh Lake was bluish-black, and the island was black.

Lynette muttered, "Ghosts." This was a place of ghosts. Ghosts that were only memories. Ghosts that were dreams.

She had lived with ghosts for a very long time, now.

She turned her head, focused on Many Pines, a half mile off, around the bend of the lakeshore. It looked like a ferryboat lit up on a river at night with the little bay behind it. *Memories make us warm,* she thought.

There were people between her and the inn. They were moving as slowly as a glacier, as gracefully as a soft snow. And they were as white in the darkness as the belly of a carp.

"Ghosts," murmured Lynette Meyer.

She had made room at the inn for ghosts.

TWO

Jean Ward closed her eyes in the darkness and let the man touch her. It had been too long, far too long, since she had let him touch her this way, and though she couldn't remember his face, she could remember his hands moving with such inhuman skill over her body.

"Jack," she muttered.

He did not answer. His hair touched her neck and she shivered. She smiled. The smile broadened. "Jack!" she cooed again, and then again.

This was not simply ecstasy. This was elevating. She could barely stand back from it and view it.

"Jack, don't stop!" she murmured.

But he did. Though just for a moment, only for a breath. Then his hands were on her again, caressing her again.

But there was a difference.

His hands were rougher. As if they had aged. As if the skin had dried and hardened.

Still, their touch was wonderful, elevating, and she cooed "Jack" again and again as the hands moved over her, "Jack," whose face and occupation she could not remember, "Jack," who had always lingered so sweetly and so gently in her head, like her memory of something tasty.

"Warm," she heard.

The hands were very rough. As rough as cement. They hurt now and she wanted him to pull away. "Let's talk," she said.

"Warm," she heard.

"Let's talk," she said. "Please let's talk." She opened her eyes. The only light was what filtered in from outside—a soft bluish glow from arc lamps around the parking lot. She saw a face in that bluish glow. It was a face she did not recognize, a face that was as flat as glass and as translucent as snow. She shook her head, "I don't understand."

"Warm," said the face before her.

"I don't understand," she said, and barely heard her own voice, as if it were a voice speaking in another room.

She saw water around her.

"Warm," said the face before her.

"I don't understand," she said.

"Warm," said the face before her.

She saw water all around her, and far, far above, the muted, creamy glow of sunlight or moonlight. "Who are you?" she said.

"Warm," said the face before her.

She shook her head. She sought to rise from the bed, but she felt cold move into her, as if her body had been opened up down the middle and ice was being poured in, and she could not move.

She saw water around her. She heard her voice plead, like a recording of her voice, "Please, please," and her body opened up, the cold poured in.

"Warm," she heard.

She saw water around her. And far, far above, the muted creamy glow of the sun or the moon.

"Warm," she heard.

"Warm," she said.

She heard someone knocking at her door. "Jean?" she heard, but she did not answer.

"Warm," she whispered.

"Jean?" she heard again, more insistently. "Open the door, open the door!"

"Warm," she said, and saw water around her, the

creamy muted glow of the sun or moon far, far above, the tingling coolness of crisp sheets on a warm day, the sting of snow.

"Warm," she said again.

"Jean, please."

She stood.

She went to the door. She opened it.

She went into the hallway, down it, out another door, and into the night.

"We have to go," Jeff Glynn said.

Amy Glynn, in a rocking chair near the bed, gave him an inquisitive smile. "Go? Where? I like it here." Her smile stopped. "You go."

He shook his head. "Not *that* again. Amy, there is something *wrong* here, can't you feel it?" He shook his head again, stared at the ceiling. "Of course not. You're part of it."

"I'm part of nothing, dear," she said. "Part of nothing. I like it here. It's comfortable. I feel . . . safe. I feel at peace."

He sighed. "*That* is bullshit!"

"Listen," Amy said, "I didn't want you to come along in the first place."

"I'm aware of that."

"But you did. You *always* do what displeases me. And you never, ever, *ever* listen. Well, listen now, sweetheart, because I've got something very important to say to you." She paused very briefly; then, "I have a friend."

Jeff's mouth fell open. "A friend?"

"A male friend."

"A male friend?"

"Do you have echolalia? For the first time in our relationship you start listening to me and when you do you repeat everything I say. Yes, a male friend. A good, kind, gentle man—"

"It's Arnaut Berge, isn't it!? That bastard—"

"It's not Arnaut."

"Who? Who is it?"

"I don't know."

Jeff's face grew quizzical. Then he smiled, as if relieved. "I understand, now. This is a . . . fantasy. You're telling me about one of your fantasies."

She shook her head. "He's no fantasy, Jeff. He's as real . . . as real as you are. More real than you because *he* listens to me."

Jeff harrumphed. "This is fine, this is great. Here we sit, the happy couple, finances are good, we've got a nice home, a wonderful child, and here we sit talking about some *lover* you've got—"

"He's not my lover."

"Oh, sure, and the moon is made of green cheese."

"He listens to me. He listens, he doesn't interrupt, he's kind, he's gentle—"

"And what does *that* mean."

"What does what mean? Gentle? It means he's gentle *looking.*"

"Gentle looking, gentle looking." Jeff threw himself forward in his chair. He clasped his hands in front of him, planted his elbows on his knees, stared hard at the floor. "Is it me? Is it something I've done?"

"Yes," said Amy.

He looked at her, flabbergasted. "Yes?"

"Of course it's you. Who else would it be? You don't care about me. You never did."

"That's not true—"

"But all that's moot. I want you to go." "I'm expecting him."

"Sorry?" Jeff said, giving her an exasperated smile. "You're *expecting* him. Expecting who? Your lover? I don't believe this."

"I told you, and I meant it—he is *not* my lover. He's

old enough, for God's sake—he's *old* enough to be my great-grandfather. My grandfather, anyway."

"And you don't even know his name?"

"Who needs names? He listens to me, that's all I'm interested in."

"I'm not going."

She shrugged. "Stay then."

"Is he a guest here, Amy? Is your lover registered here at the inn?"

"I assume so."

"And now you're not denying it, are you?—that he's your lover. You're not denying it!"

There was a knock at the door. Jeff's head snapped toward it, then back at Amy. "I'm going to tell him you're not here."

"He'll know better." She gave him a smug smile.

"Amy, this is ridiculous." Another knock. "This is beyond ridiculous. You can't have a lover—my God—we have a *house,* a life together—"

"I don't have a lover. I have a friend."

Another knock. Jeff got up, shoved his hands into his pockets. He shook his head, "I'm confused, darling. I should want to . . . beat the hell out of him—"

"No, you shouldn't. And you mustn't. It would be cruel. He's old, as I said."

Another knock, then, quickly, another.

Jeff looked pleadingly at Amy. "Can you call to him to go away; can you do that?"

"Why? He's my friend. Go let him in."

"I can't let him in. I won't."

Another knock. Jeff started to the door. He stopped, looked back. There was another knock. "I'm sorry if I'm acting . . . strange about this. I know I should be more assertive, more . . . manly—"

She laughed quickly.

"But it's true," he said.

"Nothing's true. Everything changes." She nodded. "Go open the door."

He looked blankly at her for a few moments. Then he went and opened the door.

Arnaut was there. He looked wild-eyed. "I need your help," he said. "Please help me."

HISTORY

"Mary, it's your mother. It's Martha."

"Yes, Daddy. What about her? I just talked to her, we were going to play tennis."

"Something's happened, Mary. Something awful. Something I prayed would never happen, but it has, because I brought her here, and now this place has taken her, and it will take us all—"

Mary Berge watched as a tear stained the diary page. At the top of the page she had written, "THE EVENTS OF A DAY IN JULY." Below that, in smaller, very fastidiously formed letters, "The Death of Martha Berge by Accident." It was a week after her mother's death and Mary was putting down what she could remember. The conversation with her father was first, though the words she was using were not his words, they were the paraphrase of his words. Trying to remember exactly what he had said, she thought, would be like trying to remember the precise solution to a complicated maze. She wondered now, as she often did, what kind of mind he had that could make such mincemeat of the language he had grown up with. *Damn him,* she thought, surprising herself. *Damn him, damn him.*

She added to the page, "Your mother has been drowned in the lake, daughter. The lake has filled her up and caused her death." *That,* Mary knew, was verbatim. She could not help but remember it any other way.

And so, with that taken care of, she could note more mundane things: "Day partially cloudy, warm, several deerflies buzzing. A man appeared from his room in his underwear when mother was brought in. He stood in his underwear for a long time watching. I wanted to yell at him to go away and put clothes on but I knew that would just attract attention to him, so I stayed quiet.

"The boat that brought mother in was blue and white. It had a cracked windshield, and a very big outboard motor with the name 'Evinrude' on it in gold. When it brought mother in, a seaplane flew over low and tilted its wings. The seaplane was green. It flew on to the island at the center of the lake. It disappeared beyond the island. The name of the man who flies the plane is Mr. Darby.

"Mother's face was an awful white, the color of restaurant plates. She looked like wax. She looked like she was a Kewpie doll, and I remembered when I saw her that she used to nod at women who looked like Kewpie dolls and she used to say, 'That woman looks like a Kewpie doll.' Now *she* does.

"Daddy has been dragging himself from here to there this past week as if it is a great great effort that he would rather not do.

"He misses her terribly."

"Look for who?" said Jeff Glynn.

"Jean Ward," Arnaut answered. "She's outside."

"So?"

"She's in danger."

Jeff stared dumbly at Arnaut for a few moments. Clearly the man was in distress, but just as clearly he was making no sense at all. "How?" Jeff asked.

"The lake," Arnaut answered.

"She went into the lake?"

Arnaut nodded quickly. "I think so." He stopped nodding, put a hand hard on Jeff's arm, looked him squarely in the eye. "The lake wants her. It wants us all, our humanity, ourselves. It creates. It holds us."

Jeff grinned nervously. "Sure," he said.

"It has wanted us always."

Jeff nodded. "Yes," he said.

"Always!" insisted Arnaut.

They heard a scream.

Arnaut cocked his head toward its source—the area of the lakeshore. "Martha," he whispered.

HISTORY—SEPTEMBER, 1979

"Two months. The trees are changing. Becoming gold and red. It's happening early this year.

"Daddy prays. I don't know if it's really prayer. He's not a religious person. I don't think it's really prayer. I think it's something else, like wishing. He's wishing for Mother to come back. He stands alone in the gazebo and looks out at the lake. Then he mumbles to himself with his head down, like someone praying. He does this at night, late, when the people staying here are mostly asleep. But I see him.

"I can't hear any words. I leave my window open. I can see the gazebo from it, I'm pretty close to it. I leave my window open because he would hear me open it otherwise. But when I watch and listen I only hear him mumble and it makes me sad.

"TWO AND A HALF MONTHS AFTER THE ACCIDENT.

"Daddy said to me, 'Lakes are for wishing, daughter.' He smiled like he was keeping a secret. Then he said, 'And islands are for wishing on.'"

THREE

The entity that had once been Catherine Mosiman settled into Amy Glynn. The entity that had been Max Mosiman settled into Samantha. And the entity that had been Anita Mosiman looked on, pleased that its children were warm once again.

They settled in as unobtrusively as a dormouse settling into its winter nest. Their hosts noticed little. A sudden chill, as if a door had been opened and then quickly, quietly closed. A queer shifting of the light, as if their eyes possessed a nictitating membrane—as the eyes of snakes do—and it had come down. Then the light returned to normal.

And now that there was warmth, there was life. And they could go home.

Amy Glynn looked at Samantha, asleep in her arms. She smiled. What greater joy was there in life than to watch her infant sleep? She wondered what dreams a creature so young could have, if any at all, and she cooed, "What do you dream of, baby dear?"

The idea came to her all at once that Samantha might dream of floating in the waters of the womb, where there was constant food and warmth, and where there were no questions and no concerns, where time saw only the sprouting of fingers and toes, where the quick tapping of her heart was not a measurement of slow death but of growth toward life, where there were no needs and there was no cold, no crying, no sucking desperately at the air where a nipple should be.

"Is that what you dream of, baby dear?" Amy

whispered. "The waters of the womb?" She smiled an apology. "I can't put you there. I'm sorry."

Home to their house on the island.

Then it struck her how ironic it was that the waters of the womb were the source of life, that the waters of the womb gave life, and nurtured it, and that the cold waters of the earth did the same, that they teemed with life, and were so necessary, so indispensable to life itself, to her, to Jeff, to Samantha.

She watched Samantha bring a clenched fist up to her face, watched her closed eyes shut very tightly for a moment, then watched, relieved, as she relaxed.

Amy shook her head, "I'm so sorry, I'm so sorry," she whispered. "Was that a dream of death?" A tear formed in her eye and dropped to Samantha's pink receiving blanket. Another tear formed. She brushed it away. "What can I do for you, my child?" she said softly. "What can I give you but insecurity and tears and cold?"

Inside her, the entity which had once been Catherine Mosiman stretched out to the length of cities, the breadth of clouds, the weight of dust.

And the entity which had once been Anita Mosiman looked on, pleased, expectant, warm with love.

Amy stood. "Better not to dream of death," she whispered to her daughter. "Better to dream of the waters of the womb." She started for the door. She stopped halfway. She cocked her head. There was a mirror positioned obliquely to her left and she could see three people in it. She saw herself and she saw Samantha. She saw the face and naked body of Anita Mosiman, and she said, "I know who that is." She smiled at her reflection. She said, "It is myself."

Samantha let out a short, high-pitched cry, as if she were being pinched. Amy looked at her. A tiny balloon of spittle appeared on the child's lips and was quickly withdrawn on an inhale.

She would be waking soon, Amy realized; she was beginning to fuss, beginning to slide out of her awful dreams and back to the real world, where death waited to lie across her face and take her breath away. Amy shook her head. "We can't have that. The waters of the earth will soothe you again, baby dear." Because what difference was there, really, between the waters of the womb and the waters of the earth? None. Only a difference of place and temperature.

She went to the door, opened it, went down the hallway to the exit door, opened it, felt a slap of cold air on her face, hugged her infant daughter tightly to her breast. From the darkness beyond she was aware of voices shouting, and dimly she knew that one of the voices was Jeff's.

She stepped out of the inn. She whispered to her child, "The waters of the earth will soothe you, baby dear."

HISTORY—1986

Francis Carden was uncomfortable in a rowboat, not because he couldn't swim but because he didn't trust his strength to stay with him should it become necessary to row a long way in a hurry. So he was happy to beach the boat on the western shore of Dog Island. He'd been working at Many Pines for a short time and it was the first chance he'd gotten to go out on the lake alone. He'd have preferred the powerboat, but it was in use by water-skiers, and the tour boat was being overhauled.

He got out of the rowboat, secured it on shore and climbed the short, muddy slope which led to the island proper.

He'd been told about the island. In Eagle Bay, people referred to it as "Mosiman's Island," because of the people who had once lived there, and then had died there.

He saw Arnaut Berge almost at once and he raised his arm to call to him. He stopped. Arnaut was in a clearing fifty feet away, his back turned, head down, hands apparently clasped in front of him. It was an attitude of prayer, Carden realized, or an attitude of meditation.

Carden watched him for several minutes. Arnaut did not move.

At last, Arnaut raised his head, turned and walked toward Carden. Carden smiled, waved, called, "Hello." He got no answer. Arnaut moved through the clearing and quickly past him, eyes fixed. He descended the short, muddy slope that Carden had come up; he turned to his left. Carden followed a short way. He watched as Arnaut rounded the southeast corner of the island. Moments later, Carden heard the sound of a motor, and moments after that, Arnaut reappeared piloting a small boat back to shore.

Lynette Meyer could not see Arnaut's face well. Light from the inn was feeble here, at the far end of the line of cottages; it was a dull blue-black, the color of the lake itself. His face, she thought, looked like the mask of a face. His mouth was open, and words were coming out, but his lips did not appear to be moving. His eyes were wide and large, but they were black ovals in the rectangle of his head. He had grabbed her hard by the shoulders and she had told him several times, "You get your hands off-a me."

"Where is Martha, where is Martha?" he asked again and again.

"You get your hands off-a me," Lynette told him again. She still had the axe in her left hand, its head pointed down. She realized that she was not far from using it on this man who had had the balls to grab hold of her.

"I'm not trying to hurt you," he said.

"Well, I sure as hell am gawna hurt you."

"No need," he said. "Martha came out here. Martha. My wife. You've seen her?"

"I ain't seen her."

"She . . ." He paused. His grip weakened on her shoulders. "The lake wants her. It took her once, now it will take her again. I know this."

"You don't know shit, Mr. Berge. It ain't the damn lake. It's the damn island!" She twisted away from him. She lifted her right hand so it was pointing in the general direction of Dog Island. "It's that damn island, Mr. Berge! It's the damn island, it's always been the *damn island! That's* what killed your wife, Mr. Berge. *That's* what killed those poor people. That *goddamn* island is *alive!* It wants whatever it can get. It makes *ghosts!*"

He shook his head. "No. You're wrong. That is at right angles—"

She swung at him with the side of the axe. The flat blade clipped him on the chin. He went down on his knees. She stared at him a moment. "It's the damn island, Mr. Berge," she whispered.

He fell face forward into the snow-covered sand.

Lynette walked very slowly, with purpose—axe swinging gently—toward the inn.

Arnaut awakened an hour later in what he saw as sunlight on what he felt as warm sand. He heard what he supposed were the muted sounds of his guests enjoying themselves on the beach. He sat up. He saw people swimming—two small girls being watched over by their mother hovering close by, a boy in his teens doing the back float. The boy was out farther than was safe, Arnaut thought, and wondered if Barbara, the lifeguard and waterskiing instructor, would call to him to come back in. Near the boy, a blonde woman was doing a skillful breaststroke that was leading her in Arnaut's direction. Arnaut watched her, pleased by the fluidity of her motions. He folded his knees up to his chest, clasped his hands in front.

"That's far enough, young man!" he heard. He looked. He saw a stout woman in a tight red swimsuit pointing stiffly at the boy who was doing a back float. "Do you hear me, Richard? Richard? Answer me now, young man, or so help me, I'm going to go and call your father." Richard glanced over, waved, turned around and started to swim back.

Near the stout woman, a tall, slightly built young woman wearing a pair of jeans and a cream-colored blouse was carrying her infant into the water. *That's strange,* Arnaut thought, because the woman was wearing shoes. He watched as she waded into the water, hesitated, looked back, waded further in, stopped again—the water was at her knees, now—and smiled at a man running toward her. The man was shouting; "Amy, no! Amy, stop!"

Arnaut turned his attention back to the woman swimming. Only her head was visible—she was treading water, Arnaut supposed. The sunlight on the water behind her made her face only a mask of darkness, but Arnaut supposed that she was looking at him.

She disappeared.

Arnaut pushed himself to his feet.

To his left, the man who was running shouted, "Amy, what in the name of heaven are you *doing?*"

Arnaut walked slowly toward the beach. "Martha?" he whispered.

The woman reappeared in the water, her arms flailing.

Arnaut ran. "Martha?" he screamed. Beneath him,

the warm sand changed to snow. "Martha!" He got to the beach, ran through the shallows, through the thin ice, dove in. He began to swim, his eyes on the woman all the while, sunlight dappling the water around her. She went under again, came up, went under.

He heard, from behind him, on shore, "I'll help you, Jeff. I'll help you!"

Then, a woman's voice, "God, oh my God, help us!"

"I'm coming, Amy. Don't let go of Samantha! Don't let go, don't let go!"

Arnaut continued swimming. His strokes were quick, graceful, strong through the frigid water. Above him, the sunlit sky became cold and star-filled.

"She's stopped," he heard. Then, "I've got them. I've got Amy and Samantha. Thank God, I've got them! They're safe!"

The heat left Arnaut's body quickly; the frigid water sapped his strength. His strokes grew slow and awkward; his hands slapped into an area of thin ice, but he pressed on.

From behind, from the dark shore, he heard, "Arnaut, come back!"

His strokes stopped. He went under, came up, began to swim again, his eyes on the woman ahead of him in the water, her face masked by the night.

"Arnaut, please come back; we can't come after you!" It was Francis Carden's voice.

Arnaut went under.

He felt hands on him, felt the water close over him. *Martha!* he screamed, far, far back in his consciousness. *I'm coming to you! Martha!*

Too many hands, he realized. There were too many hands on him. More than simply Martha's. A *world* full of hands.

Light from the inn filtered dimly through the dark water. He saw two faces before him, each a flat, white, nearly featureless mask.

He opened his mouth to speak, to say his wife's name again.

Water flooded into his lungs.

He hung suspended between the surface and the bottom of the lake for one minute, two minutes, aware of the hands on him, aware that life was leaving him.

Until, at last, there was only one pair of hands. And they caressed him.

And tugged him gently away, toward the island.

FOUR

At first, Mary Berge wanted an end to it. She wanted it all sewn up, wanted it concluded. She wanted a corpse to view and wanted to weep over it. Then she could put it to rest.

But she couldn't put it to rest. There was no corpse to view and weep over. Wherever it rested, it rested beyond the view of her eyes, so it beckoned to her when she thought about it. And she thought about it often. She couldn't help it.

She spoke to her father and he spoke back. She told him that his words made a Rube Goldberg kind of mess of the language; he told her that he didn't know who Rube Goldberg was.

Then he evaporated. Sometimes she reached for him, to touch him, but she never succeeded.

She went to the island early the next autumn, after she had closed the inn. She walked the paths that Ben and Anita Mosiman had walked, and Max, and Joe Archer, and Catherine, and Linda Kennedy and her husband. She grew to wonder about the place, because she felt it hugging her, just as it had hugged others.

She grew to wonder about herself, too—about her grief, about wishing, loving, and about living. And about her father. Whether she had ever really known him. Or ever really could know him. Whether he would not always be a mystery to her, and she to him.

Whether he wasn't an island, too.

She spoke to him often about these things.

But he spoke to her only once, with the voice of air and memory. "The earth promises life," he said, his words slow and clear and perfect. "All we have is life."

And after a while, as the island hugged her, she grew to believe it.

THE BEST IN HORROR

☐	51572-2	AMERICAN GOTHIC by Robert Bloch	$3.95
☐	51573-0		Canada $4.95
☐	51662-1	THE HUNGRY MOON by Ramsey Campbell	$4.50
☐	51663-X		Canada $5.95
☐	51778-4	NIGHTFALL by John Farris	$3.95
☐	51779-2		Canada $4.95
☐	51848-9	THE PET by Charles L. Grant	$3.95
☐	51849-7		Canada $4.95
☐	51872-1	SCRYER by Linda Crockett Gray	$3.95
☐	51873-0		Canada $4.95
☐	52007-6	DARK SEEKER by K.W. Jeter	$3.95
☐	52008-4		Canada $4.95
☐	52102-1	SPECTRE by Stephen Laws	$3.95
☐	52185-4	NIGHT WARRIORS by Graham Masterton	$3.95
☐	52186-2		Canada $4.95
☐	52417-9	STICKMAN by Seth Pfefferle	$3.95
☐	52418-7		Canada $4.95
☐	52510-8	BRUJO by William Relling, Jr.	$3.95
☐	52511-6		Canada $4.95
☐	52566-3	SONG OF KALI by Dan Simmons	$3.95
☐	52567-1		Canada $4.95
☐	51550-1	CATMAGIC by Whitley Strieber	$4.95
☐	51551-X		Canada $5.95

Buy them at your local bookstore or use this handy coupon:
Clip and mail this page with your order.

Publishers Book and Audio Mailing Service
P.O. Box 120159, Staten Island, NY 10312-0004

Please send me the book(s) I have checked above. I am enclosing $_____
(please add $1.25 for the first book, and $.25 for each additional book to
cover postage and handling. Send check or money order only—no CODs.)

Name _____

Address _____

City _____ State/Zip _____

Please allow six weeks for delivery. Prices subject to change without notice.

BESTSELLING BOOKS FROM TOR